PRICE OF PASSION

Ann had ignored the warnings of her native good sense, the instinctive fears of her untouched innocence, when she had surrendered her heart to the man who called himself Michael James Black.

Now in the great abandoned ruin of the house that once had been the proudest mansion of the Phenwicks, Ann writhed in the ropes that cruelly bound her, and stared with horror into the merciless face of the leering satanic stranger who held her captive.

Gone now was the rosy aura of infatuation, the dazzling dawn of the intoxicating joy that she had known so briefly. In its place was a single chilling certainty:

Love had promised her heaven.

And led her straight into hell. . . .

Other books by Katheryn Kimbrough
available from Popular Library:

A SHRIEK IN THE MIDNIGHT TOWER

The Saga of the Phenwick Women:

#20
KATHERYN KIMBROUGH'S
Saga of the Phenwick Women

ANN, THE GENTLE

POPULAR LIBRARY • NEW YORK

Published by Popular Library, a unit of CBS
Publications, the Consumer Publishing Division
of CBS Inc.

February, 1978

Copyright © 1978 by Kymko Associates

ISBN: 0–445–04168–4

*Affectionately dedicated
to
Dearie-Dear*

CAST OF CHARACTERS

MICHAEL JAMES BLACK
An attractive young man who, having no memory of his past, is found on the New Jersey shore.

SALLY ORNBY
The widow of the late John Frederick Ornby and mistress of Falmouth House.

ANN ROSE ORNBY
Her pretty, gentle daughter, who believes she is destined to become a Phenwick woman.

FREDERICK ORNBY
Freddie is Sally's son. Extremely close to his sister, he has shared her dreams and adventures in the old house.

Lilly Gore
The housekeeper of Falmouth House.

Zebidiah Robbins
A wealthy widower of Portland, Maine, who has four children and is seeking to marry a second time.

George Tomlin
Handsome young business associate of Robbins'.

CRANDALL ORNBY
Cousin to the late John Frederick Ornby and head of the Medallion company in Portland.

Benita Ornby
His attractive, sensitive wife. She has never had children of her own.

STUART PHENWICK
The ruling member of the Boston dynasty of Phenwicks. Handsome and compassionate, he is a good businessman.

NANCY PHENWICK
Widow of the late Peter Phenwick and dutiful mother of his four young sons.

THADIUS PHENWICK
The eldest son, recently re-

5

CAST OF CHARACTERS (Continued)

THADIUS (*cont'd.*)

turned from service in the navy during the Civil War. He is good-looking and outgoing, but not without his problems as he attempts to adjust back into civilian life.

JOHN PHENWICK

Nancy's second son. Differently attractive from his brother Thad, he is a scholar.

PAUL PHENWICK

Nancy's third son. In his teens, his rebellious spirit is beginning to show; yet he is devoted to his family.

DANIEL LOUIS PHENWICK

Nancy's youngest son.

Giddeon Phillips

An old fisherman who finds Mike on the beach and takes him in as a temporary replacement for his own sons lost in the war.

Amanda Phillips

His shrewish wife.

CAPTAIN RODERICK WELLINGTON

An injured and maimed Union officer. With part of his body shot away, he returns to New York bitter and disillusioned.

THELMA WELLINGTON

The captain's duty-bound wife. A vital, attractive woman, she faces a life of incompletion with her heroic husband.

Tim Duggan

An Irish immigrant laborer, who befriends Mike when they work side by side.

Kate Duggan

His wife.

ANNIE DUGGAN

His plain-faced daughter.

SAM DODSWORTH

The man to whom Annie Duggan is promised. A violent person, he reeks of the atrocities

	he has experienced during the war.
HARRY STILES	A male nurse who attends Captain Wellington. His perverse ways make him vulnerable to certain situations.
DR. JOSEPH ORNBY	The devout physician and psychologist, who is a cousin to the Phenwicks.
DR. AUGUSTUS ORNBY	His brother, also in the same profession.
Jennings	The Wellingtons' butler.
AUGUSTA PHENWICK	The first of the Phenwick women.
CLAYTON LATSHAW	The designer and architect of Falmouth House as well as creator of the other houses Augusta had had built.
LEONA	A black and gray tabby who lives at Falmouth House.

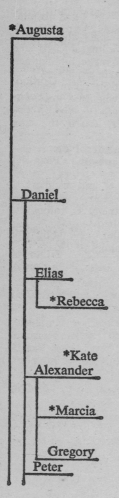

*Augusta

Founder of the family, married to Barrywell, then to Joshua Phenwick. The three children by Barrywell were murdered by their father; Daniel Charles was the only son of her marriage to Joshua. She later adopted Edward and Jane Munsk, whom she raised as Phenwicks. Augusta maintains an eerie hold over the surviving members of her family.

Daniel

Augusta's only son who lived to adulthood. Father of Elias (by Kate Mumford); married to. *Margaret O'Plaggerty; father of Alexander, Peter and Rachel.

Elias

Married to *Patricia Kelburn; father of Rebecca.

*Rebecca

First married to Johnny Ornby; second marriage to Robert Cathcart; mother of Kate Phenwick.

*Kate

Married to John Collier.

Alexander

Married to Susannah Phenwick; adopted two children: Marcia and Gregory Wing.

*Marcia

Married to Stuart Phenwick; mother of Daniel Charles II and Ann Marie.

Gregory

Married to *Ilene Dumphy.

Peter

First married to Helen Barnfather; father of Augustus,

8

Daniel (con't)

Peter (con't) — Joanne, Prentise and Joshua. Second marriage to *Nancy Cox; father of Thadius, John, Paul and Daniel Louis.

Augustus — Married to Lillian Webb; father of Stuart and Gordon.

Stuart — Married to *Marcia Phenwick; father of Daniel Charles II and Ann Marie.

Gordon — The strange dual-natured son.

*Joanne — Only daughter of Peter. Unmarried actress.

Prentise — Married to *Harriet Pettijohn; father of James, Frances, Louis, Martha, Patrick Sam and Tom.

Joshua — Married to *Olivia Pritchard; head of Medallion Enterprises in London; father of *Ophelia, Leon, Ruth Carrie, Elizabeth and David.

*Rachel — Daniel's only daughter. Died in her teens.

Edward (Munsk) — Adopted son of Augusta; married to *Patricia Kelburn; father of David and Susannah. (Actual son of John and Lydia Munsk.)

David — Edward's only son, killed in War of 1812.

*Susannah — Edward's daughter; married to Alexander (Lex) Phenwick; foster mother of Marcia and Gregory.

* Denotes Phenwick women about whom books were written.

Augusta (con't)

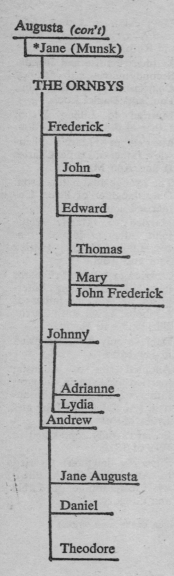

*Jane (Munsk) — Adopted daughter of Augusta; married to Jeffrey Ornby; sons: Frederick, Johnny and Andrew. (Actual daughter of John and Lydia Munsk.)

THE ORNBYS

Frederick — Jane's eldest son; married to Henrietta Ellsworth; sons John and Edward.

John — Married Dorothy Wren; children: Millicent, Crandall and Virginia.

Edward — Married Sarah Hadley; children: Thomas, Mary and John Frederick.

Thomas — Married Zelda Casey. No children.

Mary — Died in teens.

John Frederick — Married Sally Battell; children: *Ann Rose and Frederick.

Johnny — Father of Adrianne and Lydia by his first wife; second marriage to Rebecca Phenwick. No children.

Adrianne — Murdered in England.

Lydia — Unmarried.

Andrew — Married to Livinia Hendricks; father of Jane Augusta, Daniel, Theodore, Angela, Bertha and Jeffrey.

Jane Augusta — Married to Eustace Clark. No children.

Daniel — An attorney. Wife: Mellissa Kesler; children: James, Henry, Thomas and Sarah.

Theodore — (Dr. Ted.) Wife: Louise

10

Theodore *(con't)*	Lacy; children: Joseph, Augustus, Collin, Mary Rose and Ruth.
Joseph	A physician. Wife: Sheila Dumphy.
Augustus	A physician. Wife: Nell Willet; children: Charles and *Louise.

Prologue

The drums of war rumbled their staccato dirge from the Gulf of Mexico to the Canadian border. The dead and dying lined the roads, cluttered the primitive hospitals, while the wail of the mourners grew louder and louder. Little was the faith in the immortality of man and the continuation of life. If only I could have told them. But I doubt they would have listened. Times of sorrow are devoid of reason. And long after the dead were buried, the sorrow lingered, the emptiness remained.

What was the use of that war? Of any war? I suppose it was the inability of people to reason because they are so highly motivated by greed. Lack of love, some have said, lack of compassion. Brutality raged in the name of freedom; brother fought brother and died side by side. The cost of fear comes high.

I did what I could on this side to assist the many who found themselves awakened to a new existence. Nay, if the truth were truly known, it is an old existence, one in which time and space have new meaning or no dimension at all.

Yet the lineage of Augusta Eugenia Phenwick continues, persists in widening circles of emotion, heartache and triumph. I do not mourn or grieve. Yet I linger and watch and wonder how much longer my vigil must endure.

My adopted daughter, Jane Ornby, has long since been on this side of the veil—as they say. She lived long and grew feeble in earthly mantle. We touched in an exchange of expression that is difficult for mortals to conceive of. Then she went her way, perhaps to keep an eye on her children and grandchildren; still she had many of her own lessons to learn and much work to do here.

I had given Falmouth House in Portland, Maine, to Jane. Even before Jane made her transition, her heirs had begun to scatter until only her great-grandson, John Frederick Ornby, remained at the lovely house I had had constructed overlooking Back Bay. Another of Jane's great-grandchildren, Crandall Ornby, continued with Medallion Enterprises in Portland, constructing ships. While there was still an affiliation with Medallion of Boston and London, the firm in Portland had basically become independent and was no longer under the direct guidance of the Phenwick family.

John Frederick Ornby left his wife, Sally, and his two children at Falmouth House and went to war. That was 1862. He was killed in 1863, the target of a Confederate soldier's bullet. His widow elected to remain at Falmouth House, where she wanted her children to be raised. I doubt if she ever gave up all hope that John Frederick would return to her—at least not for a year or two after she received word of his death. She wanted her pretty, gentle little daughter and her handsome, endearing son to be raised in their father's house.

I found myself continually attracted back to Falmouth House and to that little girl, around whom I showered the scent of violets whenever possible.

Chapter 1

1864

Amanda Phillips had a hard face, a difficult smile. Grown plumpish over the years, she was bitter with a predominant sense of futility. The war had left her and her husband, Giddeon, impoverished. Her sons were dead. Her daughters had married and had disappeared, losing all contact with her. She managed her chores and did her best to make ends meet, to raise vegetables and prepare the fish and other sea life Giddeon caught. The best of his catches went to market, Amanda had to do with what was left. She often cried, remembering her family; but she wept when nobody could see her tears.

Early winter the year before, Giddeon had found a young man's body washed up onto the rocks as he was preparing to go out for the morning catch. The young man wasn't dead, but he was close to it.

Giddeon took him back to the weathered house, which was little more than a shack, and asked his wife to put the young man in a bed which had once been occupied by their eldest son. Amanda grudgingly complied with Giddeon's wishes. That boy was not her son, nor could he ever take the place of the lad who had been lost to war. Still, beneath that hardness, she found a touch of compassion and nursed him to health.

"Who are you?" Amanda had asked when the young man eventually regained consciousness.

"I don't know," he replied. He had a funny trace of an accent, soft-spoken.

Amanda was certain that he was a Confederate soldier, although the few pieces of tattered clothing he wore were not part of a military uniform. "You a Southerner? A Confederate?"

The youth shook his head. "I don't know who I am. In fact, I'm not certain I'm alive."

"You're quite alive," Amanda returned, scowling. "You sound to me like a Confederate soldier, and I oughta blow your brains out."

"Why?"

"Why?" She snorted contemptuously. "To repay the death of my sons. An eye for an eye."

"I don't understand. Is there a war?"

Amanda glared fiercely and padded away from the bed.

When Giddeon returned that day, he was pleased to see that the young man had become conscious. A compassionate man, no matter who the boy might have been, Giddeon wanted to see him back to perfect health.

"He has no memory, Mother," Giddeon said after interviewing the patient.

"Either that or he's playing dumb!" Amanda returned through closed teeth. "What do you intend doing with him?"

"Why, he's too feeble to climb out of bed," Giddeon explained. "If he has no memory, he has no home. Once he's on his feet again, he can help me. We must share God's bountiful goodness with him."

"God's bountiful goodness? You are a fool, Giddeon. I've always said that, and I'll continue to do so until the day you die," she scorned. "Well, do what you please.

16

But if I ever discover for certain that he's a Confederate soldier, I'll kill him on the spot. Do you hear me, Giddeon?"

"Yes, Mother, I hear you."

Life had become tedious and dismal for Giddeon Phillips. He had put much hope in his sons, certain that at least one of them would work alongside him. He could not give up when word came of first one, then of the other two being killed. When he had found the youth's body, a new glimmer of hope had begun to be kindled within him.

"Years ago," Giddeon said one evening as he sat beside the young man's bed, "I had a dear friend by the name of Michael James. We were as close as two men could be. He accidentally drowned while he was fishing. I don't believe I wept as much over my own sons as I did over Michael James. Since you can't remember who you are, I would be honored if you would take the name of Michael James."

"Michael James," the youth mused. "I would think the name would cause a black shadow to disturb you."

"No, no," Giddeon quickly replied. Then he chuckled. "But if it would make you feel less ill at ease, you could be called Michael James something or other."

"Black?"

"What?"

"Black. Michael James Black. I believe I would like to simply be called Mike, if you don't mind."

Giddeon chuckled louder. "Mike Jim Black, hey? All right, so be it."

As the simple nourishment given by Amanda began to take the emaciated look from him, Mike took on a bright color and the saggy hollows of his face and body began to fill in. He was quite good-looking, almost handsome. He had a vivacious smile and a cheerful outlook

17

when he wasn't perplexed about his shadowed past. Dark hair and steel blue eyes accentuated his well-shaped face. When he was finally able to walk, he moved gracefully yet with a masculine stride. Because he knew his soft speech disturbed Amanda, he desperately strove to develop a speech pattern similar to Giddeon's.

Through the winter Mike worked side by side with Giddeon. He learned to fish, to handle a boat, to make and set traps. He had quick learning ability and seemed to thrive on work.

"I suppose you often wonder who you are," Giddeon said one afternoon after the work was finished and the two were sitting down on the wharf. Giddeon whittled when he wasn't otherwise occupied. He liked to keep his hands busy.

"Oh, I wonder often," Mike replied, staring at gulls soaring on the horizon. "But it really doesn't bother me any more. At the risk of sounding a fatalist, I suspect there was a reason for me losing my memory. Maybe I had become so disgusted with my former way of life that I wanted to escape from it. That would be convenient, wouldn't it?"

"You mean you purposefully set about to forget who you were?"

"I don't think it was conscious," Mike responded. "But I've given it much thought, and I imagine that something within me directed me to forget. Maybe one day I'll meet someone who can set me straight about such things." He laughed. "I don't believe I was a fisherman before—but I enjoy fishing now."

Amanda Phillips had remained distant from Mike. While he had changed his way of speaking, she could not forget that he once spoke softly like a Southerner. That thought bothered her. Another thing that disturbed her was the fact that Mike spent so much time with Giddeon.

18

Her husband seemed to prefer the youth's company to her own. That was understandable. She and Giddeon had grown apart over the years. Now that her daughters were gone, she chose to sleep in one of their old beds rather than with her husband. That estrangement seemed to draw them further and further apart and she was envious of Giddeon and his friendship with Mike.

As spring began to flower, Amanda's bitterness increased. Actually she found herself excited by Mike's presence and that worried her. She was past such desires, she thought; still they came. Since she couldn't love him, she took the opposite emotion and professed openly to hate him for no apparent reason.

"Amanda's a strange woman," Giddeon confided in Mike. "She's been a good mother—and, in her younger days, she was a good wife. Not that she's not a good housekeeper and manages well with little, but she is of little personal solace to me. I'm beyond the point where I need her to occupy my bed all the time—but sometimes— Well, that's something that shouldn't be discussed, isn't it?"

"If you wish to talk about it, Giddeon, you should do so."

"No. No, that is a very private matter," the older man said. "Come along, we had best get back to the house before she works herself into a rage because we're late for supper."

Mike walked with his hand on Giddeon's shoulder. Surely he had a father of his own somewhere, but for now Giddeon was the most fatherlike person he knew. He was also Mike's best friend.

As they climbed the incline toward the unpainted, patched house, Giddeon clutched his chest in reaction to a sharp pain. He moaned and seemed to lose his balance.

"What is it, Giddeon?" Mike inquired, catching him in his arms to keep him from falling.

19

"It's a pain. I reckon you'd better just put me down and let me rest here on the sand," Giddeon gasped.

Mike helped him down, comforted him as best he could, then ran to the house.

"What have you done to my husband?" Amanda demanded to know. She had been watching from the window. "What ails Giddeon?"

"He has a pain in his chest. I had better go fetch the doctor."

"Fetch the doctor? We ain't got money to get no doctor!" Amanda scolded.

"I'll make arrangements with the doctor," Mike said. "You go tend to Giddeon."

Giddeon was forced to bed for two weeks. During that time Mike did his best to tend to the fishing, the cleaning and the marketing. Amanda kept a sharp eye on him, suspicious that he had purposefully done something to cause Giddeon's attack and that Mike was about to swindle them—out of what? They had nothing. Still it was the principle. And it was also the fact that she felt as she did toward Mike.

Once Giddeon was back on his feet and able to go about his usual tasks, Amanda continued to watch her husband and the younger man with contempt. By then she had manufactured a case against Mike, convincing herself that it was he who had made life so miserable for her. Giddeon preferred his company and showed great concern for his well-being. And Amanda was taken for granted.

Mike always accompanied the Phillipses to church on Sunday, riding in the back of the buggy and sitting beside Giddeon in the pew.

On a Sunday morning in April, Amanda looked up from her place in the pew to see a Union soldier in uniform, seated with his parents. She recognized him as

Tom Hicks. Later, while Giddeon and Mike were holding conversation with the preacher, she ambled over to where Tom Hicks was standing. He had known two of her boys.

Amanda drew Tom's attention to Mike and, as she did, she began to explain her suspicions about the young man. Tom was a lieutenant, a good soldier and naturally suspicious himself.

"What were you talking to Tom Hicks about?" Giddeon questioned Amanda as they drove home.

"He was a-telling me about how he was in battle and barely escaped with his life," Amanda replied. "Tommy's a good boy. And his mother later told me that he had been wounded. That's why he happens to be at home. He's recovering from the wound. You'd never know it to look at him." She cast a side glance back at Mike.

"Something's wrong," Giddeon said shortly after they reached the house and the horse was tied out to graze.

"Wrong?" Mike asked.

"I feel it in my bones," Giddeon related. "It's a queer feeling I get every so often. And for some reason, I keep thinking it has something to do with you."

"With me?"

"Like you were in danger."

Mike laughed. "How would I be in danger?"

"I don't know." Giddeon removed currency from his pocket and handed Mike three bills. "I want you to take this. You may need it."

"I don't want your money, Giddeon."

"I owe it to you. I know you worked for the doc to pay for him taking care of me," Giddeon stated. "I owe you more than that. But that's all I've got right now. You keep it, you never know when it might come in handy."

Mike argued, but Giddeon insisted he take the money.

Later that evening, about sundown, Mike looked up from the book he was reading in his room on the second floor. A band of six soldiers was riding over the rise toward the house. A feeling of apprehension came over him. Before he could close the book, Giddeon arrived at his door in a state of agitation.

"Them soldiers are coming for you, Mike," Giddeon said. "The old lady told me what she said to Tom Hicks. You'd better go down the back way and run along the beach."

"Why run?"

"Because Amanda has suspicions of you, Mike. I don't know what's put such fool thoughts in her head, but they're there all right. I know it," Giddeon explained. "There's no time to go into details. Just get yourself away from here."

"Why? If I run, they'll be certain I've done something wrong."

"You've got no way of proving who you are—even if you knew," Giddeon said, pushing the youth toward the door. "Go north, go farther north to New York or beyond. There's a war going on. And anyone who has suspicion around them, even if they're perfectly innocent, could find themselves in a prison stockade."

"I don't understand, Giddeon."

"Don't bother to, just go. I know of what I speak. Another three minutes and it'll be too late. I'll stall them here at the house."

Perplexed, Mike gathered a few things and hurriedly went toward the back of the house. There was no time for goodbyes or last words of encouragement. He could hear Amanda and Giddeon arguing downstairs. Waiting until he heard the horses at the front of the house, Mike trembled as he ran toward a brush-covered sand dune and hid behind it.

Only taking time to catch his breath and gain his bearings, Mike soon found himself running down to the shore. His boots splashed in the water as he sped fifty yards up the beach. Then he leapt onto rocks and scampered over them, hoping he had not left a visible trail.

Chapter 2

He had lived with the Phillipses for less than six months, yet Mike had learned much from Giddeon, especially in ways of survival, hunting, fishing and protecting himself against the elements. On several occasions Giddeon had spoken of his desires to go West as a pioneer; his wife had constantly objected to such an adventure. With his children grown, Giddeon had abandoned such notions as a reality; still he dreamed of what it might have been like. The old man had imbued Mike with many of his ideas.

Mike had skillfully eluded the Union soldiers who had come searching for him. He lay low for the daylight hours and did not venture out until nearly sundown. Keeping to the shore as best he could, leaving it only when he reached marshy areas, he headed north. Hazy moonlight brightened the way after he had made a meal of fish and wild strawberries.

As he walked through the night, the same questions returned again and again. Who was he? From where had he come? Now, why was he being pursued? Was he a Confederate? If so, had he been a soldier? What had caused that shroud of darkness to fall over his mind, cutting it off from all memory of the past? Furthermore, what was his destiny? He felt a strong magnetic pull toward something: but what? Maybe it was Fate that had actually driven him from the comfort of Giddeon Phillips' home. Then again, perhaps it was Fate that had led him to Giddeon in the first place. Certainly without Giddeon's help and the lessons he had taught him, Mike would not have been nearly as self-sufficient as he had become.

In thinking back, Mike reached the conclusion that Giddeon was aware that they would only be together for a short while—as much as the old man would have liked Mike to stay with him and take the place of his sons. Giddeon had often pointed the direction to New York, and once he had drawn a primitive map of the New Jersey coastline, Staten Island and Manhattan Island. It was grossly inaccurate, but it did give a general direction for Mike to follow. Giddeon must have had some kind of premonition that Mike was destined to go to the most populated city in the United States. Situated well north of the Mason-Dixon line, Mike could easily become lost in the melting pot of immigrants from all over the world.

If only Mike had an inkling of his identity. Yet at that time that which concerned him most was to get as far north as he could.

After traveling several days, existing as best he could off the land, and rarely encountering any other persons, Mike reached Perth Amboy, from where he could see the southernmost end of Staten Island. There he was able to scratch up a few odd jobs which paid him enough to purchase a new suit of clothing and the fare to cross over to Staten Island and buy transportation to the northern part of the island. He also saw a better map than the one Giddeon had drawn. There was ferry service from Staten Island to Manhattan. He observed the relationship of New York to such other cities as Philadelphia, Newark, Hartford, Connecticut, and Boston, Massachusetts. Of all the names of the cities he came across, the one that seemed to have a familiar ring to it was Boston. The name kept returning to him and he wondered if that place was to be his ultimate destination.

At the northern end of Staten Island, Mike met a middle-aged woman who was deeply distressed over her husband's health. Her man was a blacksmith and he had had an accident. Work was piled up, but he could not do it, nor could he find a suitable person to work for him. Mike took advantage of the opportunity. He was not a blacksmith by trade, but he could learn quickly. In two months he was able to save enough money to go to Manhattan and live in modest comfort until he was able to establish himself there. By then the owner of the shop had recovered sufficiently to return to work. Mike was offered a position if he would stay on. He declined it.

The hot, muggy weather of summer greeted Mike at the Battery on the southern tip of Manhattan Island. His two months' labor as a smithy had increased his strength, and when he walked about in his shirt sleeves, the wind blowing against him, he exhibited a strong, manly physique.

He soon found a job working on a water wagon, delivering water to the fashionable homes up above Prince Street. Mike had taken a room above a saloon in a street predominantly occupied by Irish immigrants. The accommodations were cheap and included breakfast. The Shamrock tavern was a lively place in the afternoon and after dark. Mike would purchase a bucket of beer and take as long as two hours to finish it as he sat and observed the clientele. One bucket was his limit, after which he would climb the stairs to the small third-floor room, where he would sleep unclothed with the window wide open. The heat was often oppressive, but he worked hard and fatigue caused him to sleep.

The man who worked alongside Mike on O'Brien's water wagon was a red, beefy-faced, bullish fellow by the name of Tim Duggan. Duggan was powerfully strong, a hard drinker who boasted of his strength, especially at times the effects of liquor got to him. Scrappy and often downright mean, there were few who challenged his might, and those who did lived to regret it. Mike was discerning enough to realize it was best to get on the right side of Duggan from the outset.

"Sure now, ya look like a bleedin' limey, ya do," Duggan commented the first time he met Mike. "Still with th' name o' Michael James Black, ya could be—at least part Irish, lad. An' since ya don't know ifn ya are or ya ain't, I'll pretend ya are."

Mike laughed. He immediately took a liking to the brawny, beer-bellied Irishman. And since he had no prejudices that he was aware of, he set out to become friends with the man.

They worked long hours, taking little time to rest except when they were riding one place to another. The sweltering days of summer made work difficult. But Duggan warned Mike that the snows of winter and the slushy streets could be far worse. It was best to learn to cope with the heat and enjoy it. Mike didn't understand. Often the men worked shirtless, especially when they were loading the barrels onto the wagon. Mike had grown tough and somewhat brawny. The sun had turned his skin to a golden tan which accentuated his handsome features.

Mike often thought back to the days immediately after he had first been found on the rocks by Giddeon Phillips and how pale and scrawny he had appeared then. What a transformation had taken place. During those summer days, he usually went to the public bathhouse after finishing work, where he soaked in a tub of hot water and went to the room where heated rocks caused the dirt of the city to wash from his pores. He often scrutinized himself in the large wavy mirror that hung on one wall of the bathhouse. Tan above, white below, he watched the steady change in his body brought about by long hours of labor.

"What d'ya do o' a night?" Tim Duggan asked one Saturday afternoon as they paused in the shade of an elm in a small square.

"Sleep," Mike replied.

"Alone?"

"Yes."

" 'Tis a pity," Duggan observed, then smiled. "What ya need is t' find yourself a nice lass, ya do. Sure now, a man as manly built as ya oughta be quite a lad with th' ladies. I still have me a time or two in spite o' me ol' woman. I used t' tell th' priest about it, but I figure it ain't none o' his business. Tell ya what, why don't ya drop up t' my place some night after dinner an' I'll take ya around an' show ya th' places t' meet lasses who're accommodatin'."

Mike was not certain he was ready for such adventures. Giddeon had warned him that women would cost him money, and Mike was trying to save as much of his wages as he possibly could. New York was all right, but he didn't want to remain there forever. More and more the thought of going to Boston came to him. But he didn't want to be considered odd in Duggan's eyes, so he accepted the invitation.

The Duggans lived on the second floor of an old brick building just off Broadway. At best it was in an Irish ghetto, dirty and in a poor state of repair. The walls were paper-thin; the sound of yelling penetrated from apartment to apartment. Repulsive odors were everywhere. Children swarmed like flies: dirty urchins with sad, hollow eyes. They touched Mike's heart.

The Duggans' accommodations were meager. Kate Duggan did her best to keep a presentable house, but with seven children at home, it was constantly in a state of turmoil. Broken furniture had long gone unmended. The floors were scrubbed clean, but deep stains could not be removed.

Kate was a large woman with stringy hair and big rosy

cheeks. She looked a perfect match for her husband and, Mike thought, she could probably pack a substantial wallop to match Tim's. She stared with hard, suspicious eyes, squinting to get a closer look at the stranger. She scrutinized and formed opinions.

"Th' best I kin offer ya is a cup o' tea an' a piece a bread," Kate said.

"Thank you anyway, Mrs. Duggan, I've eaten," Mike returned.

"Suit yourself, laddie. 'Twas offered," Kate grumbled and shuffled toward the kitchen where dishes were piled in the sink.

Mike sat uneasily in the shabby parlor, if that is what it could be called. He used a yellowed piece of newspaper to fan himself. Little eyes watched him. He felt self-conscious.

"I brung ya a cup o' tea all th' same," a sweet voice said. "Me mither said ya didn't want it, but I brung it anyway."

Mike looked up into the pert, pretty face of a girl of seventeen. She was undoubtedly Tim Duggan's daughter; his features were in her face. But where they appeared rough and bloated in Tim's face, they were small and almost refined in hers. "That was very kind of you, miss."

She giggled and turned pink and flustered. " 'Tis th' least I could do, sar."

"My name is Mike," he introduced.

"I'm Annie, th' second daughter. Pleased t' meet ya."

"I'm pleased to meet you, too, Annie."

Annie blushed even more, running her hands over her wrinkled cotton frock. Her dark red, natural curly hair looked tangled. She was self-conscious of her appearance. Yet she had caught a glimpse of Mike and she was fascinated by what she had beheld. She had to meet him, to speak with him. And now that she was in his presence and he was scrutinizing her as one might investigate a

29

piece of merchandise, she was embarrassed and uncomfortable.

"Well now, would ya look what's a-goin' on in here!" Tim Duggan exclaimed as he entered the room, hoisting up his trousers. "Annie, lass, what're ya a-doin' gawkin' at Mike Black like that?"

"Just a-gawkin', Da."

"Well, go on with ya. He ain't got time for th' likes o' you."

Annie edged her way from the room and stood behind the bedroom door, peeking through the crack.

"Annie's me second daughter," Duggan explained. "She don't know how t' fix herself up much. Just as well, too, since she's kinda spoken for."

"Spoken for?" Mike questioned, interrupting the speculative thoughts he had been entertaining.

"A lad by th' name o' Sam Dodsworth, who's gone t' war, wants her," Tim said. "He ain't much, but th' best th' likes o' Annie can hope for. He's a carpenter by trade, so he ought t' be able t' take care o' her. Come along, lad, ain't no use us just standin' here jawin' about Annie. Lord, she ain't no prize."

Mike looked back as Duggan went ahead of him through the door and out into the musty-smelling hallway. Annie was out of sight.

Mike found Duggan's sordid forms of entertainment not at all to his liking, but he felt obliged to make a show of interest. When he finally escaped Tim, he walked around and ultimately headed toward the Hudson River. He couldn't get thoughts of Annie from his mind. Beneath her unkempt exterior, he could not help but believe there was a pretty face and a gentle soul.

Duggan was grouchy the next day. A bucket of beer for lunch made him groggy and Mike ended up doing the bulk of the work. Only once did Annie's name come up.

Duggan grumbled. "She ain't much good for nothin'.

She can't hold a job. She's a dreamer, that's what she is. Th' best thing for her is t' marry Sam Dodsworth—when he returns—an' raise her a mess o' kids. That's all th' likes o' her is good for."

"Does Annie love this Sam Dodsworth?" Mike questioned.

"That's a helluva question, lad. Annie wouldn't know what love was ifn it come up an' knocked her on th' head."

"Do you?"

"Do I what?"

"Do you know what love is, Tim?"

Duggan swiped a beefy hand over his face. "That ain't no kinda question t' ask me, lad. I don't even know th' meanin' o' th' word."

Mike sighed. "Nor do I."

Later that afternoon, while they were making the last stop at the Wellington house, Mike overheard a row among the servants. One of the chargirls had been dismissed from service because of negligence. The girl departed in a fit of profanity and unladylike behavior, slinging parting remarks demeaning the character of the lady of the house.

Mrs. Roderick Wellington, a handsome woman in her mid-thirties, had directly taken the girl's abuses. She was used to that sort of thing. Because of the nasty necessity of dismissing the girl, Mrs. Wellington was in the basement floor of the house where Mike and Tim were depositing the barrels of water.

Mrs. Wellington was in the process of gathering her composure when she came upon Mike. His tight-fitting cotton shirt was wet with perspiration; his tanned, well-built chest could be seen defined beneath it. He ducked his head in the lady's presence and scurried about his work.

"You! Water man!" Mrs. Wellington called. "I wish a word with you."

31

"Me, ma'am?" Mike asked.

"Were you listening to my conversation with that dreadful girl?" she asked.

"No, ma'am. Still I couldn't help but overhear that there was an exchange of words between you," Mike replied. "I'll get on with my work."

"You'll wait until you're dismissed," Mrs. Wellington stated. "You'll come up to the sitting room on the first floor when you've finished so that I may pay you."

"Duggan collects the money, ma'am," he commented, "I only do the heavy lifting."

"I'm aware that Mr. Duggan collects the money," Mrs. Wellington returned. "But today I'll give the money to you. You'll find the stairs just there. I'll be waiting for you."

"Yes, ma'am. Oh, and ma'am, if you're looking for a girl to replace the one you just let go, I know a young lady who is seeking a position," Mike said.

"We'll speak of that upstairs." Mrs. Wellington lifted her skirts and hurriedly walked away.

"What does she want t' pay you for?" Duggan asked after Mike related his conversation with Mrs. Wellington.

"That is a mystery to me," Mike replied. "But she did seem interested when I mentioned I knew a young lady to replace the one she let go."

"You do? Who?"

"Your Annie."

"My Annie? Work here?" Duggan questioned incredulously.

"It would be a step up for her," Mike commented. "And it might be precisely what she needs."

Duggan shrugged. He knew that it was necessary for Annie to have employment. He couldn't afford to feed his family on what he made—not and have anything left for his own entertainment.

Mike stopped to wash his hands and face in the

32

watering trough. Neatly combing his hair and adjusting his clothing as best he could to look presentable, he made his way to the first floor of the elegant brownstone house.

"So there you are," Mrs. Wellington stated as Mike edged his way into the room. "What is your name?"

"My name?"

"I'll not give payment to a man whose name I don't know."

"It's Mike Black, ma'am."

"Hmm." She stepped toward him, one hand on her hip, the other clinging to the long strand of beads that hung about her neck. "You're not Irish, are you?"

"I don't know," Mike replied honestly.

"Your parents—?"

"I don't know who they are either."

"Were you raised an orphan?"

"I don't mean to appear to be insolent, ma'am, but I don't know that either. I could be a foundling of poor parentage, or a prince, for all I know. I have no notion of who I was a year ago."

"You've lost your memory?" Mrs. Wellington asked.

"Yes, that seems to be the case, ma'am."

"In the war?"

"I don't know."

"It's a possibility, isn't it? You certainly don't speak like a common street person," she observed. "And you have a refinement of beauty that must have come from good breeding."

"I wouldn't know about that," Mike remarked.

"What wage do you make as a water man?"

"What wage?" Mike stammered. "Three dollars a week. Seven days."

"I'll give you five dollars a week, including a place to stay and all your meals, if you'll come to work for me," Mrs. Wellington said.

"What sort of work for you, ma'am?"

33

"Handyman. You can drive a carriage, can't you?"

"Yes."

"And you're strong enough to handle the lifting of heavy objects and to shovel coal." Mrs. Wellington circled around him, gazing interestedly at his back side as well as his front.

"I thought it was a chargirl you let go," Mike said uneasily.

"It was. But I let my handyman go just yesterday for outrageously flirting with that same impudent girl," Mrs. Wellington explained. "Oh dear, it is such a chore for me trying to run this house with Captain Wellington away at war. I was never very good at that sort of thing. You don't drink, do you?"

"I usually have a bucket of beer in the evening after my work," Mike answered.

"Beer is hardly drinking," Mrs. Wellington returned. "The man whose services I terminated yesterday was a notorious drinker. Whiskey, that was his downfall. I don't mind if a man drinks—provided he drinks his own liquor, not mine—I'm referring to hired help now. Naturally I offer gentleman callers a bit of libation, that's proper—my husband's instructions. The captain has been away three years. I receive letters, of course, and I write daily—or at least every other day. Why are you staring at me like that?"

"You seem, if you'll pardon me for observing, to be nervous, ma'am," Mike commented, a wry smile crossing his lips. "You seem to be jumping from one subject to another."

"Impudent!"

"Am I, Mrs. Wellington?" he asked.

"Perhaps not, Mr. Black—uh—Mike." She stepped to the window and pretended to look into the street below.

"About the money for the water."

34

"What? Oh, yes. It's there on the table." She didn't
look back.

"I'll just take it and go."

"No, wait!" She pivoted about, her skirts swirling as
she did. "You didn't give me an answer about my propo-
tion to you."

"Which proposition?" He tried not to smile.

"About the position I offered you."

"Five dollars a week?" Mike raised his eyebrows
meditatively.

"Six," she hurriedly inserted. "But for that amount—
and food and lodging—you'll be expected to do little
extra things. I believe I can trust you."

"Trust me?" He chuckled. "Are you such a good
judge of character, ma'am?"

"I try to be." She walked toward him, hand on her
hip. "Well?"

"If you'll give Annie Duggan—she's the daughter of
the man I carry water with—a chance at replacing your
chargirl," Mike said, "I'll come to work for you."

"What is this Annie person to you?"

"Only my partner's daughter who desperately needs
work."

"Well . . ." She circled Mike again. He could almost
feel her eyes burning through him. "Annie Duggan?
She's an Irish girl, then?"

"Yes."

"Oh, very well. But I warn you, I won't put up with
hanky-panky among my domestics," Mrs. Wellington
stated.

"Did you say *among* them, or *with* them?"

"Now you are being insolent," she said, glaring.

He smiled and his eyes twinkled.

Mrs. Wellington smiled, too. She had to look away.
"When can you begin?"

"When do you want me?"

Mrs. Wellington put her hand to her mouth, her index

finger between her teeth. "The handyman's room in th[e] basement is ready anytime you can come."

"Annie can start work tomorrow," Mike said. "Bu[t] I'll have to give my employer notice until the end of th[e] week. It wouldn't be right to leave him short-handed."

"That is most considerate of you," Mrs. Wellingto[n] remarked. "Most young men just up and leave an em[-] ployer when a new position comes along." She went t[o] the window. "Very well, send this Annie person aroun[d] tomorrow. I'll give her a trial. I will count on you start[-] ing work next Monday."

"Thank you, ma'am."

"Don't forget your money on the table—for th[e] water."

"Yes, ma'am."

"Oh, and Mike," she said, turning back to him. "D[o] you own a white suit?"

"No, ma'am."

"Wait." She went to her purse on the desk and too[k] three dollars from it. "Here, purchase yourself a whit[e] suit and come tomorrow evening that I may see you i[n] it."

"Do you require me to wear white?"

"No, not to work in, of course," Mrs. Wellingto[n] replied. "But if you look well and presentable, perhap[s] you can escort me to church. You're not Catholic, ar[e] you?"

"No, ma'am."

"Good, neither am I." She smiled.

"Yes, ma'am. I'll purchase a white suit and come t[o] call tomorrow evening," Mike said as he opened the door.

"And you must come to the front door tomorrow evening," she instructed, "not to the servants' entrance. You're not my servant yet." She laughed giddily.

"Excuse me, ma'am," the butler said, appearing the[re]

36

other side of the opened door. He handed her a tray with a card on it.

Mrs. Wellington took the card. "Stuart?" Her eyes flashed to Mike. "You may go now, Mr. Black."

"Yes, ma'am. Good day." Mike bowed slightly and left the room.

"Very well, Jennings," Mrs. Wellington announced as she turned her attention back to the butler, "you may ask Mr. Phenwick to come to me here."

"Yes, ma'am."

Mike had been just outside the door when Mrs. Wellington made her pronouncement. He hesitated a moment, then moved away as Jennings appeared in the hallway. After going to the end of the hallway and the head of the back stairway, he stopped on the pretense of adjusting his boot. From there he observed the handsome figure of Stuart Phenwick before he entered the sitting room.

Hurriedly he went downstairs to relate the news to Tim Duggan. For the moment he put consideration of Stuart Phenwick from his thoughts.

Chapter 3

Two dollars and fifty cents seemed an exorbitant amount to pay for a white suit, including a shirt and cravat. Mike purchased a pair of off-white boots for the remaining fifty cents given him by Mrs. Wellington. He dipped into his own savings for enough to buy a suitable hat to wear with his new outfit.

His employer had been displeased when Mike announced he was quitting as of the end of the week. A slight raise was offered because Mike was a good worker; but it was declined. Even Tim Duggan tried to convince Mike to remain as a water man.

Annie was hired as chargirl, but it was not a live-in position. She was gone from the Wellington house by the time Mike arrived that evening. Jennings opened the door to him, looking down his nose as he did, since he was knowledgeable of the position Mike had been offered. The butler knew of Thelma Wellington's curious interest in certain young men. He said nothing as he showed Mike to the entrance hallway and the bench upon which he was to wait.

"Mrs. Wellington has a caller at the moment," Jennings finally said as he reached the stairway.

Mike examined his appearance in the large beveled mirror behind the bench. The white suit was well-fitting, snugly clinging to his form to accentuate his fine physique. The dry goods salesman had assured him that it was not too tight and that it gave him a handsome appearance. Mike tried the hat at several angles, then removed it and combed back his long locks.

Staring into the reflection of his own eyes, Mike wished he could see behind them into the past. Not knowing who he really was disturbed him. He felt quite comfortable in fine clothing and he took poses that were quite natural for him to assume.

Mike's preening was interrupted by the appearance of a handsome gentleman who was descending the stairs. He smiled broadly, in such a personable way that Mike felt compelled to smile back. As he did, he was certain he recognized the man.

"How do you do, sir," the man said. "You must be the Mr. Black Thelma is awaiting."

- "Thelma?"

"Mrs. Wellington."

"I'm Mike Black."

"Permit me to introduce myself. I'm Stuart Phenwick."

"My pleasure, Mr. Phenwick."

"And mine, Mr. Black." They shook hands. "I've brought Mrs. Wellington word from her husband."

There was an awkward silence.

Stuart smiled. "Captain Wellington has been wounded and he has been hospitalized in Baltimore. He is too badly injured to return home for several months." He stared into Mike's face and got a puzzled expression. Suddenly he snapped his fingers. "I know why you look familiar. You bear a remarkable resemblance to my Uncle John."

"I do?"

Stuart laughed. "Uncle John has recently turned eighteen years old."

"Eighteen?" Mike questioned. "But you—"

"Uncle John would be my father's half brother. I was practically grown when John was born," Stuart explained. "If you're ever in Boston, you must come and meet Uncle John, so that you can see the resemblance for yourself. Perhaps there isn't any really, and it's just my imagination playing tricks on me. Oh well, I must be off—and Mrs. Wellington is waiting for you. Good evening."

"Good evening." Mike watched Stuart's reflection through the mirror. Then he glanced back at his own. "Phenwick?" he said aloud.

Thelma Wellington was waiting, poised in a satin-covered chair. She was fashionably attired in a pink and maroon dress, which looked a bit heavy for the warmth of the evening. Still she appeared remarkably cool and comfortable. Her bearing was almost majestic.

"Ah, there you are, Michael. What kept you?" asked Mrs. Wellington.

"I dallied for a word with your Mr. Phenwick," Mike replied.

"Ah, dear Stuart. What a wonderful person he is! And such a very dear friend. He stopped on his way from Washington to Boston especially to bring me word from my husband. But never mind that. I must say I am duly impressed with your appearance, Michael. I've had many a handyman, but I've never had one as truly handsome as you."

"You make me blush, Mrs. Wellington."

"I should hope so," she returned with a coy smile. "You should always wear white. It does remarkable things for you."

"Are you impressed with the wrappings?"

"The wrappings would be ineffectual without the contents within them," Mrs. Wellington returned, lifting herself from the chair and maneuvering her skirt so that it whispered as she stepped around him. "Most impressive."

40

"If I have your approval, then I'll excuse myself."

"No. Goodness, whatever for?"

"I was of the impression you only wished to inspect my appearance," Mike said, his eyes innocently watching her.

"Well, of course, that," she replied. "But I thought we could have a chat. May I offer you a drink?"

"Not unless you have beer."

She started to object, then laughed. "Oh, yes, I did say something about my employees not drinking, didn't I? But tonight we could pretend you're not an employee— for technically you're not until next Monday. Isn't that so? Of course it is, Michael. I should like to get to know you better."

"You would?" He was intently staring at her.

"Now don't tell me you've never dressed in fashionable attire before," she said after her eyes slid from his and swept over his handsome appearance. "They fit too well and you wear them with elegance."

"If I have, Mrs. Wellington, I don't remember. I am suffering from amnesia, and I don't recall who I am or any of my past," he explained simply.

"Yes, so you said before," Mrs. Wellington commented. "Mr. Phenwick tells me it will be months before I can hope for my husband to return. Even then he is liable to be a hopeless cripple the rest of his life. He has lost a leg, part of his hip and—well, other sections of his anatomy. I want to weep, but I can't. I'm still a very vital woman with depths of desire and very real romantic ideas. If Roderick—oh dear, I can't speak of it." She began to cry.

Mike watched her, feeling helpless to comfort her; nor could he find words to suit the situation. "Mrs. Wellington—"

"Oh, Michael," she cried. "Don't think it terrible of me, but I need to be held right now. I bravely accepted the news from Stuart and wouldn't permit him to comfort me

41

in my travail. Now the full impact of his words has touched me and I need to be held before I swoon on the spot." She swayed back and forth and seemed to grow limp.

Mike stepped to her. He hesitated before he raised his hands to steady her. She fell into his arms and wept bitterly against his chest.

As the days began to cool in the autumn of 1864, both Mike and Annie had settled into the routine of their work at the Wellington house. Annie had never held a job for such a long period in her life. It wasn't the work she cared for, but she was intrigued with the idea of working in such close proximity to Mike. Often during the day she managed to be where he was.

When Mike could take the time, he had long chats with Annie Duggan. Clean and in her service uniform, Annie's beauty became more apparent. She was basically a sweet girl with a gentle disposition. And the emotional feelings she was developing for Mike could not be disguised.

Mike encouraged her interest because he was very much impressed with her. When she was finished with her day's work, Mike would offer to ride home with her on the horse-drawn streetcar and walk with her from the stop. Sometimes he would take the streetcar back, other times he would walk, especially if nothing further was expected of him during the evening.

During those periods of cogitation, Mike believed that he was falling in love with Annie. She meant much to him, occupying his thoughts. Yet, because he had questions about himself, disturbing thoughts, he was uncertain that he was ready to consider marriage. Perhaps he had a wife somewhere waiting for him to return. That notion had occurred to him more than once. He might even have children. With such contemplation he felt it would be wrong for him even to broach the matter of his romantic feelings for Annie.

Then there was the matter of Thelma Wellington. Mike knew beyond a doubt that she, too, was emotionally involved with him. His tasks as handyman were minimal, but he was often required to spend long hours in her company. She bought him clothing on the pretense it was to make him presentable in her presence when he accompanied her in public. She gave him little gifts and increased his salary: for occupying his time.

Thelma became bright and giddy when in Mike's company. She only took on signs of gloom when she received word of her husband, or when Mike was away and she knew he was with Annie. She wished to discharge the girl, but she was doing an admirable job.

"I have never seen you so radiant," Stuart Phenwick commented when he arrived for a visit with Thelma Wellington in October. "Can such a youthful charm be provoked by thoughts of your husband's return?"

"I suspect 'provoked' was a poor choice of words, Stuart," she replied. "If you mean 'caused by,' well, I'm afraid I would have to deny it."

"Deny it? But, my dear Thelma, Roderick is living in anticipation of his return home," Stuart explained.

"And I'm living in dread of it," she returned.

"In dread?"

"I sent a whole man away to war," Thelma sighed. "Only part of a man will be returning to me—and, I fear, not the better part."

"His love is as strong or stronger than ever," Stuart related. "His mind is sound, considering all he's been through."

"But his body, Stuart, his body," Thelma sobbed. "If my husband can't be a husband in the fullest sense of the word, I can't—" She broke into deep sobbing. Stuart comforted her. "I love Roderick, I always have, perhaps I always will. But I am a vital woman, Stuart. I need a man who is just as vital and alive. Am I to live out the rest of my life as a prisoner with a cripple for a jailer? The

43

thought of even seeing his maimed body distresses me."

"Then you are a paradox, Mrs. Wellington," Stuart said softly. "How can you appear so gay in anticipation of Roderick's return and say these things . . . ? Unless . . ."

Thelma looked up at him. "Unless, Stuart?"

There came a light rap at the door. A moment later it was opened and Mike appeared. Both Thelma's and Stuart's eyes went to the handsome young man.

"Forgive me, Mrs. Wellington," Mike said, "I didn't realize you were occupied."

"Stay, Michael," Thelma instructed. "Stuart Phenwick is an old and dear friend. And I trust an understanding friend. Are you, Stuart?"

"I try to be."

"You've met Michael, haven't you?" she asked.

"Yes, in passing."

"Michael is not only a handyman, he is handy to have around the house," Thelma stated. "I've no doubt you catch my meaning."

"I'm beginning to."

"Michael has a problem," Thelma continued.

"Please, Mrs. Wellington, I—"

"Don't interrupt, Michael." She turned to Stuart. "You see, Michael's suffering from amnesia. Michael Black is simply a name he has taken in lieu of not knowing his own. I mention this to you because perhaps you can assist him."

"What? In regaining his memory?" Stuart asked.

"Yes, indirectly. You've mentioned your cousin in Boston, the doctor."

"Dr. Joseph Ornby? Yes, and his brother Dr. Augustus Ornby. They both deal with physical and mental illnesses," Stuart said.

"Maybe one of the good doctors can be persuaded to come to New York and examine Michael."

"It would be more convenient for Michael to go to

44

Boston," Stuart explained. "Both my cousins are extremely busy, especially now with war victims taking much of their time. Surely there are similar types of doctors here in New York."

"Why don't you excuse me for a few minutes and speak with Michael?" Thelma asked, feeling the need of letting the men become better acquainted.

"She's in love with you, isn't she?" Stuart stated shortly after Thelma Wellington left the room.

"I suspect she is."

"And from your tone, I suspect you're not emotionally—"

"How could I possibly be? She's a married woman. I'm her servant. And, for all I know, I may have a wife and family elsewhere," Mike returned. "Furthermore, she's a woman several years my senior. It's an impossible situation."

"And are you emotionally attached to someone else at this time?" Stuart questioned.

"I am—somewhat. Again, I have not permitted myself to lose control of my reason," Mike said, "for the same reason I gave—except Annie is younger than I am."

"Ah, Annie it is." Stuart smiled understandingly. "My friend, I was deeply in love with my first wife. Marcia gave me two beautiful children. My daughter is named Ann Marie. After my wife's passing, I had a lingering affair with a married woman—who was my uncle's wife. I fathered a child with her—a son who is still somewhere in Georgia, a child I've never seen. Now I am married a second time. I deeply love Ruth. Each of those three women were as different from the other as they could possibly be. Still I believe I loved each of them. Some men are capable of many loves, others of only one—and still others of none. I envy the second group and pity the last."

"Why have you told me this?"

"Because, as for me, I thought I could never love anyone but my first wife. I was ready to kill myself when

Marcia died," Stuart explained. "But time healed the wound." He glanced over at Mike. "I suspect you are a man without great financial means or you wouldn't be employed as a domestic. Your Annie is also a domestic, I take it. Do you really love her?"

"I don't know. I think I do when I reason with my emotions."

"And what are your feelings about the girl when you're in Mrs. Wellington's presence?" Stuart asked.

"I don't know that I give Annie much thought at such times, unless her name is brought up."

"Ah."

"I don't see what you're driving at."

"When I first encountered you, and when I saw you again this evening," Stuart continued, "I would never have guessed that you were anything but a gentleman of means—certainly not a domestic. Your attitude, your carriage, your manner of speech are not those of a common person from menial environment. No, on the contrary, you are something quite better than that."

"I take that as a compliment."

"Well then, suppose you were to marry your little Annie," Stuart suggested, "and one day discovered your past to be one of affluence. What would become of your Annie then—especially if you had married her? Even if you didn't have a wife lurking in the past, wouldn't your Annie be out of place in an alien world?"

"You were about to suggest an alternative, I suspect."

"Enjoy your Annie, have fun with her—and do the same with Mrs. Wellington. I'll speak to her for you, if you like. She can make it well worth your while if you will become her paramour."

"Her lover?"

"Aren't you now—in a sense?"

"In a sense?"

"I know women well enough to know what is going through Thelma's mind. I see how she looks at you. I

46

saw the expression in her face when I first came in this evening. Any idiot could see what had caused that in her. It wouldn't be a matter of marriage, because she has a husband. Although he's an invalid, chances are he will live for many years."

"My God! What are you suggesting?" Mike questioned.

"Captain Wellington will never again be able to function as a man. I know that for a fact," Stuart explained. "Yet now more than ever he needs Thelma's love. But she is a woman who needs the fulfillment of a man, complete and whole. The Wellingtons are very wealthy people. They can afford whatever price you may ask. You can still have your Annie on the side and your little romance."

Mike closed his eyes. "Can I? Am I really that sort of man, Mr. Phenwick? You don't know me. Furthermore, you don't know Annie. She is in love with me. Too true. But, alas, she has been spoken for. It's an impossible situation. She may not love her Sam Dodsworth, but he is a soldier. One day he'll return and my 'little romance' with Annie, as you call it, will be over. So you see, I'm a man both without a past and a present—as far as knowing anything lasting about me."

Stuart put his hand on Mike's shoulder. "I'll do whatever I can for you, Michael. Think about what I've said. Life is too short to be miserable."

Chapter 4

Bearded, balding, despondent Roderick Wellington was confined to the second-floor room in the fashionable brownstone house. His eyes wore a tired expression, weariness was written in the downturn of his lips. Vitality was gone from his voice. Day in and day out through the winter months, he would either remain in bed, propped up with pillows, or sit in a large chair by the front window where he could look down into the street. To get from the bed to the chair, he had to be carried by Mike. A male attendant had been hired to look after his needs, but the man lacked the strength of Mike.

"It would have been a simple matter," Roderick stated to Mike one morning after being moved from the bed to the chair, "for them to have let me die on the battlefield. My horse had been shot from under me and I was so badly wounded I couldn't free myself from the weight of the dead animal on my leg. I was certain I was dying then. How much better it would have been. I wonder if we aren't meant in this life to experience certain agony; or perhaps this is a retributive matter because of my earlier misuse of power. Hindsight is little more than rationalization, I suspect."

"The doctor says you are basically in good health, sir,"

Mike commented as he arranged pillows behind Wellington.

"In good health? With one leg and hip gone?" Roderick snorted contemptuously. "Oh, yes. There's not even a place to attach a wooden leg. And my poor wife. At least if I were dead she could marry again and discover a modicum of happiness through the rest of her life. I'm nothing but a burden."

"You're a hero, Captain Wellington," Mike said.

"That's not quite true, either, boy. I was given a captain's commission not for my military knowledge, but because of my social position," Wellington explained. "My dreams of heroic bravery were only that: just dreams. I was well protected behind the lines, where I had a grandstand seat to watch the men of the blue and of the gray fall like insects in the exchange of gunfire and the clash of swords. The Confederates got the upper hand on us and we suddenly found ourselves surrounded. It was every man for himself as we tried to find openings in the lines to retreat. I was little more than a sitting pigeon. Both my horse and I seemed to have been hit at the same time. God in heaven was merciful to the poor horse, not to me."

Harry Stiles, the captain's attendant, entered the room. Mike was excused.

February was coming to an end. Snow was on the ground. The streets were slushy and slick with ice. Mike shoveled snow and cleared paths to each of the doors. He spent several hours a day in the carriage house, grooming the animals, feeding and tending them. If Annie finished her work in time to coincide with Mike's time in the carriage house, she would go to be with him. Often she would just stand and watch while he worked.

"Sure now, Mrs. Wellington has been naggin' at me again," Annie complained. "I get th' floors so sparklin' clean ya kin practically see your face in 'em. An' I polish up the woodwork so that it plum shines. Still she nags at me. Phoebe, the upstairs girl, says there's only one reason

49

Mrs. Wellington scolds me so—it's because o' you, Mickey."

"Because of me?" Mike asked, scowling.

"Phoebe says she knows for a fact that Mrs. Wellington fancies you as much as I do," Annie continued. "Is that true?"

"Part of my job is spending time with Mrs. Wellington," Mike explained. "Lately she has me accompany her more and more to places she used to go with the captain before the war. A lady can't go places unescorted."

"But Mrs. Wellington is very fond o' you, ain't she?" Mike sighed. "It would seem that way."

"And are you fond o' her?"

"She has been very kind and generous. But love can't be bought."

"You don't love her, do you?" Annie asked.

"Why do you ask me such things, Annie?"

"Because I believe I love you very much, Mickey," she replied.

"We're only meant to be friends, Annie, I thought we had decided that," Mike said. "Your father has taken me aside any number of times to remind me that you have been spoken for by Sam Dodsworth."

"I don't love Sam Dodsworth," Annie pouted. "Sam spoke to Da about me, and it was Da who promised me to him. I had nothin' to do with it."

Mike smiled understandingly. "Your father even gave me a pistol to protect myself against Sam Dodsworth."

"Because I told Da I liked you very much and I prefer you to Sam," Annie remarked in a matter-of-fact way. "I know you must like me very much or you wouldn't have got me a position here at th' Wellingtons'."

"I had only just met you when I arranged for you to work here," Mike returned. Then he dropped what he was doing, wiped his hands on his trousers, went to her and took her in his arms. "Yes, little Annie, I do like you very much. I think of you most of the time."

50

"Even when you're with her?" Annie questioned.

Mike closed his eyes as a vision of Thelma Wellington came to him. "You must understand that I'm paid to do what I do with Mrs. Wellington."

"Paid to make love to her?"

Anger mounted in Mike. In retaliation, he forced his mouth to hers. He kissed her and she responded. Almost as if they were dancing, he led her to where the straw was piled, their lips still held together. Moments later they were no longer standing as their passion crescendoed.

Stuart Phenwick arrived in New York during the first week of April 1865. He had been down to Washington, D.C., for Abraham Lincoln's second inaugural on the fourth. His principal reason for being in New York was to meet his Uncle Thadius, who had recently been discharged from the navy. While he was in that city, Stuart felt compelled to call on Captain and Mrs. Wellington.

"The war is all but over," Stuart announced as he sat in the second-floor room with Roderick Wellington. "If things go as planned, Lee is expected to surrender any day now."

"The war will never be over for me, Stuart," Wellington replied. "I'll carry the horror of it to my death."

Handsome, serious, somewhat withdrawn, Thadius Phenwick listened to the conversation and talk of war. He, too, had witnessed his share of combat. Seeing the maimed captain gave the young man a strange sensation, and he longed to escape from that room. He ultimately excused himself and left Stuart to chat with Wellington.

"John?" Thad asked as he saw the silhouette of the tall man and the outline of his face in the dim glow of lamplight. "Is that you, brother John? Stuart said he— Oh, I beg your pardon."

Mike had stepped toward Thad. "Were you speaking to me?"

"In these shadows, I mistook you for my brother. But

51

of course, he wouldn't be here in New York—not unless he came with my nephew," Thad explained. "I'm Thadius Phenwick."

"I'm—" For a moment another name almost came to Mike's mind. What was it? "I'm Michael Black. I work for the Wellingtons."

"Ah, so you're the Michael Black of whom Stuart spoke." Thad tried to lighten his tones. "I should have known instantly. He told me you resembled my brother John. I was always very close to John. It's been a long time since we've seen each other."

"I've often wondered if I had brothers or sisters," Mike commented. "If so, they're probably lost to me forever."

"There was a man aboard the ship on which I last served," Thad related, "who lost his memory for nearly six months before it returned."

"Did he recall what he did during those six months he was without his memory, once it returned?" Mike asked. "I've often wondered about that—I mean with myself, should I regain knowledge of my past."

"I can't answer that. I should imagine that he did." Thad chuckled. "Funny, I never thought about that."

"That's because your memory is intact."

"Sometimes, after what I've been through, I wish it weren't. Still I wouldn't want to forget my mother and my brothers. I have three brothers. My father had a grown family before he married my mother—he was much older than she. That's why Stuart is so much older than I—and still I'm his uncle."

Thad and Mike got acquainted and a kind of friendship began to develop.

"I have a terrible premonition," Thelma Wellington said a short while later when she was alone in the sitting room with Stuart.

"A premonition?"

"That something awful is going to happen, and this

52

brief interlude of happiness will come to a sudden end."

"Interlude of happiness?" Stuart questioned.

"What more can it be?" Thelma returned. "I pay Michael well for his service, and I do believe he has some feeling for me—still he is merely hired to do what he does. And I see a distant look in his eyes. Ever since you mentioned your doctor cousin in Boston, I know he has thought of going there to be treated by him."

"It would be well if he did."

"No! I don't want him to know who he was! I want him to be just as he is now," Thelma stated. "Even with his association with that little Irish girl—I can abide that. But if his memory were to return, we well could both lose him."

"Would it be such a drastic tragedy if you did?" Stuart asked.

"I think I would put a pistol to my temple," Thelma replied.

"Then you've fallen deeply in love with him?"

"Deeply, Stuart, deeply."

"Oh dear, I had no idea it would go this far."

"Because you're not a woman, Stuart, you don't know."

Stuart took her hand and held it for several minutes. "My dear, dear Thelma, you've put yourself into a very difficult situation, haven't you?"

"More so than you can know." Thelma looked away as tears came to her eyes.

General Robert E. Lee surrendered at Appomattox Courthouse on April 9, 1865. President Abraham Lincoln was assassinated on the fourteenth of April. One month to the day after that, Tim Duggan was interrupted as he loaded the water wagon at O'Brien's.

Tim's reaction of surprise mixed with alarm could not be disguised. Setting the keg on the wagon, he moved uncertainly toward the large man who still wore the uniform of a Union soldier. Tim was a large man, but he appeared less imposing beside the firm, hulky structure of Sam Dodsworth. Sam had a full beard and bushy eyebrows. His hands were huge with thick fingers. There was no mistaking he was a man of powerful physical strength. Teeth showed when he laughed, and he often laughed although the sound was just as often menacing.

"Glory be, Sam Dodsworth!" exclaimed Duggan as he stared strangely at the man. "Ya've come home from war, have ya?"

"The war is behind me," Sam said in a deep, gruff voice. "I've put it from my mind. My quest is to come back to collect my debt from you, Tim Duggan."

"Your debt?" Tim was perspiring from work; Sam's nearness caused him to sweat all the more. "You mean—?"

"I've wenched myself from one end of the country to the other," Sam stated. "Now I've come home to settle down an' raise me a family. In short, I've come to get Annie."

"Things have changed since you've been away, Sam."

"Changed." Sam glared. "A debt is a debt, Tim Duggan, an' nothin' changes that until the debt is paid."

"I'm full aware a th' debt I owe ya. Sure now, ya know I'm an honest man—at heart," Duggan said. "I've other daughters—younger an'—"

"I don't want any but Annie, an' I've come to claim her," Sam snarled. "Where is she?"

"She ain't here, Sam," Tim returned, leaning against the wagon and trying to look casual. "She hardly ever comes around O'Brien's. 'Sides, she's workin'."

"Workin'? Where?"

"Up at th' Wellington house. She's a chargirl—an' that's about th' best th' likes o' her kin expect to do."

"She'll not work again until she's given me a houseful of kids," Sam stated, removing his blouse to put his heavily muscled arms on display. "You'll tell me where this Wellington house is an' I'll go collect my bride an' make arrangements with the priest. We'll have a big celebration an' everyone'll get drunk. Hey, Tim!"

Tim Duggan was not afraid of many men; but Sam

Dodsworth was one who caused him to tremble in his boots. Hesitantly he gave Sam the address of the Wellington house.

No more had Sam Dodsworth strode out the gate than Duggan ran to Chauncy O'Brien's office and explained that he had to take an hour or so off to tend to important business. O'Brien was not receptive to the idea and suggested that whatever Tim had to do it could be done on his own time. Was anything so important that the water man would dare to risk his job?

Annie had finished her work early and went to the stable as she usually did in the afternoon. She tried to be secret about her movements, but the entire household, including Thelma Wellington, knew of the girl's daily visits to the stable and the rendezvous she had with Mike.

Mike greeted her warmly as he usually did. He had a singular kind of love for the girl. Mrs. Wellington believed he went to Annie out of pity for her, and that they had an immature exchange of emotions, nothing more. How could any man, particularly one as handsome and seemingly intelligent as Mike, be completely charmed by the likes of Annie Duggan? Yet Thelma Wellington's was an impossible situation, too. And until Captain Wellington made his transition into another dimension, Thelma had to content herself with things as they were. If Annie provided a means of pacifying Mike in some way, then Thelma would put up with it.

"Ya been workin' hard today, Mickey?" Annie asked as she watched him curry the beige mare.

"No harder than usual, Annie," he replied lightly.

She touched his back. "I've thought o' you th' whole day, aye, that I have, lad. It was all I could do to keep me mind on me task. Twice Jennings had to scold me an' threaten with exposin' me to Mrs. Wellington. Jennings thinks I'm lazy. It's not the case . . . I'm in love."

Mike turned to her, opening his arms. She fell into them. "Oh, Annie, Annie, you are such a silly little thing."

55

"Do you love me, Mickey?"

He kissed her. As he did, Annie put her arms about him and let her hands slide over his back. The excitement generated by his kiss was interrupted as her fingers ran over the pistol tucked in his waist.

"What is this, Mickey?" she asked, pulling her head back from his.

"A gun. It's one Tim gave me."

"Why're ya carryin' it?"

Mike smiled warmly down into her face. "There have been prowlers lately in the neighborhood. Captain Wellington suggested that I carry it when I'm here in the stable, or when I take Mrs. Wellington out in the buggy. Now that the war is over people are acting peculiarly. I reckon it's because ex-soldiers haven't quite gotten out of the habit of fighting." He chuckled softly. "I'll put it aside, if you'd like me to."

She kissed his cheek. "Ya kin put it aside when ya go to pull off your britches."

Nearly fifteen minutes later while the young couple were involved in romantic adventure, they were bluntly interrupted by a banging on the stable door. Mike scampered to his feet and pulled into his trousers. "Stay back, Annie. I suspect it is Jennings. I'll handle it."

No more had Mike lifted the bar from the door than it swung open. Sam Dodsworth was standing full in the doorway, arms akimbo.

"You Mike Black?" the big man asked.

"I am."

"Where's Annie Duggan?"

"Who are you? Why do you want to know?" Mike questioned.

"In the first place, I'm Sam Dodsworth," he announced, reaching over and pinching the flesh on Mike's chest. "And ifn Annie's in here, ya'd better have a good reason for not wearin' your blouse."

"It's hot—summer—"

56

"I damn well know it's hot," Sam returned, boldly striding into the stable. He straight-armed Mike aside. "Annie Duggan, come out. I know you're in here."

"Look, mister, you're trespassing in here," Mike shouted as he regained his balance.

Sam snorted and made his way toward where the straw was piled. "Annie's spoken for—by me. That bein' the case, I reckon it's not me who has been trespassin'."

Mike stepped to where he had put the pistol, held and cocked it as Sam got dangerously close to where Annie was hiding. "Don't go any nearer, Dodsworth."

Catching a glimpse of the gun, Sam hesitated before he pivoted around. "You wouldn't pull a gun on me ifn Annie weren't in here."

"I might. You're trespassing. This is the Wellingtons' stable and I've been ordered to keep all intruders out. Now either you get or you'll force me to shoot."

Sam inched closer to Mike. "Do you know how many Confederate soldiers I killed durin' the war?"

"I ain't much interested."

"Well, I lost count anyway." Sam stepped to within arm's reach of Mike. "When ya kill that many, one man more or less ain't gonna make much difference."

Mike was trembling. His finger was frozen at the trigger. "Stay back, Dodsworth, I'm warning you!"

Sam raised his hand, connected with the pistol and snatched it from Mike's hold. "I'll take that, Mike Black. Now stand aside and let me collect that which belongs to me."

As Sam turned back and went toward the straw, Mike ran around in front of him to bar his way.

"You stay back, Mr. Dodsworth!" Mike ordered.

"I'll count to three, Black," Sam growled, "then I'm pullin' this trigger. One—"

Annie emerged from behind the straw, holding her dress to her. "Go away, Sam! Ya ain't wanted here!"

"I knew ya was here, Annie, an' I knew what ya was up

57

to with this fella. It's your old man that should put a bullet through his head."

"I'm here 'cause I want to be," Annie exclaimed. "I love Mickey, an' I never could love you."

Sam fumed. "Two . . ."

Annie went to Mike. He tried to protect her with his body; but he faced Sam. Annie slid under his arm and got in front of Mike as Sam said, "Three."

Sam's coordination was slightly off. He pulled the trigger before he realized Annie was in the way of his target.

Annie fell limply into Mike's arms. He eased her gently onto the straw before he charged at Sam. In a moment Mike had the pistol and was frantically on his way to the bench where he had other bullets. Sam could tell that Annie had been badly wounded. He was suddenly frightened. Before Mike could reload the gun, Sam ran out the door.

"Mickey . . ." Annie cried.

No more had Mike reached the wounded girl and put his hand to her forehead than she breathed her last. Sightless eyes stared up at him. He wanted to cry, but his most pressing emotion was desire for revenge. Seeing there was nothing more he could do for Annie, he dashed to the door and practically ran head into Jennings.

The stiff butler looked beyond the man. He could see Annie and that she was bleeding. "You shot her?"

"No!" Mike fell against the doorsill and looked back at the motionless figure of Annie Duggan. "He did. The man who ran out shot her."

"What man?" Jennings asked. He put his hand to the gun and removed it from Mike's hand. "The gun has been fired, but it has been reloaded." He held it on Mike as he went to examine Annie.

"I tell you I didn't shoot her," Mike insisted. "I wrenched the pistol from the man who did."

"What man?" Jennings repeated. "Stay right where

you are while I have a look at the girl." He touched her. "She's dead. You killed her."

The accusation rang through Mike's head. He panicked. Jennings had never liked him. Now it was his word against the butler's. In that frightened moment, he thought of the consequences of what might happen if Jennings were to accuse him publicly of murder. If he wanted to, the butler could drag the Wellingtons into the matter; while he believed the Wellingtons would stand by him, the whole situation would reek of scandal and Mike would still stand accused of killing Annie Duggan. Then there was the matter of Tim Duggan. What sort of revenge might he seek, especially if Sam Dodsworth put pressure on him? Would Tim believe Mike? Even if Tim wanted to, would Sam Dodsworth permit it? Confusing thoughts bounded against his brain.

"Stay right there with your hands in the air," Jennings ordered as he took a closer look at Annie.

Self-preservation became paramount in Mike's thoughts. Even if Jennings was a good marksman, in that moment he was distracted; Mike might have a chance of escape. Swiftly he dashed from the stable and threw the bar across the outside of the door.

Running barefoot from the stable into the basement of the house, Mike went immediately to his room. He slipped into his good pair of boots, put on a blouse and got his money from the place where he had hidden it. His pulse was frantically pounding as he left the room and hurried toward the front of the lower floor of the house and out the service entrance. He could hear the sound of Jennings banging against the stable door.

Once in the street, Mike walked at a quick pace, but he tried to appear less terrified than he actually felt. His legs were trembling and a terrible gnawing sensation was in his stomach. For a few minutes he felt as if he were going to be sick.

Heading north on Broadway, Mike kept a steady

speed, hoping not to draw attention to himself. He tried to rationalize what had happened and determine what he must do. To run away would only be verification of his guilt; but not to run could place him in an awkward situation where he could not prove his innocence.

There was only one course he could take. He had saved enough money to purchase a railway ticket out of New York and still have enough to live on for a period of time. His first thought was to go West, where he could become lost in the wilderness of the frontier. He had often given consideration to such a venture, but going it alone presented him with many reservations. If he only had one friend with whom he could travel, or if he had married Annie, they could have joined up with a wagon train. A man could not even consider going West by himself, not unless he was of an entirely different nature than Mike.

Chapter 5

Second thoughts about running away began to plague Mike. Wouldn't it be better for him to go back to Tim Duggan and explain what had happened? But Mike didn't know the reason behind Tim's promise of Annie to Sam Dodsworth. And the more he thought about it, the more he convinced himself that Sam must have had a strong hold over Duggan—and probably still had.

Perhaps if Mike were to return to the Wellingtons, they would help him. Still how much could he trust Roderick Wellington, who was envious at best of Mike's youthful body, whole and exciting to his wife? Roderick had been outwardly friendly, but there was no guessing what depth of emotion ran against Mike in Wellington's mind. Thelma Wellington would be virtually helpless to Mike against her husband's wishes.

Mike considered various possibilities over a bucket of beer in a saloon near the train station. The first conclusion he reached was that he had to get out of New York as soon as possible. Then a picture of Thadius Phenwick came to his mind. Stuart Phenwick had been kind to him. Thadius had seemed to want to be his friend. Furthermore, he had developed a curiosity to want to see John Phenwick, who allegedly bore a resemblance to him. And he desperately wanted to meet the Doctors Ornby to seek their help. Before he finished the bucket of beer, he had decided to travel to Boston and look up the Phenwicks.

The Boston train left at 6 P.M. Mike was aboard it, riding coach. The monotonous clackity-clack of the wheels did not numb his thoughts until the train was well out of New York and moving steadily through Connecticut.

The tempo of the wheels over the tracks rekindled old questions in his mind, especially about his background, his past. Yet was who he was as important at that time as where he was going? Thoughts of death came to him. Chances were his own family had long since given him up for dead. And might he still not be hanged for the death of Annie Duggan? Would death be so awful? And, he wondered, if the soul continued on after death, would he then know who he had been before he was stricken with amnesia? Considering his amnesia, he was glad he had chosen to go to Boston since he had given much thought to the possibility of the Phenwick cousins, the doctors, helping him overcome his mental condition.

Boston had become a large, bustling city. Mike was surprised to discover that it was like New York in many ways. He remembered that the Phenwicks owned Medallion Enterprises, a large shipping firm with increasingly diversified interests. It seemed logical to Mike to attempt to locate the company at the waterfront.

The older Medallion buildings at the wharf were used for warehousing. Only a small office was kept there. Mike was instructed how to reach the principal headquarters up on Tremont Street.

As Mike headed in the direction he had been given, he was surprised when a carriage pulled up alongside him. The driver called to him, beckoning him to the vehicle.

"Did you want me?" Mike asked.

"The lady inside did," was the reply.

Mike stepped to the carriage door and squinted in. "Hello."

The door swung open. The lady's full skirt was spread over the seat. She was quite pretty with nice features. Elegantly attired, she sparkled with jewelry. "Why do you hesitate, John? Get in and I'll give you a lift," she said in a well-modulated voice.

"How do you do, ma'am," Mike said. "I appreciate the offer, but my name isn't John."

"Oh, come now." She leaned forward for a better look.

"My name is Michael Black," he informed her.

"It's been some time since I last saw John Phenwick," she commented. "I can see on second glance that you're not quite John Phenwick. But you do have a remarkable resemblance to him. Are you related to the Phenwicks?"

"I don't believe I am," Mike replied. "Are you?"

"I am the widow of Gordon Phenwick," she stated.

"Funnily enough, Mrs. Phenwick, I was headed toward the Medallion office in Tremont Street."

"Well then, Mr. Black," she said, "won't you get in and I'll instruct that you be driven there."

Millijoy Phenwick had become a grand lady, who seemed perfectly at ease with wealth and affluence. She ran her eyes seductively over the handsome young man as he sat beside her. Her interest in him was in no way disguised.

"You're not from Boston, are you? I can tell by the way you speak," Millijoy commented.

"I've recently come from—from New Jersey," Mike explained, thinking it best not to mention New York for the present.

"Nor do you sound to be from the South," Millijoy continued. "I'm too well aware of the way Southerners speak. Do you know the Phenwicks?"

"I've met both Stuart and Thadius Phenwick," Mike replied.

"Ah, then one day you must have Thadius bring you to call on me at Triumph House," Millijoy said. "Thadius is a dear boy. I've seen him only once since he returned from the war. He's changed—become a man in many ways. In other ways, he's still the little boy I first knew."

Mike thanked Millijoy for the ride and promised to come visit her if he could find the opportunity. The lady puzzled him. While she reminded him somewhat of Thelma Wellington, he had to admit that he had never before met her equal.

Thadius Phenwick welcomed Mike with a friendly greeting and immediately took him into the privacy of an inner office.

Mike explained the circumstance that had brought him to Boston.

"There's no reason why I shouldn't believe you," Thad said. "Although I must admit it would appear that circumstances were against you. Stuart is away at the present time, tending to business. He'll know better how to deal with this situation than I."

"Your brother John—?"

"Johnny's over at Cambridge, going to school," Thad replied. "I'm the adventurer, Johnny's the student. He'll be home on the weekend."

"I should like to meet him, since I was again today mistaken for him," Mike related.

"You must come to the house and meet my mother and other two brothers," Thad said a short time later. "Mother will be pleased to make your acquaintance. And I will be curious to see if she thinks you resemble Johnny. The fact is, when we first met I hadn't seen my brother for nearly two years. Since I've been back, and have seen him, I must honestly say I see only a vague similarity in your face and his. Johnny has changed. I suppose he says the same of me." He laughed.

Later that afternoon Mike accompanied Thad to

Peter House. It had been a warm day. The well-shaded house looked inviting.

Nancy Phenwick had not been warned of company. Gracious and outgoing, she soon made Mike feel at home. The lovely lady tried to read the question in her eldest son's face. "What is it, Thadius?"

"Do you notice anything about Mike?"

"Notice anything?" She shrugged. "He's quite handsome. Is that what you mean?"

Fifteen-year-old Paul Phenwick arrived at that moment. An eagerly enthusiastic lad, he went directly to his mother. "It's Lulubelle Abercrombie," he remarked, interrupting the conversation, "she's asked me to her house for supper tonight. I said I'd have to ask you first, although I was certain you would say yes."

"It's rude to interrupt when we have a guest, Paul," Nancy commented sternly, in the role of the proper Bostonian mother. "Where are your manners?"

Paul shrugged. "Since when are my brothers company?"

"One should take care not to be rude to one's brothers," Nancy explained.

Paul took a closer look at Mike. "Oh. I thought it peculiar for John to be home. You should have more light in here."

"Paul, this is my friend Mike Black," Thad introduced.

"You thought he resembled—?" Nancy questioned. "Yes, I can see where you might have thought that. Well, Mr. Black, since you look so much like my son, I suspect I should bid you welcome as one of the family—so to speak. You're certainly handsome enough that Johnny should be flattered to think you were mistaken for him."

"A mother cat can always tell her kittens from those belonging to another cat," Thad commented, "even when nobody else can."

"Meaning?" Nancy asked, raising her eyebrow. "Surely you're not suggesting I have feline qualities."

"It was only an example." Thad laughed. "Well, Paully, who is this Lulubelle Abernathy of whom you speak?"

"It's Abercrombie," Paul corrected his eldest brother.

"You know the Julius Abercrombies, don't you, Thadius?" Nancy asked. "I've known Minnie Abercrombie for years—that is, Mrs. Abercrombie."

"I'm afraid I don't, Mother," Thad returned. "You forget I've been away from Boston for some time."

"Obviously Paul is too anxious to dine with the young lady and her family," Nancy said, "to be congenial at our table tonight. If Mr. Black will take Paul's place—"

"Of course he will, won't you, Mr. Black?" Paul stated.

Mike smiled broadly. "I accept the invitation."

Later that evening Nancy suggested that Mike spend a while as guest in their house. There was sufficient room.

"I met a relative of yours today," Mike explained as he was shown to the guest room.

"A relative?" Thad questioned. "There are Phenwicks all over Boston. Or was it a Phenwick? I suspect there are actually more Ornbys here than there are Phenwicks."

"Ornbys?"

"I used to know the genealogy," Thad replied with a light ripple of laughter. "My great-grandmother adopted two children when my grandfather was a boy of ten or twelve: Uncle Edward and Aunt Jane. I forget what their real last names were. They became Phenwicks. Aunt Jane married a Dr. Ornby—do not ask me which one—and her son—Andrew, I believe it was—came to Boston. Several of his sons and grandsons have become doctors."

"Dr. Joseph and Dr. Augustus?" Mike asked.

"Yes, those are the two I know. How do you—?"

"Your—well—Stuart Phenwick mentioned they might be able to help me with my memory," Mike explained.

66

Thad laughed. "Stuart's my nephew. But don't try to figure it out, just take my word."

"All right." Mike laughed too.

"It's unfortunate you didn't arrive in Boston two days earlier," Thad said after assuring Mike he would take him the next day to meet both Joseph and Augustus Ornby.

"Why so?"

"Another of my nephews was here: Jim Phenwick from Savannah," Thad related. "Jim's just about my age. He recently married Miss Dorothy Wilkes of Charleston at the same time that my niece married Henry Ashton. Both my niece and her husband, the Ashtons, are from England."

"There are Phenwicks in England?"

"It would seem they're from all over the place, wouldn't it?" Thad laughed merrily. "I've nieces and nephews I've never seen. Cousin Ophelia—that's the new Mrs. Ashton— once aspired to be an actress like my half sister Joanna."

Mike suddenly had a startled expression.

"What is it?"

"That name, Ophelia, isn't it unusual?"

"My sister-in-law, half brother Joshua's wife, once aspired to be an actress," Thad explained. "Ophelia was the name of a Shakespearean character she portrayed. I suppose she just missed being called Juliet or Portia."

Quietly Mike repeated the name Ophelia as a picture momentarily flashed into his mind. It was of a ship.

"What is it, Mike?"

Mike explained the picture. "I suppose I've seen a ship called the *Ophelia*."

"Possibly. There's not a Medallion ship called that— yet. But I suspect Joshua is enough attached to his eldest daughter to name a ship after her one day. I hope you'll be comfortable in this room."

"What—? Oh yes, after the places I've slept in the past —that I can remember—this is practically like a palace,"

Mike responded, but his thoughts were busy trying to recapture the image of the ship that had entered his mind.

Next day as Thad and Mike were heading toward the offices of the Doctors Ornby, Mike interrupted a banal line of chatter with a question about Ophelia Ashton.

"Ophelia's a real beauty," Thad explained. "But she did undergo rather harrowing experiences—actually several. She and her brother were in transit, crossing the Atlantic, when their ship was blown off course by a hurricane—or at least a tropical squall—into southern waters and was fired upon by a Confederate vessel. She, Henry Ashton and a couple of other people ended up on a deserted island after several frightful days adrift. Ultimately they were picked up and Ophelia and Henry were taken prisoners to be held for ransom. Jim and Adam Truff—mostly Adam—managed to help them escape."

"And the others aboard the ship?" questioned Mike.

"I fear most of them were lost at sea," Thad said. "The first mate reached shore with some survivors, but to my knowledge, none of the others have been found. Tragedies at sea are common enough in peacetime. I came close to danger several times when I was in the navy. I don't like to think about it."

Augustus Ornby was away seeing patients at the hospital. Joseph was busy, but he would be able to make time to see his cousin and Mike Black. The kindly doctor listened carefully to Mike's story.

"And you absolutely do not recall anything that happened before you were found by Giddeon Phillips?" Joseph asked, stroking his beard.

"Nothing."

"Would you object to me trying to hypnotize you?" Joseph said.

"I don't know that I can be hypnotized. But please try."

Joseph was able to put Mike under, but the young man seemed to have a subconscious block as well to events that occurred prior to the time he was found by Giddeon Phillips.

"It's not a lost cause," Joseph commented after he had brought Mike back to consciousness. "But it's something we'll have to work with. Augustus has done more with this sort of thing than I. If you have time, we'll both examine you. Perhaps it would be best if we three—you, too, Thadius, if you like—were to get together of an evening. I've patients waiting and a very busy schedule. Tomorrow evening around eight would be good."

"I'm afraid it's a hopeless cause," Mike commented as they walked back to the Phenwick house. "Maybe I'm not meant to know who I was."

"What do you mean by that?" Thad questioned.

"Maybe it's Fate or Destiny," Mike commented. "I've thought that I might have lived some sort of terrible existence prior to losing my memory. If I had been headed in a wrong direction, leading the life of a criminal, for instance, perhaps the powers that be stepped in and changed the course of my life."

"You mean like guardian angels and that sort of thing?"

"Possibly." Mike stopped and stared into Thad's face. "Do you believe in Fate, Thad?"

"I don't know that I do. We were raised devout Christians. We have faith in the power of the Almighty."

"Do you actually, or are you only repeating what you've been taught you *should* believe?"

"A curious question."

"I may have been taught the same things," Mike said. "In that case, perhaps I'm fortunate to have lost the memory of such."

"I don't follow you."

"Everything I believe—even about myself and my existence—is based upon what I've been able to sort out for myself," Mike replied. "I've attended church with the Phillipses, as well as with Mrs. Wellington, but in most cases I had the feeling of being completely detached from

69

what the preachers had to say. Even Mrs. Wellington listened subjectively from attitudes drilled into her by her forebears from her childhood, perhaps her infancy. At what point does one begin to learn and comprehend anyway?"

"I still don't quite get what you're aiming toward."

"Take you, for instance. If you didn't know that Paul was your brother—that you had been in some way separated during childhood, and you were to meet years later, do you suppose you would know you were related?"

"I hadn't thought of that."

"You and Paul don't have a great resemblance to each other. Paul seems to resemble your mother while you, I suspect, look like your father. You've the Phenwick look that Stuart has."

Thad thought a moment. "I see what you're driving at."

"You were trained from childhood to know Paul as your brother. Yet you even mistook me for your brother John. Again, you had been taught through familiarity what your brother John looked like. It's the same thing with religion. You've been taught concepts of God and Jesus Christ—but are they truly your concepts, or are they those of your parents, relatives, friends, ministers and goodness knows who else that might have influenced you—especially during childhood? Whereas I've no memory of childhood lessons, therefore I can be objective in thinking of such things as Fate—and God, if you will. When I think this way, I wonder if I would not be better off to remain in the dark about my past."

"I wonder," Thad remarked as they drew near to the house, "if when your memory returns such a philosophy will be in conflict with what you were earlier taught."

"*If* it returns."

"It's an interesting theory," Thad mentioned. "Supposing, however, you were to discover that you had no sort of religious teaching as a child, wouldn't that negate your theory?"

70

"It might."

Thad and Mike continued their philosophical conversation into the night, exchanging thoughts, presenting hypothetical theories and possible answers, in the course of which they grew closer together as friends. Both young men were affected by the other's thoughts and opinions. Thad needed that sort of thing after being two years away from Boston and his grim adventures in the war.

The following night Joseph and Augustus Ornby received Thad and his new friend at their office. While the Ornby brothers had a certain similarity of features, they could have been mistaken for unrelated strangers if they had not been introduced as brothers. If he had a brother someplace, Mike wondered, and they were to meet one day, say twenty years from now, would either have an inkling that they both had been born from the same parents?

Augustus scrutinized Mike with keen, close-set, dark eyes. "If you never discover your true identity, Mike, you had better persuade Thad to adopt you as his brother. You've not met John yet, have you?"

"No, sir."

"You could easily take John's place," Augustus speculated.

"I think not," Mike returned. "From what I've heard of John Phenwick, he has a distinct personality all his own. Certainly he has an education that I could never duplicate in full."

"True. I stand corrected," Augustus said.

"But Mike does have a sharp wit," Joseph inserted, "not unlike John's."

"It's a matter of environment, then, isn't it?" Augustus returned.

"One man might have the same formal education as another," Mike added, "but he cannot have experienced the same personal events, nor is one apt to react in the same way to facts given him."

71

"Ah, yes," Joseph remarked. "He has you there, Aug. Take us, for instance. Our father gave us similar educations. But Augustus chose to spend a longer time at studying than I. Being older I returned to Boston to work with Father, while Aug remained abroad."

"Yet there is a hereditary factor inherent in each of us that is similar," Augustus inserted.

"But only vaguely, dear brother."

This time Augustus put Mike under hypnosis. Again the young man was only able to be taken back to the time he was found on the rocks by Giddeon Phillips. But in the course of regression, Mike went into minute picturesque detail of the events that had happened in New York.

"Do you have a wife somewhere, Mike?" Augustus asked while the subject was still under.

"No."

"Are you certain of that?"

"Yes."

"Where is your home? The home in which you were raised?"

"I don't know."

A pounding sound came on the front door.

"Who the devil—?" Joseph said softly and slipped from the room. He opened the door as noiselessly as possible.

Paul Phenwick was standing outside. Breathless and wearing an expression of urgency, he gasped out a question. "My brother and Mike Black are here, aren't they?"

"Why, yes, Paul. What is it?"

"They're looking for Mike."

"Who is?"

"The police."

"For what reason?"

"I overheard a conversation between a police investigator and Mr. Julius Abercrombie, who you know is on the police commission. I was calling on Lulubelle, who I find ever so nice. Anyway, I overheard that a warrant is out for Mike's arrest, that he had been trailed from New York to Boston. So far they don't know that he's staying at our house. I surmised it would be best if I came and warned what was happening."

"Good boy. You'll have to wait a few minutes. Mike is under hypnosis," Joseph informed him.

When Mike was conscious again, Paul repeated what he had told Joseph.

"I don't understand how they could have traced me here," Mike commented in reaction, "unless someone followed me from the Wellington house on that day Annie was killed."

"Then it would be best for you to get out of Boston as soon as you can," Thad suggested.

"Am I to always be a fugitive?" Mike questioned.

"Thad is right," Augustus said. "You have no way of proving your innocence. Perhaps Stuart can do something about the situation, but I can't see it would do you or anyone else any earthly good to have you put in custody and perhaps railroaded into a trial where you're judged guilty."

"Railroaded?" asked Mike. "How?"

"Think a minute," Thad said. "Sam Dodsworth is a veteran of the war, a hero, no doubt. Public sentiment at this time is with the men who have fought for the cause of democracy. It's your word against Dodsworth's. Be objective. Under the circumstance, whose word would you take?"

"I see."

"And if your Annie's father prosecutes, well—"

Mike was frowning. "Where could I possibly go?"

"Portland," Joseph said.

"Portland?"

"Portland, Maine," Joseph augmented. "Thad can take you by carriage to Wakefield tonight. There you can catch a train in case the Boston station is being watched."

"Tonight?"

"Joseph is right," Thad stated. "I'll go back now with Paul, pack your things and bring the carriage around to pick you up."

"In the meantime," Joseph stated, "I'll draw up a letter to introduce you to the Ornbys in Portland. Cousin Crandall operates the Medallion company. Cousin John lives at Falmouth House. He'll surely take you in until you can get settled. Once this blows over you can return to Boston and we'll continue where we've left off."

Speaking of railroading, Mike thought, but he said nothing. He nodded his head in agreement. Thad and Paul left. Joseph went to compose the letters. Augustus remained to attempt to draw Mike into further conversation.

Chapter 6

The night was dark, cloudy, with periodic misty interludes as the carriage sped toward Wakefield. They were practically the only travelers over the ten-mile stretch of road.

Arriving at Wakefield shortly after midnight, Thad went directly to the station, checked the train schedule to Portland, purchased a ticket and arranged for hotel accommodations near the small station since the train did not leave until morning.

"You needn't stay over, Thad," Mike protested. "You've done enough for me already."

"I *do* need to stay over. I'm far too tired to drive back to Boston tonight," Thad returned. "Besides I want to make certain you get safely aboard the train. I'm half-tempted to put the carriage in the stable and ride up on the train with you."

"That would be a useless waste of time," Mike said. "I can manage."

They went for a stroll about the town before retiring.

"I'll make arrangements to have a bank draft wired to you in Portland," Thad stated. "It may not be there until the first of the week, but it will give you sufficient money to operate on while you're there. I've only met my Ornby cousins in Portland once. They probably wouldn't remember me any more than I remember them. The only thing I do recall about that city is the monstrous old Falmouth House which was built by my great-grandmother. Many of the Ornbys have left Portland, I understand from Joseph, and I don't know of any Phenwicks there."

"I can't understand why you're being so kind to me, Thad."

"Why? Kindness was taught to me by my father," Thad replied. "You might say that is part of my religious heritage."

"I note a touch of sarcasm in your tone."

"Heaven forbid."

They both laughed.

"Seriously, I am concerned for your well-being, Mike. Maybe it's the resemblance you have to my brother that makes me feel a kind of kinship to you. I don't know what it is, I only know the feeling is there. And don't worry about the money. Maybe someday you'll be able to give me something in return. Whether you do or not is unimportant; I know that one receives for what he gives, and the gift doesn't always return from the person to whom the original gift was given."

"I feel inadequate . . ."

"Stop it. Feel adequate because you're my friend—or simply because you're another human being. Actually, you're doing me a favor by accepting my gift. A wise old sailor taught me that."

Mike was embarrassed, yet most appreciative of the deed as well as the friendship behind it. He would not feel quite as alone in the world from that time on, not as alone as he had felt in the past.

The two young men shared the same room in the hotel that was convenient to the rail station in Wakefield. The hotel was actually an old, renovated house. The two cots were comfortable enough considering the accommodations, but Thad had difficulty falling asleep. Shortly after he did, he was awakened by Mike's moaning and restless tossing.

"No! No!" Mike said loudly and flopped over onto his belly.

"Mike?"

No answer.

Thad was nearly able to fall off to sleep again when Mike mumbled incoherently. "What is it, Mike?"

Mike breathed raspily, heavily. "I can't find her."

"Can't find whom?"

Another long period of silence.

Just as Thad began drifting off again, Mike softly mumbled: "Ophelia . . ."

The next morning Mike was awake before dawn. He let Thad sleep until he had washed and dressed.

"Did you have nightmares last night?" Thad asked as they went to the station.

"I don't remember. Why do you ask?"

"You talked in your sleep." Thad explained what he had heard.

"Ophelia? That's queer. Why should I have mentioned that name?"

"Don't you recall that's my niece's name?"

"It is? I was thinking you had said it was Portia," Mike commented.

"No, Ophelia." Thad stared at him for a minute. "Her brothers are named Arnold and David."

Mike stared blankly at him, then cocked his head when it seemed that Thad was attempting to get a reaction from him.

"Arnold was lost at sea," Thad added.

"And David?"

"He's still at home with his parents. He was quite a bit younger."

The train was on time. The young men shook hands as Mike prepared to board. The steam puffed, the whistle blew and the wheels began to move.

Mike had a sudden thought. "Wasn't he called something else?"

"What?" Thad yelled back, running alongside the moving train.

"Wasn't he called something else?"

"Who?"

The train had begun to pick up momentum.

Mike's voice was lost in the sound of the train whistle.

"I can't hear you."

"Never mind."

Thad waved as he watched the train seemingly grow smaller as it blended in with the line of the tracks. Then he went to get the carriage to drive back to Boston.

Mike stood at the rear platform and gazed until he could no longer see Thad or the station building. Why did it seem he was always running? Was that to be the scenario of the rest of his life? What a dreadful thought! First New Jersey, then New York and now Massachusetts. Had his life before amnesia been the same? If only he knew.

A strange thought came to him. Perhaps he was running because some unseen force was attempting to lead him back to his origin. Could he have originally been from the state of Maine? In his condition, anything could be a possibility.

Before Mike left the rear platform as the train picked up speed, he felt deep regret for having to leave the hospitality of the Phenwicks of Boston. He had become close friends with Thad. Nancy had welcomed him as though he were another son. Even Paul and Daniel Louis had been outgoing as they strove to make him feel at home. Ironically he had never encountered John Phenwick, the one for whom he had been mistaken. How was it possible that two complete strangers could have a similar appearance? One day he would make a point of meeting John.

Two sparkling, nearly black eyes stared out from the second-floor window of the huge, ominous-appearing old mansion in Portland. It was situated high on the hill over-looking Back Bay. Dainty hands pushed aside the Irish lace curtains. A gentle spring rain had been falling for nearly an hour. The clouds were rapidly moving away and patches of blue were beginning to appear in the east. The window was open. The girl stood back just far enough that she could observe but neither be seen from below nor get wet. Long dark hair was braided and twisted into a net at the back of her head. The pretty face and well-shaped features might have been captured in Dresden china. She wore a low-cut mauve satin gown, trimmed with lace and pink ribbons. A tiny cameo hung at her throat.

Her younger brother had chanced by the open door to her room, saw her curious staring from the window and entered. He was fourteen, she was sixteen. They were the only children of the late John Frederick Ornby. Most of their life had been spent in that old house. They were each other's companion. The boy was bright-looking, but lacked the extraordinary beauty of his sister. His coloring was lighter and his eyes were a gray-blue.

"What do you see?"

"Oh, Freddie," his sister said, acknowledging his presence. "A cart is coming up the hill. It's Jake and he has a passenger."

"A passenger?"

"I suspect we're about to have a visitor."

"Can you see who it is?"

"Not from this distance, silly. Don't crowd me, Freddie. I was here first. Besides, this is my room, not yours."

The children watched as the cart pulled up to the front gate, stopped and let the passenger off. Mike walked around to pay Jake for his service and remained at the gate while the man turned the cart around and headed back down the hill. He was wearing a broad-rimmed hat and a whaler's slicker, which was all the protection he needed from the diminishing drizzle of rain.

Mike turned to look up at the monstrous old rambling house. Thad had explained about the eccentricities of his great-grandmother and her custom of building huge houses. Falmouth House appeared in need of repair. Weeds grew high around it and the ancient trees could stand a good pruning. He noticed the Irish lace curtains move on the second floor, but did not give it any but passing thought. Bolstering himself, he pushed open the large gate and shut it after he had entered.

"I can't tell much what he looks like with that big hat over his face," Freddie commented.

"He's tall—at least he's not short."

"What difference does that make?"

"And he carries himself well."

"Shall we go down and get a better look?" Freddie asked.

"Not until after he rings the doorbell. It wouldn't be proper. But we can stand at the bedroom door," his sister said.

The doorbell rang. The perpetually tired, heavy padding of Lilly Gore's footsteps could be heard going in the direction of the front door. The children went to the upstairs hallway.

Lilly Gore was in her mid-forties, a large woman who, upon first meeting, appeared to be mostly bosom. She wore a gray apron over her black dress and a gray cap to match, an appropriate costume for a domestic. She puffed and gasped for breath as she opened the door.

"Yes?" Lilly automatically wiped her hands on her apron.

"I was told this is Falmouth House," Mike said. "I've come to see Mr. John Frederick Ornby."

"You're too late," Lilly wheezed. "Mr. Ornby's been dead nearly three years. Ay-ah, he was killed in the war."

"Oh, I'm sorry to hear that. Is Mrs. Ornby in?"

"She's in, but I don't know that she's a-seeing."

"I have a letter from Dr. Joseph Ornby of Boston," Mike stated with a broad smile.

"I'll take the letter to Mrs. Ornby, but don't get your hopes up, young fella." Lilly rubbed her nose with the back of her hand, gave Mike a quick once-over and scuffed back down the hallway and out of sight.

"As soon as Lilly's in the next room, Freddie, you go down and see what he wants."

"Aren't you coming?" Freddie asked.

"Not until you find what he's after. It isn't proper for a young lady to be so outwardly curious."

Freddie chuckled as he skipped down the steps. A moment later he jerked open the front door.

"Mrs. Ornby—oh, I was expecting—"

Freddie grinned. "I'm Master Ornby. I'm the man of the house. You've come to see my mother?"

"I've recently come from Boston, where I was staying with Mrs. Nancy Phenwick and her sons," Mike explained. "I understand the Phenwicks are distantly related to you."

"What is your purpose for being here?" Freddie questioned.

"I believe I should discuss that with Mrs. Ornby."

"I said that I was the man of the house."

"Quite right." Mike was well aware of the importance of becoming acquainted with family members. It was certainly undesirable to antagonize any of them, especially a young lad like Freddie. "Dr. Ornby sent me to see your —that is—to be introduced to your family. I've recently arrived in Portland and don't know a soul here."

Lilly came padding back down the hallway. "Mrs. Ornby will see you in the sitting room. You show him the way, Freddie. I've got bread rising in the kitchen."

"My name is Michael Black—Mike. I take it, then, that you're Freddie Ornby."

"I am." Freddie smiled. "Come with me, Mike. What brings you to Portland?"

81

"Oh, that's a long story, my friend, a long story," Mike replied.

Sally Ornby wore black. Youthful beauty still lingered in her face, but lines of sorrow were well-etched there. Sad eyes stared at Mike and thin lips made only a faint attempt at smiling. She glanced up from Joseph's letter. "Mr. Black?"

"Mrs. Ornby." He bowed and tried to cover his nervous, awkward feeling. "I fear my arrival is most inopportune. Apparently your late husband's cousins in Boston were unaware of Mr. Ornby's departure."

"My husband had only casual communication with his family in Boston," Sally said. "Dr. Joseph and Dr. Augustus both have been to pay us a visit here at Falmouth House—but that was several years ago. Mr. Ornby went to Boston on two different occasions of which I'm aware. Undoubtedly he had closer contact with the doctors than I have had. Furthermore, in response to what Dr. Ornby has written herein, we have had little contact with the Phenwicks. Oh, there are portraits of ancient Phenwicks hanging about the house. I would have gladly had them packed into the basement, but Mr. Ornby was sentimental about his ancestry."

"May I extend my sympathy over the loss of your husband, Mrs. Ornby. Had I known I would not have come," Mike stated. "I have a letter to Mr. Crandall Ornby of the Medallion company, but I came directly here."

"Under other circumstances, I would offer you our hospitality, Mr. Black," Sally remarked, picking at her fingers as she did. "I fear we are the less affluent members of the Ornby family. Mr. Ornby made several bad investments. Frankly, I'm too proud to go to Mr. Ornby's cousin, Mr. Crandall Ornby. It is a personal matter.'"

"Mother, can't we ask Mike to take tea with us?" Freddie asked.

"Tea?" Sally looked absently at her son. "Why, I suppose we can do that. Lilly's making fresh bread."

"That would be most kind of you, Mrs. Ornby," Mike commented. "I've eaten little since morning. And it appears I will have to walk back to the center of the city."

"Very well, it is settled then," Sally said. "Won't you take a seat?"

"Thank you."

Sally looked beyond Mike toward the door. As he was preparing to sit opposite the woman, Mike turned back to see what had attracted her attention. The sixteen-year-old girl standing there was the loveliest creature he had ever seen.

"You've met my son, Frederick, Mr. Black," Sally mentioned. "May I present my daughter? This is Ann Rose."

"Miss Ornby," Mike nodded and went toward her with an extended hand.

"Mr. Black, it is my pleasure." She gently accepted his hand. "Mother calls me Ann Rose. I prefer just plain Ann, if you don't mind."

"Just as I prefer being called Mike."

Ann smiled sweetly. "I was standing outside the room and overheard that you've come from Boston and our cousins there."

"Yes, your cousins Ornby and Phenwick," Mike inserted.

"Ah, yes, the mysterious Phenwicks of Boston," Ann commented, moving to take a seat beside her mother. "It would be best, Mother, if you were to send Freddie now to inform Lilly that we will have tea."

"Yes, of course." Sally motioned to Freddie. "It will be a while. Hot bread and butter will be delightful—and the bread has to cook yet."

Freddie darted from the room.

"What brings you to Portland, Mr. Black?" questioned Ann.

"I hope to take a position at the Medallion company."

"I'm certain Cousin Crandall will take you on. The last time he came to visit, he complained of not having sufficient help," Ann related. "He doesn't come often."

"Cousin Joseph mentioned in the letter that you are interested in genealogy, Mr. Black," Sally said, folding the letter and placing it on the table beside her.

"He did?" Mike looked surprised. "Dr. Joseph hadn't mentioned he was including such information."

"Then you're not interested in genealogy?" Sally questioned.

"Well, I am in a way. You see, I consider Thadius Phenwick to be my best friend and he mentioned on several occasions that he would like to know more about the Portland aspect of his family," Mike contrived. "Naturally, I told him I would scout about and see what information I could get for him. That's the extent of my interest in genealogy."

"If Cousin Thadius—he is our cousin, isn't he?—is so interested in the Ornbys of Portland, why doesn't he come himself?" asked Ann. "Furthermore, if you and Cousin Thadius are such good friends, why didn't you remain in Boston with him?"

"Really, Ann Rose, that is a personal matter which should not be your concern," Sally scolded.

"Perhaps one day Thad will come to Portland." Mike stared from Ann to Sally, then glanced back as Freddie returned. "May I confide in you?"

"If you wish, Mr. Black." Sally glanced only briefly at Freddie before she turned her gaze back to Mike.

"I am suffering from amnesia. My past is a complete mystery to me further back than a year ago," Mike explained.

"How terrible!" exclaimed Ann.

"Do you feel you have some distant connection with the city of Portland, Mr. Black?"

"No, not necessarily, Mrs. Ornby. Sometimes I feel like

a leaf that is caught in the wind; I simply go where it carries me," Mike said. Then he laughed. "Don't think me peculiar. I use that as an example simply because that is how I feel at times. Perhaps I'm willing to accept a certain destiny—I can't really say. But I hope that circumstance and the higher powers will somehow lead me back to a point of origin."

"You don't remember anything about your past?" questioned Freddie. "Then how do you know your name?"

"I don't know it. Mike Black is simply a name I've taken as a means of identification."

"How fascinating," Ann declared, sitting forward on her chair. "Oh, that's very interesting. Life must be a complete adventure for you."

Sally glared at her daughter. Ann was becoming too absorbed in the man. "If you'll excuse me, Mr. Black, I wish to change for tea. Ann Rose, come along with me."

"Aren't I dressed properly for tea?"

"I wish you to help me change."

"Very well, Mother." Ann rose. "Don't tell anything more about yourself until I return, Mr. Black."

"Ann Rose!"

"Yes, Mother."

Ann glanced back at the man and smiled as she glided from the room in the company of her mother.

"Mother has not been herself since—well, since we received word about our father," Freddie explained. "We all stay pretty much to the house."

"Sealed off from the outside world?"

"I think that is how Mother would like it to be."

"And what of your education?"

"I go to school. So does Ann—at least she did. Mother keeps her at home to be with her," Freddie stated. "We can't afford to keep servants any more—only Lilly, and that's because she works for practically nothing. We have some money, but we must be frugal. I'll work at the

85

Medallion office this summer—and, if I'm acceptable, Cousin Crandall may permanently take me on."

"Maybe we'll be working side by side, Freddie."

"That would be something, wouldn't it?" Freddie laughed. "Would you like to see the portraits Mother mentioned?"

"The portraits? Oh yes, the Phenwicks."

Freddie led Mike across the entrance hall to the music room. The interior was musty-smelling and appeared to be rarely used. Part of the furniture was covered and the windows were tightly closed. Attention immediately went to the large portrait hanging opposite the door.

"By the style of the dress, I suspect that is one of the older ancestors," Mike commented as he eyed the imposing portrait.

"She was the first Phenwick woman to live in America," Freddie related. "Her name was Augusta. I recall old Lydia Ornby telling tales about her. I was very young at the time. Ann could tell you better than I. She has an excellent memory." He glanced up at Mike. "Oh."

"Don't feel bad," Mike said with a laugh. "I have an excellent memory too, for as far back as I can remember." He looked up at the likeness of Augusta Phenwick. A frown crossed his handsome brow. "I've seen two portraits similar to this one in Boston. I suppose they're all copies of the original."

"Cousin Kate Cathcart has the original at Phenwick House in Greenfield," Freddie explained. "That was the one painted by Clayton."

"Clayton?"

"I don't know his last name." Freddie beamed mischievously. "Didn't you know? We have a ghost at Falmouth House. Don't tell Mother I told you. She doesn't like people to know."

"A ghost?"

"Yes. Clayton. He's only seen on the third floor or down in the basement," Freddie said. "I've encountered

86

him—well, I think I did—just once. But I've had some awfully spooky feelings when I've been upstairs—or down below. Ann claims to have seen him on several occasions, but I think she exaggerates."

"How strange, a ghost."

"Cousin Crandall believes that because of the ghost none of the other Ornbys would have Falmouth House as a gift," Freddie stated. "But my father was raised here and used to brag that he and Clayton were great friends. Well, that may or may not be, since I suspect Ann got her tendency to exaggerate from Father."

Mike found the statement humorous. "And you didn't inherit that tendency?"

"Well—perhaps, but not too much."

Tea was served at four.

Ann kept staring at Mike, then quickly looked away whenever he would turn his attention to her. Rarely had she had the opportunity to be in the presence of handsome young men. And there was something about Mike that had captured her interest.

"Have you thought of selling the house?" Mike asked after he had finished the third roll offered him.

"Oh, I couldn't sell Falmouth House," Sally stated. "My husband was born here."

Mike looked to Freddie, who pointed upward, indicating the third floor.

"But isn't it far too large for you to take care of?" Mike questioned. "Surely the three of you and your house-keeper must rattle around in this place."

"We keep much of it closed off," Sally returned.

"Couldn't you rent out rooms?"

"Who would come all the way up this hill to find a room when there are sufficient accommodations in town?" Sally asked.

"It was a thought." Mike smiled, suddenly feeling un-easy. "It's time I was preparing to find me a room for the night."

"Couldn't Mike—?" Freddie started to ask.

Sally scowled. "Mr. Black will have to be hurrying along then. It's mostly a downhill walk."

"Yes, I observed that it was as we came up the hill," Mike said. "It's been a pleasure meeting you folks and taking tea with you."

"You will come again, won't you, Mr. Black?" Ann asked.

"I don't like to come uninvited."

"We don't give invitations, Mr. Black," Sally said coldly.

"But you will be welcome anytime you care to drop by," Ann included. "Won't he, Mother?"

Sally thought a moment. "Why, yes, I suppose so."

"You've got weeds that need hoeing and trees that need cutting," Mike commented. "Perhaps on my days off you'll allow me to come and tidy up around the place. I enjoy working out of doors. And you can repay me with a hot meal, if you like."

"That would be a wonderful idea, wouldn't it, Mother?" Ann questioned.

"And I can help Mike," Freddie declared.

Sally didn't like the idea. There was something about the man that disturbed her. Was it because she was reacting to him because he was a desirably handsome young man and she had been widowed for three years? Or was it because she detected an expression in her daughter's face that worried her? "We'll see."

Mike took Sally's hand and bowed low to kiss the back of it. "Thank you for your hospitality, Mrs. Ornby. I hope I haven't disrupted your routine of things."

"Not at all, Mr. Black. You're welcome," Sally returned. "And, if you like, once you're settled, you may come and help tidy up the yard."

"That would be my pleasure."

"Freddie will see you to the door."

"Miss Ann," Mike said as he took the girl's hand and

placed a kiss on the back of it, "I must say I am already delighted that I have come to Portland. I am honored to have been in your company this afternoon."

Ann smiled sweetly. She wanted to say something. But after flickering her glance toward her mother, she thought better of saying anything.

"He's right, Mother, we could rent rooms," Ann said as Freddie showed Mike to the door.

"It would be too much trouble," Sally returned. "Besides, we're not destitute yet."

"We could let a room to Mr. Black—"

"That would be out of the question."

"Or the old gardener's house which hasn't been used in years."

"Impossible, Ann Rose."

"Why?"

"Because he is a virile young man, and you—well, I know best."

"Mother! What a thing to say!" Ann stared hard at Sally.

Sally sighed. "It's inevitable. You're becoming a young woman and there's not much I can do about it. But I'll not put temptation in your way, nor will I encourage you growing up too soon."

Ann stared deeply into her mother's eyes until she could no longer stand the tension. Abruptly she turned and ran from the room.

"Ann Rose—?" Sally sighed. That terrible empty feeling she knew so well returned and she sat back in the chair.

"I'll walk part of the way with you," Freddie suggested as they reached the gate.

"That would be kind of you, but it's not necessary," Mike replied.

"You mustn't think badly of Mother," Freddie said as he walked beside the man. "She's been through a lot."

"I don't think ill of her. She has every right to be

cautious. After all, for all she knows, I could have myself written the letter allegedly from Dr. Joseph Ornby."

"Did you?"

"No."

"Well then—"

"I'm a stranger in your midst," Mike said. "In fact, I'm still very much a stranger to myself."

They walked in silence for a few minutes.

"Will you get in touch with me and let me know where you're staying?" Freddie asked. "I have a feeling that we will become good friends, don't you?"

"I hope so, Freddie, I do hope so."

Chapter 7

Crandall Ornby was a man of forty-two. Bald with the exception of a fringe of brownish blond hair in a horse-shoe shape about his head, he had small features which didn't seem quite right for his head. Paunchy, with a tendency to accumulate weight around his hips, he none-theless attempted to walk with dignity and authority. His thick moustache connected with his sideburns, and he wore tiny eyeglasses only when they were absolutely necessary. He looked over the top edge of the eyeglasses after reading the letter he had been given.

"I know Joe Ornby quite well," Crandall said, reaching for a cigar. "I have spent time in Boston. Most of my dealings have been with Stuart Phenwick, and twice I've been to London to do business with my cousin Joshua. You wouldn't know of the London Phenwicks, I suppose."

"No, I'm certain I don't," Mike returned.

"Joe wants me to give you a job. What can you do?" asked Crandall.

"I've been a fisherman, a water carrier, a stableman and a—well, general handyman," Mike explained. "I may have done other things."

"Joe writes that you're suffering from amnesia," Crandall mentioned as he scanned the written words on the paper. "I trust that's not a kind of contagious disease."

"I've a loss of memory," Mike related.

"Oh yes, I was certain I had encountered the word somewhere." Crandall chuckled to cover embarrassment. "I'm not one of the more studious Ornbys, but I do well in business. What choice did I have? The Medallion company fell into my lap and I had to learn to operate it and make it pay, or lose it." He studied Mike. "You look strong enough. Can you cut wood and drive nails? We construct ships, you know. With the fatalities of war, there is presently a demand for more vessels. I need carpenters. Are you interested?"

"I'm willing to learn anything," Mike replied.

"Good. Then you can begin work tomorrow," Crandall stated. "Do you have a place to stay?"

"I've taken a room nearby, a short walk from here."

"Then you have some money."

"Yes, thank you."

"From the way you speak," Crandall said, "I suspect you have leadership ability. I'll keep my eye on you. One day you'll meet Mrs. Ornby, my wife. I trust her judgment. If she's impressed with your skill, I may consider you for a better position. But it's best to work a season or two with the other men so that you learn the work."

"I enjoy hard work, sir," Mike commented.

"Good. Then you'll be here at seven in the morning." Crandall waved his hand as if dismissing the young man. Then, after Mike was gone, he rose from behind his desk and went to the window to watch Mike make his way up the street.

Mike quickly learned what was required to handle the job he had been given. Furthermore, he curiously observed what others did. Soon he was helping out wherever he was needed. He could lift as well or better than most of the men and he was always fast to give assistance before it was asked for. The men respected him, looked up to him with quiet admiration. He made friends with many of them and encouraged them to find ways to improve their work.

Six weeks after Mike had been hired at Medallion, Crandall Ornby returned to his office after an inspection tour to discover he had a visitor. The clerk had announced that Mrs. Ornby was waiting to see him. He was surprised to see not his wife, but Sally Ornby waiting in his private office.

"Sally?" he questioned. "Excuse me, my hands are dirty."

"Cousin Crandall."

"What brings you down to the wharf?" he asked as he rinsed his hands in a basin of water. "I regret I haven't had time lately to come and call on you, Sally. Benita was saying just the other day that we hadn't heard from you in some time. I thought she was going to invite you for tea."

"Your wife did send around a note about tea. I didn't accept the invitation," Sally said. "Mr. Ornby, I've worn widow's weeds quite long enough, don't you think?"

"I should have thought you would have cast those silly things off long before this," Crandall returned. "With all due respect to late Cousin John Frederick, a few weeks of mourning seems to me to be quite sufficient. You're still an attractive woman. Were I in your place, I would be considering another marriage."

"You're a man, Mr. Ornby. It's quite a different matter for a lady. Besides, I have two children who require my attention—and, I might add, my affection," Sally explained.

"Ah, dear Annie and Frederick."

"Ann Rose is becoming quite a young lady."

"I must come and meet her," Crandall stated. "Perhaps I can introduce her to some proper young men of social background. At the present time, however, there is an abundance of eligible young ladies. It's always that way after a war where so many men have been killed."

"I hadn't come to you with concern over Ann Rose."

"Of course not. Then what is it, Sally?"

"I'm desperately in need of funds, Mr. Ornby," Sally admitted. "I've no one else to turn to in my plight."

"I can arrange for you to have a loan against your Medallion stock. I regret it isn't paying you larger dividends at the present time." He lightly touched his moustache as another thought came to him. "Why don't you try to sell Falmouth House? Surely you and your children don't need all that room."

"My husband was very fond of Falmouth House," Sally stated. "I don't believe he would want me to dispose of it."

"But you can't live there forever," Crandall protested. "Why, once your children are grown and married, you'll be all alone in that old monster."

"That is not the case. You know John Frederick in his will left the house to Ann Rose—not to me. Those were my wishes. We had discussed it. It's her house, not mine. Which brings me to the second request I wish to make of you, Mr. Ornby." She lowered her head as she attempted to muster courage. "I would like you to introduce me to some respectable older man—that is, a man of affluence —preferably a widower—"

"Ah, I see." Crandall smiled broadly and smoothed his moustache. "There are not that many wealthy men in Portland. I'll speak to Mrs. Ornby about the matter. Benita dallies among society far more than I." He cleared his throat. "Believe me, I don't want Falmouth House under any circumstance, but I'll use it for collateral in return for a loan. Something can be arranged."

"That's very kind of you, Cousin Crandall."

"How soon do you need the cash?"

"Immediately."

"Ah. Well, in that case, why don't you wait here and I'll go fetch my banker to bring you funds and the necessary papers to sign. After that is taken care of, we'll discuss the other matter."

Crandall felt more compassion than responsibility for his cousin's widow. He would be as generous as he could possibly be with her. Yet he was shrewd enough a businessman that an out-and-out gift of money was out of the question. He did not want to be seen at the bank with Sally for fear that word of it would get back to his possessive wife. And there had been a time when Benita Ornby had been jealous of her husband's interest in Sally.

After waiting ten minutes in Crandall's office, Sally became restive. She rose and paced. Finally she decided to leave the cigar-smoke-permeated room to get a breath of fresh air. She wandered through the building where other offices were, then went outside in the direction of the docks and the construction area.

An autumn chill was in the air, but it was not uncomfortably cold. She stood where she could observe the construction of a ship's hull. The actual work was being done in a large shed-like building.

The sight of the men interested Sally. She stared at them, not realizing that she was being observed.

"It is you, Mrs. Ornby," Mike exclaimed as he stepped to where she was standing. He wiped his forehead with his shirt sleeve. "You must excuse my appearance."

Sally blinked. "I don't believe—why, it's you, Mr. Black."

"I'm pleased you remembered."

"I thought you would have come to call on us before this."

Mike smiled. "I was of the impression that you weren't too anxious to have me return to Falmouth House."

"What ever gave you that notion?"

"Your attitude, Mrs. Ornby." Mike ducked his head.

"Like any mother, I'm protective of my children," Sally stated.

"And you have your suspicions of me, is that the case?"

"You came to us a stranger."

"Has time made me any less a stranger?"

95

"The fact that you're successfully in the employ of my late husband's cousin seems to make you less of an alien, as it were," Sally said. "I think I should tell you my attitude has altered since we last met—out of necessity it has had to be revised."

"May I ask what you mean by that?"

"I'm putting away my widow's weeds, Mr. Black."

"Of necessity?"

"You might say that. Even a mother robin takes measures to see that her young are properly nourished."

"I should think Miss Ann Rose and Master Frederick would not flourish too greatly on worms."

Sally laughed. "You have an interesting sense of humor."

"Sometimes crude—"

"But it shows you do have a light side to your disposition," she commented. "Am I keeping you from your work?"

"As a matter of fact, you are."

"Then I must excuse you," Sally said. "Please come to Falmouth House to call on us, Mr. Black. I assure you I'll not be as inhospitable this time."

Mike strode forward after saying goodbye to Sally, aware he was being watched. He wanted to win her approval as a person without making himself too attractive to her. Still he knew he would have to obtain Sally's consent before he would be permitted to get better acquainted with Ann. Why were older women so often attracted to him, he wondered, as if they were magnetized to him?

The man directing the hoist had not seen Sally standing where she was until the bundle of canvas began to swing. Before she could be warned, Sally stepped sideways into the range of the bulky parcel. The man yelled. It was too late.

Moments later Mike carried Sally from the construction area. Compassionately he placed her on a bench in

96

a reclining position and examined for broken bones. Orders were given to a young boy to fetch a wet cloth.

"What's going on here?" Crandall questioned as he arrived with the short, stout banker.

"Mrs. Ornby wandered out into the construction area," Mike informed him, "and became the target of a swinging bundle of canvas. I don't believe she's severely hurt, just knocked unconscious."

"Your wife, Crandall?" the banker asked.

"No, the wife of my late cousin, the lady of whom I spoke to you," Crandall replied. "She'll have to be gotten to a doctor."

"Or the other way around, Crandall," the banker suggested.

"What was she doing in the construction shed anyway?"

Mike shrugged. Instinctively he knew the answer.

Sally was only stunned. A doctor was not necessary. The loan arrangement was made.

Two days later Sally received an invitation to dinner at the home of Crandall and Benita Ornby. At the time Sally thought it unusual that her children had not been included. Then it occurred to her that her cousins by marriage had definite reasons for not asking the children.

On the day of the dinner party, bundled in their warmest clothing, Ann and Freddie Ornby took the buggy to town to shop for a few needed items. Among other errands, they were to pick up a cape which Sally had had tailored.

"While we're here," Freddie suggested, "why don't we stop by the Medallion office and see if Cousin Crandall will consider letting me work for him on Saturdays?"

Ann smiled, as she suspected her brother had somehow picked up her thoughts. She had been attempting to come up with a reason to stop by the Medallion company. The best she could think of was to thank Cousin Crandall personally for the loan he had made to her mother. She had other motives.

"Lovely! Absolutely lovely!" Crandall exclaimed as he

viewed Ann. "I always believed you to be an attractive child. You're hardly a child any more, are you?"

"I turned seventeen in October," Ann replied, smiling brightly.

"I'll be fifteen in December—the fourth," Freddie stated. "And I would like to work here at Medallion on Saturdays until next summer. Then I'd like a regular job."

"Well now, I believe that can be arranged, Cousin Frederick," Crandall said. "And what can I do for you, Cousin Ann Rose?"

"At what age do you think it proper, Cousin Crandall," Ann asked, "for a young lady to begin to think about marriage?"

"I should imagine she begins to think about it around the same time she realizes she is developing into womanhood," Crandall said wryly. "But I would say it was proper about the same time she meets a young man who is interested in her."

"I stopped going to school at the time of the death of my father," Ann explained. "We've stayed pretty much to Falmouth House. How does one go about meeting a suitable young man? I have to ask this of you, Cousin Crandall, because Freddie here is the only other male relative I have—that is, close male relative who lives in Portland."

"I was speaking to your mother about just such a matter recently," Crandall related. "But she was of the opinion that you were still too young to consider such things."

"Perhaps I'm too young to marry, but I don't think I'm too young to look around and consider the matter. Do you?"

"Ah, dear Ann Rose," Crandall commented as he took her hand. "I regret I haven't a handsome son just a year or two older than you. That would be the solution to all of your family's problems, wouldn't it? I mean, if you were to marry one of my heirs— Well, that's not possible, so I don't even know why I'm mentioning it."

"I hadn't seen you for so long, Cousin Crandall," Ann

said, "that I thought it would be a good idea to get reacquainted. Now surely you'll have a thing or two to speak to Freddie about concerning his new position. If you don't mind, I'll just browse around."

"Yes. It's not wise for you to go out into the construction area," Crandall warned, "but if you do, watch yourself. Remember that is where your mother had that slight accident."

"I'll be careful, Cousin Crandall." Ann smiled sweetly and left the office.

"I must say I can't get over how your sister has grown up, Frederick," Crandall stated. "She has become a real beauty."

"She's the same old Ann that I've always known."

"Yes, but you are too near to the forest to see the trees, lad." Crandall laughed. "I should think it would not be difficult at all to find a nice, handsome, wealthy husband for your sister."

"And what if she wants to marry for love?"

Crandall frowned. "If I were a young lady and in her position, I would learn how to love wherever opportunity knocked."

"Yes, Cousin Crandall, but you're not a young lady." Freddie smiled. "What sort of position will you have for me?"

Ann sauntered through the cold hallway as if the temperature were several degrees warmer. She had one goal in mind. Her attitude of anticipation seemingly kept her from noticing the cold as she stepped into the construction shed. The noise was deafening. Curiously she walked around examining various aspects of the activities. She obviously attracted attention as the men slowed their work to ogle her.

"This is no place for a woman!" a man shouted. "Go on, get out of here! These men have to work and it's dangerous for them to be distracted!"

Ann smiled back at the sound of the man's voice. She waved and started to retreat.

A strong hand touched her shoulder and propelled her about.

"It *is* dangerous—" Mike stopped in mid-sentence. "Miss Ornby?"

"Mr. Black?" She tried to sound surprised.

"Your mother was struck when she came in here not long ago," he said.

"Yes, I know. And she was carried to protection by you, wasn't she?"

"Yes. I did what I could."

"Why haven't you come to Falmouth House to call?"

"Let's not stand here. Come back toward the offices."

Ann permitted him to lead her in the suggested direction.

"You didn't answer my question. I thought you were going to come and hoe weeds and prune the trees," Ann said, her eyes holding steady on his face.

"I've been working long hours. And I was afraid I might not be welcome in your home."

"But you should have known you would be welcomed by both Freddie and me," she commented. "We have so few—if any—friends."

"Then I apologize for not coming to call," he sighed. The closeness and the beauty of the young lady caused him to become self-conscious of his own dirty appearance. "You must forgive the way I look, Miss Ann."

"You can't help being as handsome as you are," she returned.

"I don't mean that. I refer to my dirty condition."

"You are a working man, are you not?"

"Yes, Miss Ann."

"Fact is, I hadn't noticed you weren't absolutely immaculate."

"You hadn't?"

Her eyes stared deeply into his. "Mike—"

100

"Yes, Miss Ann?"

"My mother—that is," she swallowed. "My mother is going out for the evening tonight. It's Saturday. You won't have to work tomorrow. My brother and I would be pleased if you would come to call on us. We'll have a little supper fixed for you—we have to dine anyway."

"I believe that can be arranged—if you're certain your mother won't mind," Mike said.

"Why should she mind?" Ann questioned. "Why, with Freddie present, we will be properly chaperoned."

"Were we not chaperoned, you could rest assured that I would be a perfect gentleman," Mike returned.

"I should think so. You strike me as quite a person of good breeding and manners. But I suppose one cannot judge the book by the cover, can one? You've probably been much of a lady's man before you came to Portland —and perhaps you are here, too."

"Not here, no," he denied. "But I confess I am not totally inexperienced around ladies. I don't say that to be boasting, merely to let you know that I have a normal interest in people of the opposite gender from myself. As for such activity in Portland, you may rest assured that I've led a chaste existence."

"I hadn't expected such a confession, Mike."

"I hadn't intended to make it." He laughed.

"I suppose you've come close to falling in love, haven't you?"

Mike blushed. "If you must know, there was a girl in New York—her name was Annie, too."

"Annie?" She stepped away from him. "Did you love that Annie?"

"I was quite fond of her. She died in my arms of a bullet wound. I thought in that moment that I must have been in love with her. And since, I've considered my feelings for her. She was no lady, only a scullery girl. I was lonely and she seemed to be very much interested in me."

"Like I am?" asked Ann.

101

"I beg your pardon."

"Didn't you know? Couldn't you tell?"

"I—well—I had hoped—"

"Had you?"

"Yes. Oh yes, Miss Ann."

Her look was gentle, reassuring. "Then you *will* come to see us this night, won't you, Mike?"

"It will be my pleasure."

"Mike—does it bother you that my name is Ann, too?"

"No. I'm rather partial to the name."

"You may call me Annie, if you like."

"I prefer knowing you as just plain Ann for the time being."

"I must go back and find my brother. Until tonight."

"Ann—"

"Yes?"

"Thank you for the invitation, it's most appreciated."

Ann gently laughed as she moved away from him. It didn't matter to her that Mike Black wasn't a rich man, or that he was a common laborer. She had a quiet confidence in him. Why? She couldn't explain. She only knew that she was very much attracted to him, and that her thoughts had lingered over him since their first meeting.

Mike was in a daze as he went back to work. Why hadn't he gone to call at Falmouth House? What had he feared? Reproach? His thoughts had almost constantly been on Ann. Several times he had had the opportunity to make the acquaintance of different young women in town who were attractive enough, but Ann was on his mind, deep in his consciousness. While he was plagued with remembrances of Annie Duggan and her tragic end, he could put such visions from his mind by replacing them with images of Ann Ornby. Occasionally he thought of Thelma Wellington. She had been good to him. He knew that she loved him; but he also knew he could never have loved her.

Although he had had strong feelings for Annie Duggan, now he knew that he was capable of falling in love. He put thoughts of the dead Irish girl from him and considered only his emotions for Ann Ornby.

Chapter 8

A carriage arrived at 5 P.M. at Falmouth House. The driver went to the door. Sally was waiting. She wore a brown velvet, full-skirted dress trimmed with soft lemon-colored ribbons. More extravagant-looking than she had appeared in years, Sally was filled with anticipation. Although the sight of Ann and Freddie reminded her that she was a mature woman, she felt herself quite a girl again.

"I have no idea how late I'll be tonight," Sally gushed. "And should it snow or do anything out of the ordinary weatherwise, I may just spend the night with Cousins Crandall and Benita."

"Do enjoy yourself, Mother," Ann encouraged, "and don't worry yourself about us."

"Yes, Mother, we'll manage," Freddie echoed.

The carriage door was held for Sally to enter. A hand reached from within it to assist her. Then she sat on the forward riding seat and gazed into the extraordinarily well-formed face of a gentleman. He was slender with a fine upright posture. A dark beard, speckled with gray, and heavy eyebrows gave his face character. Gray-green eyes twinkled as a smile twisted on his lips, higher on the left than on the right, and teeth were exposed.

"Mrs. Ornby?" he said. His voice had a fine timbre. "Permit me to introduce myself. I am Zebidiah Robbins.

Since I live a short distance from here, your cousins asked if I would be obliging and escort you to their home."

"I hadn't expected—" Sally demurred, unable to gaze too long at the radiant expression on his face. The carriage was shadowed. She could only imagine how he would appear in broad daylight.

Zebidiah Robbins motioned for the driver to go ahead. "I must say that Crandall was quite right; I am impressed with your beauty, Mrs. Ornby. I, like yourself, have been without the company of a member of the opposite gender for twenty-seven months."

"A widower?"

"Yes." He smiled. "I have four motherless children."

Sally returned his smile as a twitter of excitement went through her. "Are you an associate of Cousin Crandall?"

"I handle certain investments for Mr. Ornby."

Sally was so busy being impressed by Zebidiah Robbins that she neglected to recognize Mike Black when the carriage passed him as he trudged up the hill toward Falmouth House.

"Do you think Mother will be too upset," Freddie asked, "when she learns that we've entertained Mike tonight?"

"Why should she be concerned?" Ann returned. "After all, we are simply being neighborly. Poor Mike, all alone in Portland. And here Christmas is nearly upon us. We're doing a most Christian thing by having him come for supper."

"Ann?" Freddie cocked his head as he scrutinized his sister. "Are you up to something?"

"Why, what ever gives you that notion?"

"That look in your eyes and that silly smile on your lips," he commented. "You like Mike, don't you?"

"So clever of you to have guessed."

"Did you put Cousin Crandall up to inviting Mother tonight?"

"I may have made a suggestion." Ann laughed merrily.

"And I'll tell you something more. I even spoke to Kathy Robbins regarding the supper party tonight—and she encouraged her father to be present."

"Surely you don't think Mother should marry again," Freddie protested.

"If she doesn't," Ann said, "you and I may end up being an old bachelor and an old maid, my dear brother. Mother depends on us too much for her own emotional outlet. You'll understand what I mean when you're older."

The doorbell rang and Freddie was sent to answer it. The boy was perplexed; his sister's words disturbed him. Still when he opened the door to Mike Black, Freddie's apprehensions temporarily disappeared.

"How are you, Freddie, old boy?" Mike asked as he removed his slicker and overshoes. "Light flurries of snow have begun to fall. The sky was black at three this afternoon. We may be in for a bit of a storm."

"It's December. Storms do happen," Freddie returned, helping him.

"I saw a coach leave."

"It's Mother gone to Cousin Crandall's," Freddie informed him. "It's just to be the three of us."

Mike had his arm about Freddie's shoulder when the two went into the sitting room. Ann was wearing an attractively designed pink velvet dress. Her hair was fixed in long finger curls that hung down around the sides of her head. She couldn't have looked more radiantly beautiful.

"Ah, Mike," she exclaimed and glided toward him as if her feet were on wheels. "Had you arrived five minutes earlier, you would have met Mother."

"The carriage passed him as he was coming up the hill," Freddie volunteered.

"Will you have a glass of wine, Mike?" Ann asked.

"Should we?" Freddie questioned.

"Of course. We're having a party."

"A party?"

"Your birthday party, Freddie!" Ann exclaimed. "Surprise!"

Lilly Gore had been warned that Mike was to be a guest for dinner. Ann had had the servant swear to secrecy about it. The older woman complied because Ann had warned that Sally might not go to Crandall Ornby's if she knew Mike was expected. And Ann had also let the older woman in on the fact that Zebidiah Robbins was also going to be at Crandall's.

Dinner was pleasant enough. A special dessert had been prepared in honor of Freddie's fifteenth birthday. The three young people had a good time, telling stories and playing games. Ann passed the wine around several times until everyone was feeling light-headed and carefree.

Unused to wine, since it was rarely served at Falmouth House, Freddie began getting drowsy about seven-thirty. He vainly tried to keep from yawning. As the three visited in the sitting room and Mike told about his past experiences as far back as he could remember, Freddie's eyes slowly slid shut and he was soon breathing heavily in sleep.

"We seem to have lost Freddie," Mike observed.

"Freddie usually goes to bed early," Ann related. "I go to my room about the same time he does, but I read into the night—or write."

"Write what?"

"I keep a diary. I confess my life isn't all that exciting so far that I have extraordinary things to write about," she said.

"So far?"

"I have read so much," she continued, "I feel as if someday I'll have many things to write about. I've also written some short stories and poetry. I don't think my poetry is very good, but it is a means of expressing myself. I was so sad when word reached us that my father had been killed. I cried at first, then I began writing poetry about him and to him."

"You loved your father very much, didn't you?"

"We were very close," Ann acknowledged. "One day, while going through some of his old things, I discovered some of the thoughts he had written—probably when he was a young man. Father was raised in this house. Let's go to the second-floor sitting room. My father's study is next door to it. I'll show you some of his writings—and some of mine."

"Will it be all right? I mean, should we leave Freddie here alone?" Mike asked.

"We needn't worry about Freddie." Ann reached to take Mike's hand and pulled him from the room.

The stairs creaked as they climbed and Mike commented on the eerie quality the sound produced.

"But I suppose that living in such a monstrous old house," Mike commented, "one gets used to such singular sounds."

"Sometimes when I'm alone," Ann confessed, "I've become frightened until I was able to identify certain noises. Usually at such times I lock myself in my room."

Two lamps were burning in the upstairs hallway. Their dim light was hardly enough to brighten the area; still it was sufficient for them to see their way.

In the second-floor sitting room, each went about lighting lamps until a nice cheery glow was produced.

"Snow is falling," Ann remarked as she stood at the front window. "I can't tell for certain, but it seems to be coming down quite heavily. Would you mind lighting a fire in the fireplace? The logs are laid."

While Mike lit the fire, Ann got down several books in which her father had written. She read to him. As she did, Mike looked from her to the furnishings of the cozy room. It was far more comfortable-looking than the sitting room on the first floor, which was formal and used for greeting company. His attention went to a large portrait over the mantelpiece. He could not help staring at the handsome features of the young man's likeness captured in it.

"Are you listening?" Ann asked.

"Yes."

"Did you like that story?"

"It was interesting."

"What has your attention?"

"That painting."

Ann rose and went to the fireplace, where she stoked the logs. "That's Daniel Charles Phenwick. His name is on the back of it."

"Do you have any idea who Daniel Charles Phenwick is?" asked Mike as he joined her.

"He was Augusta's son."

"Ah, Augusta."

"She might be upstairs."

"I beg your pardon."

Ann laughed. "Yes, I've seen her on the third floor several times. She's not always up there. And sometimes I only sense her presence—or smell the violets."

"I'm afraid you've lost me, dear Ann."

"I found a book in the library called *The Mysteries of Rosea Hackleby*," Ann explained, "most of which allegedly was written in this very house. In the book, the author writes that Augusta Phenwick had willed herself to be earthbound to watch over future generations of Phenwick women. And when she chooses a girl to be a Phenwick woman, she periodically surrounds her with the scent of violets."

"Who does?"

"Augusta." Ann laughed. "You must think me funny. But it's the truth. I've spoken with Augusta and she actually told me that I was destined to be a Phenwick woman."

"She did." Mike looked around the room. "That being the case, since you weren't born a Phenwick, it would seem you would have to marry a Phenwick man to gain such a title."

"Yes, it does, doesn't it," Ann replied, "unless I can find a man who will change his name to Phenwick —legally and all that."

Now Mike laughed. He was certain she was having a game with him. "And where would you find such a man who would give up his own name?"

"I would think the logical place would be," Ann answered, "where a man doesn't know what his real name is—and has taken an assumed name."

"Are you suggesting—?"

"Mike," she said, going again to the window, "I intend to marry you. I've decided."

"I beg your pardon."

"You've not legally taken the name of Mike Black, have you?"

"No, not really. It's just a name I go by until—"

"But suppose you never discover who you actually are. One day you'll have to take legal action to have a proper name," Ann stated. "Why can't you be Michael Phenwick? You claim to be a good friend of Thadius Phenwick— and of Stuart. Surely they would agree to you taking their name."

Mike laughed. "Would your Augusta approve of such a measure?"

"I don't know. Why don't we go upstairs and see if she's there. We can ask her."

"Oh, now, Ann. A game is a game." He felt awkward.

"You don't take me seriously, do you?"

"Well, I do and I don't."

"I can see where you might find it difficult to swallow the story about Augusta," Ann commented, "and you may have reservations about changing your name—but of one thing I am certain, I am going to be your wife."

"You overwhelm me, Ann. It's the man's place to ask the lady."

"Who said anything about asking? I'm telling."

Before he could protest, Ann had stepped to him, put

110

her arms about him and held her lips to his to be kissed. He touched her pretty face with his fingers, outlining it before he finally pressed his lips to hers. Never had he responded to a kiss as he did to that one. Soon his arms were around her, caressing and fondling.

"I knew it would be wonderful," Ann whispered a few minutes later, "but I had no idea it would be that powerful."

"Nor I."

"Perhaps we'd better go to the third floor," Mike suggested, "before we become too romantically involved."

"Are you afraid of me?"

"No, uncertain of my own reactions. This is happening all too fast. I don't know how to respond."

"Respond as a man," Ann coaxed.

Mike turned away from her begging lips. "You don't seem to understand the terrible circumstance in which I find myself. What if I have a wife—and perhaps a family —elsewhere?"

"Have you?"

"I simply don't know, Annie, I don't know."

Ann caught his hand and kissed it. "Mike—I want you to be my husband."

"Again you don't understand. Suppose there is another and when my memory returns—if it ever does—I find myself still very much in love with her. I can't have two wives, nor do I wish to divide my love."

"You do have feelings for me. I can tell."

"Very much so. Since we first met, I've constantly thought about you," Mike confessed. "And I do have a magnificent feeling of love for you."

Ann stared into his troubled face. She kissed his cheek, then gently stroked the back of his hand. "Come upstairs. Perhaps the lady is there."

"I don't know if I'm ready to encounter ghosts just yet."

"Why not? They can't harm you."

"Why don't we just sit here a while longer by the fire and get better acquainted?" he suggested.

"Do you fear me, Mike?" Ann questioned as she sat a distance from him.

"I believe I fear myself—or at least my reactions to you," he confessed. "You're a very desirable young lady and from all indications I'm a perfectly normal young man. It's one thing to play a game with emotions—still another to permit passions to get out of hand."

"Passions?"

"Annie, my experience in the past with other young ladies," Mike said, "makes me cautious."

"You've been hurt?"

"I have learned to control my desires," Mike said, reaching to take her hand. "Let us first become friends, good friends. And, if we fall in love, then we can consider marriage and the fulfillment of all that union will mean."

Ann stared at her hand in his. A sob welled in her chest. "You're thinking of me, aren't you? I suppose I'm very foolish and immature, Mike. I want things to happen too fast, when in my heart I realize they must progress slowly."

Chapter 9

The snowfall had developed into a blizzard. Snow surrounded the frosted windowpanes. The wind was blowing with tremendous force against the house. The flames had died down in the fireplace.

"Before you put another log on," Ann said, "why don't we go up to the third floor?"

"Won't it be spooky up there with the wind blowing?" Mike questioned. "And it must be very cold."

"Are you afraid?" she teased.

"I don't know if I am or not. Very well, you lead the way."

Ann took his hand and pulled him from the sitting room. They carried a lamp and Mike took an extra candle and matches along. The wind whistled at the windows. The steps creaked beneath their footsteps. An ominous sensation came over Mike and he could not help squeezing Ann's hand tightly.

"What do you hope to accomplish up here?" Mike questioned as they reached the third floor.

"To see the lady."

"The lady?"

"When I was a small girl I came up here to play," Ann related. "It was my favorite place in the house, because nobody ever came up here. I could be alone. And in my solitude I could create whatever dreams I desired. During summer months I come up often to read or write. I don't mind the summer heat. And I like the cold. It makes an atmosphere that I find interesting. And I often see the lady."

"Just who is the lady?" Mike asked, his eyes wide as he scanned the shadowy hallway.

"She comes with the scent of violets," Ann replied wistfully.

"Your imagination—"

"Is it? That's why I wanted you to come up with me." She squeezed his hand. "Sometimes I do believe it's my imagination; yet she seems so very real to me and there is no denying the scent of violets."

"Doesn't it frighten you to be up here alone?" Mike asked.

"Oh no. I'm used to it," Ann returned. "I've been coming up here since I was a small child. I find a sense of peace and serenity—and reassurance."

"I don't understand that at all."

"I've never been harmed," Ann explained, "during my visits to the third floor. And the thoughts I have while I'm here are all very pleasant except—"

"Except?"

"Except for the time I came up here just over three years ago," Ann continued, "and I received the terrible awareness that my father was going to be killed in the war."

"Did the lady tell you?"

"No. It was a pressing thought that came while I was seated in my special room. Come, I'll show you." Ann led to a closed door. She looked up into Mike's face before she turned the knob and pushed the door open. Going ahead, she lit the lamp and placed the one she was carrying before the mirror on an ancient dresser.

The room was neatly furnished. The bed was made and topped with a lace coverlet. Curtains hung from the windows. A large rocking chair was near the bed and a table with a chair beside it was at the window.

"This is my special place. I tend to seeing that it's kept clean. In the spring and summer I have a lovely view from that window. And in autumn, the trees below turn such vibrantly rich colors. I even carry wood for the fireplace. It gets cozily warm with a fire." She smiled back at Mike, who was studying the decor of the room. "I sometimes refer to this as my dream room, for it's here I come to think and—well, to dream."

"But with so many other rooms on the lower floors," Mike questioned, "why do you prefer to be up here?"

"My father said I seemed to be attracted here even when I was a small child," Ann replied. "He used to come often to the third floor, but not to this room. When I was about seven or eight, he brought me up here one spring day and told me of the love he had for this old house. Later I discovered he made arrangements for me to inherit it if I would promise to live my life here. He didn't seem to be concerned about Mother or Freddie. You see, he, too, was convinced I was destined to become a Phenwick woman. I imagine the lady told him."

Mike was puzzled. He realized that he was in the presence of a most unusual person. Either she had a remarkable imagination, or she had an otherworldly sense of perception—or both. Yet she seemed perfectly rational. "Then actually you were deeply affected by your father's influence."

"Oh, I do believe so," Ann commented. "But I rather imagine that is why I was born his daughter in the first place. You see, his great-grandmother lived to be a very old woman. Father was very fond of her."

"His great-grandmother?"

"Her name was Jane Elizabeth Munsk Phenwick Ornby," Ann said with an amused laugh. "She was born a Munsk, and was adopted a Phenwick. Naturally she married an Ornby. Father said that she always had

115

wanted the house to be back in the Phenwick name so that a Phenwick woman would again preside over it."

"Is the lady you believe you see the spirit of your great-grandmother?" Mike asked, uncertain of what he was saying.

"No, my *great*-great-grandmother, Augusta," Ann corrected.

"The one who adopted Jane?"

"Yes."

"Then Augusta would be no blood relation to you at all."

"Quite so. And I suspect that is one of the reasons she wishes me to marry a Phenwick."

"But if, as you earlier proposed, you were to marry me and I took the name of Phenwick, I don't see where that would satisfy the situation," Mike puzzled. "I think I should write my friend Thadius Phenwick in Boston and insist he come instantly to Portland. I'm certain you would like him. And he *is* a direct descendant of Augusta Phenwick."

"There is only one difficulty with that arrangement," Ann said. "I believe that I have fallen in love with you. That puts me in somewhat of a dilemma. Therefore, the logical thing is for you simply to take the name of Phenwick. What difference could it possibly make? Your name is not Black either."

"You must let me think about this, Annie Ornby," Mike said as she went to his arms. "I don't want to be rushed into anything which I will later regret."

"What might you regret? Falling in love with me?"

"I might. I've been too recently hurt by love, albeit an impossible situation to begin with," Mike explained. "Yet I am certain that I did have a definite kind of love for Annie Duggan."

"Is that why you call me Annie?"

"I suppose it is." He kissed her. "But you are so different from the other Annie. Although I must admit she was as determined to marry me as you seem to be."

"Ah, and you fear that you might lose me, too?"

Mike held her tightly, touching his lips to hers again and again. "Just give me time, Annie. Time to sort out my thoughts and emotions. It will be a long winter, which will afford me time to get my mind in better order. We'll see each other occasionally, but the important time will be when we're apart and can consider each other with objectivity."

"Two to three months of wasted time."

"No, dear Annie, not wasted." He smiled as he put his lips to hers. "Not at all wasted. And I'll make you a promise that I'll see an attorney and look into the matter of having my name changed."

"Oh, Mike, will you?"

"Only to look into having it changed, not to go through with it until I'm absolutely certain."

"Certain? Of me?"

"No, of me." He held her to him. "My greatest fear is that one morning I'll wake up and discover I'm the person I used to be before the amnesia, a personality contrary to the one I now have. And the second fear is that I will have no recollection of all that has happened between the time I lost my memory and regained it. You must try to understand the dilemma I'm in, Annie. I'm certain I could love you very much— I—well—just bear with me and try to understand."

Ann put her head on his chest and breathed deeply. "I'll put forth deep effort, Mike, I swear I will." She trembled. "But I wonder how long I can wait."

When they returned to the second-floor sitting room, they were surprised to find Freddie waiting for them.

"Where have you two been?" he asked.

"Upstairs."

"Did you see Clayton?" Freddie questioned eagerly.

"I never see Clayton, Freddie," Ann replied. "He's

your ghost, not mine." She turned to Mike. "You see, Freddie and I have a little game about the ghosts."

"Do they really exist?" Mike asked.

Both Ann and Freddie looked startled.

"Perhaps they don't," Ann said softly.

"Clayton does—at least I think he does," Freddie remarked. "But I suppose if I'm the only one who sees him—"

Mike laughed merrily. "That's what I thought. You two are trying to put the fear of God in me, aren't you? You've been having sport with me."

"Maybe we have been," Annie commented. "Maybe."

Freddie stared into the glowing coals in the fireplace. "I went to the front door. The snow is deep. I worry about Mother. It would be best if she were to spend the night with Cousin Crandall. I don't see how a horse and buggy —or even a horse and sleigh—could make it up the hill in all the blizzard. Even if it stops falling, the snow will be far too soft to travel on until morning."

"Then perhaps she will stay with Cousin Crandall," Ann said.

Freddie turned his glance to Mike. "And if that is the case, wouldn't it be best for Mike to spend the night here?"

"Best? But would it be proper?" Mike asked.

"Why not?"

"Do you think your mother would approve?" Mike questioned.

"You could put a cot in Freddie's room," Ann suggested. "And I swear that I'll keep my door bolted. Besides, Freddie is our chaperon."

"I don't understand what all the fuss is about," Freddie exclaimed.

"You will one day, brother dear."

Mike went to the window and put his face to the pane. "Yes, it is snowing heavily. Very well, I'll spend the night on one condition."

"And that?"

"That I may sleep in one of the rooms upstairs on the third floor."

Freddie paled. "Up there?"

"Why, yes, Mike, if you like, that would be a splendid idea," Ann commented.

Chapter 10

Mike had known that look in other women's faces. How often Thelma Wellington had gazed at him with that same expression, the look that said "do anything with me that you will." And Annie Duggan had stared at him with that same fascination from the moment he had met her. There had been other women along the way, customers to whom he delivered water for O'Brien, ladies on the train. The invitation had been in Millijoy Phenwick's smile; and even Nancy Phenwick had difficulty glancing away when her interest had been aroused.

He had observed the expressions on the same women's faces when they were in the presence of other men. That look wasn't there, at least not with the same intensity of interest and fascination. Confused, Mike had stared into the mirror for long periods of time trying to discover what was so remarkably different about him. He could only conclude that the intrigue was in the eyes of the beholder. Yet something within him, in his very soul, must have attracted them or provoked such enthusiasm.

Sally Ornby had appeared nearly to devour him with her eyes, and she a widow in mourning. How quickly thereafter she emerged from that sorrowing state. Ann didn't precisely resemble her mother, but she had the same way of regarding him that Sally had. Ann's expression seemed to be augmented, and, as inexperienced as he thought himself to be, he was certain she beheld him with more than passing infatuation.

Mike had said goodnight at ten-thirty, when it appeared that Sally would not be home. Carrying a lamp, he went to the third floor and found the room which was Ann's special place. She had insisted he stay there.

He had removed his outer clothing and had turned down the bed when a jarring rap came at the door. "Yes?"

"It's me, Mike. May I come in?" Freddie called.

"Yes." Mike opened the door.

"I brought you a robe and an extra blanket," the boy announced. "Shall I light the fire for you?"

"That would be kind of you, Freddie." Mike pulled into the snug-fitting robe while Freddie put the match to the pre-laid wood. Then he arranged the pillows and sat against them, knees up, the covers over his feet.

"I saw Ann to her room," Freddie announced. "I've never seen her act so giddy and strange."

"Will you sit for a few minutes?" Mike asked, indicating the chair.

"I would like that."

"Other than to bring me the robe and blanket," Mike questioned, "what was your reason for coming up here?"

"My reason?"

"There's something on your mind, isn't there?"

Freddie blushed and nervously wiped a hand across his face. "I had a nap—and didn't think I'd be able to go right to sleep."

Mike yawned. "I was not so fortunate, and I had a hard day of work."

"Do you like Ann?" Freddie blurted.

"Yes, very much so," Mike responded.

"She likes you, you know."

"Yes, of that I'm certain."

"When I left her," Freddie related, "she was crying."

"Crying?"

"Because you said you wouldn't see much of her before spring."

"It is true. I work long hours. And I'm not used to this New England weather. I didn't say I wouldn't see her at all, only that there would be spaces between visits. I must have it that way. I've many questions bothering me."

"About Ann?"

"No, about myself." Mike pulled the covers up over his legs as Freddie went to poke the fire.

"What kind of doubts?"

"About the real me. I don't think I'm ready to marry just yet," Mike said. "And I fear if I were to come around too often and allow myself to get too close to Ann, things would happen faster than I want them to. Do you understand?"

"I think so."

"Besides, I feel Ann should have the opportunity to become a little detached from me," Mike continued. "Maybe she's only fascinated with me because she sees me. I've been told love doesn't simply happen overnight. It grows. And one's thoughts about another are as much influenced by the time they are apart as when they are together."

"Oh." Freddie didn't fully comprehend, but he tried. "Would you mind if I came to visit you during these next few months?"

"Would your mother allow it?"

"I'm certain she would."

"Why would you want to visit me?"

"Because I think you are my friend. Besides, if you're going to be my brother-in-law, I think I should get to know you, don't you?"

Mike laughed. "I suspect Annie sent you up here."

"No. I swear she didn't." Freddie's expression was earnest. "I have a few friends at school—not many. I'm not permitted to linger after school or visit my friends at their homes. Mother wants me home early. We have no male servants. I really don't have anyone with whom to talk but Mother and Ann—and Lilly. No men."

"That explains—"

"Explains *what*?"

Mike swallowed his thought. "Why you've come up to see me. You want a friend, isn't that the case?"

"Yes. Very much so."

"All right, we'll be friends. I need a friend too. I won't deny that." He yawned again. "Now, Freddie, I think you're going to have to excuse me. I'm becoming very sleepy."

"Yes." Freddie rose. "I'll go now. Sleep well, Mike."

"And you sleep well, Freddie." He watched as the boy got to the door. "There is a question I would like to ask you."

"What is it?"

"How would you feel if I were to change my name to Phenwick?"

"Phenwick?" Freddie smiled. "I think we would all like that. Goodnight."

Mike fell asleep shortly after Freddie left. He had no more than put out the lamp and adjusted himself beneath the covers than he started to lose consciousness and his thoughts began to take on a dreamlike quality.

The fire had burned down to a single glowing coal, which was hardly enough to keep the chill from penetrating the room. Mike awakened to spread his clothing over the extra blanket Freddie had brought. He wished he knew where other covers were kept, but he was not about to go searching for another one or two. He would endure the cold.

Huddling in the covers, Mike was about to fall off to sleep when he heard a faint scratching at the door. The sound alarmed him. His eyes snapped open and he stared into the darkness. When the noise persisted, he struck a match and lit a lamp.

A gray and black striped cat was outside the door. She

123

meowed as she sauntered into the room. Mike picked her up and laughed in relief.

"Well well, I have a visitor. If you're as cold as I am, you can come share the bed with me."

The cat curled up at Mike's feet as if she belonged there. The additional warmth was welcomed.

The bed was comfortable enough to be conducive to more sleep, but Mike had had just enough to rest his mind that thoughts began invading. There was no particular logic to the ideas that shot into his mind, just random pictures and words. He tossed. The cat complained but adapted to each new position.

When he was finally just about to drift off again, the cat made a throaty sound, stood up and hissed. Mike turned over. The cat hissed again. He opened his eyes.

A gray, ghoulish glow appeared to be growing brighter at the door. Mike sat up as the cat spit and suddenly scampered under the bed. Gooseflesh sprouted all over him and his throat seemed dry with apprehension. He glanced over to see that the fire had completely gone out. As he reached toward the commode for a match to light the lamp, he became aware of a pungent scent of violets. At first alarmed, it was a moment or two before he recalled earlier reference made to the scent of violets.

The unearthly glow had become lavender-hued before a faint outline of a woman seemed to form in the midst of it.

Mike dropped the match before he could strike it. His immediate impulse was to reach for his boot to use as a weapon to defend himself. But what defense would a solitary boot be against a supernatural force? What else could it be?

The lavender-gray glow persisted as Mike could distinguish the outline of the lady, her face that was almost familiar, the gown that had been styled in another era and was hemmed in darkness.

"I'm not as powerful as I used to be," the voice said.

124

"It's all these years of traipsing around and mustering the effort to materialize from time to time that's done it. Not that I'm basically weak—I'm not. I'm stronger now than I was in the past. It's just that creating a physical illusion is becoming more difficult, and, I freely admit, not all that pleasant. Never mind that. I didn't go through all of this to talk about myself."

"Who are you? What are you?"

"I can work up enough energy to give you one good, quick look. If you don't recognize me in that time, it isn't important." The apparition became suddenly brighter, more distinct.

"You're the lady in the portrait!"

The vision sighed and grew less bright. "I'm glad that's over with. That takes so much out of me. And you go by the name of Mike, don't you?"

"How did—?"

"Oh, you'd be surprised. As a matter of fact, I've been surprising people for years and years—and years."

"Why have you appeared to me?" Mike asked, feeling a little less anxious.

"Because I've chosen you to unite my family."

"I beg your pardon."

"There are powers that be who would like to gain control of this property and have my beautiful house torn down. I would become a vindictive spirit if that were to happen, I don't mind telling you that. It's time the house were in the Phenwick name again."

"Are you suggesting that I adopt the name of Phenwick as my own?"

"If your name isn't Phenwick already, I suspect that is precisely what you'll have to do."

"If—? I suppose it might as well be Phenwick as Black."

"Good, that's settled."

"No, it isn't settled. It's merely a thought. I've not accepted it."

"You shall."

125

"But I'm not a wealthy man."

"What if I were to tell you I could see that you were to become as affluent as Stuart Phenwick?"

"I would know for certain that I was having a nightmare."

"Untrue. That silly cat wouldn't have hissed and arched her back at me if I were only your nightmare. And, speaking of cats, I must relate that I've decided you're to become the lion of the Phenwick family."

"The lion?"

"Think about it, my friend. There are certain things I can't directly tell you. Just as I can't tell you exactly where you will find my riches—but you will find some of them. It's not sheer accident you've come to Falmouth House. It's part of your destiny."

"I confess you're speaking in riddles."

"All the better for you to comprehend—in the end. Many things you will have to discover for yourself—and when you do there will be no doubt that you are a true Phenwick man. I'm losing my force. It's so hard on me to do this—such a bother. Well, I've condemned myself to it, so I'll put up with it. I can tell you only one thing more, a name: Ben Strothart. *Once that name becomes significant to you, you will be led to wealth beyond your greatest imagining. Now sleep well, my big pussycat."*

The lavender-gray glow was gone. A moment later the cat crept out from under the bed and jumped onto it. The weight of the sudden invasion alarmed Mike and he reached to take hold of the animal.

Unless the cat was part of the dream, Mike was convinced he had just undergone one of the most startling and enigmatic experiences of his life. It had been so unexpected and had happened so fast. In retrospect he thought of questions he should have asked. Not that he believed in spirits, but perhaps he might have learned his true identity. He wished he knew more about such things.

Ben Strothart? Who in the world was Ben Strothart? Was that his real name?

As he held the cat and stroked it gently another phrase returned to him: *"You're to become the lion of the Phenwick family."* What in the devil did she mean by that? And why had she called him her big pussycat?

Lion . . . lion . . . kitty . . . kitty . . . ? Why was there something so very familiar about that? Cat? Pussy? Lion?

The cat stretched as she climbed away from his hold. A moment later she curled again at his feet. Mike closed his eyes and almost instantly fell asleep.

Chapter 11

Three weeks had passed since Mike had spent the night at Falmouth House. Snows were deep. He often thought of that night and his encounter with the lady both Ann and Freddie had assured him was Augusta Phenwick. Twice he had started out to call on the Ornbys at Falmouth House, but both times the weather conditions were so bad and threatening that he turned back.

Freddie had taken the sleigh when the snow was hard and packed to give an invitation to Mike to come to the house on Christmas Eve, where he was welcome to spend the night.

Ann could not put the thought of Mike from her mind. Over those three weeks she had gone regularly to the third floor in hopes of encountering Augusta, but she did not appear. On three different occasions, she imagined she got a faint whiff of violets, but that may have been her imagination.

"Are you certain Mike will come?" Ann asked her brother.

"He said he would try," Freddie replied. "How many times must I tell you that?"

"Oh, I hate the winter and being snowed in," Ann stated. "If Mike lived as near as Mr. Robbins, it would be nothing for him to come by every night as Mr. Robbins does. Better still, if Mike were to live in the gardener's house—"

"It wouldn't be wise, Ann," Freddie commented.

"Why?"

"How would he get back and forth to Medallion in all this snow?" her brother asked.

"How did the Phenwicks and the Ornbys get back and forth in years past?"

"Perhaps the winters weren't as severe as this one." Freddie had been reading before Ann had interrupted him. He turned back to the book, then looked up to observe his sister staring out the frosted windowpane. "Do you know the name Ben Strothart?"

"Ben Strothart? No. Should I?"

"I don't know. It's a name Mike mentioned. I told him it was unfamiliar to me."

On the morning of the day before Christmas, Ann went into the music room to remove the covers from the furniture and dust the woodwork. The spinet wasn't completely in tune, but it would do if Benita Ornby wished to play Christmas carols while the family gathered around. Occasionally everyone gathered at the Crandall Ornbys' for Christmas celebration. Sally had requested they all be at Falmouth House this time.

Freddie had been out cutting fir trees. He had fixed a large one to stand on the front porch to dry before bringing it into the sitting room. In the meantime he carried in boughs and smaller trees to make the house festive for the holiday. He also found holly and cranberries. The week before he had spent several days making special candles, which he placed everywhere. Together, he and Ann had strung cranberries and popcorn. The house smelled of wonderful odors. Both Lilly and Sally had been baking for three days and in the last hours before the guests were to arrive, the aroma of roasting meats mixed with the spices and other smells that made the house seem exactly like Christmas.

129

Sally had had a new red dress made for the occasion. She invited Ann to her room to help her dress. The girl would have time to get into her own new green gown once her mother was prepared.

Sally hummed and bubbled with excitement.

"What is it, Mother?"

Sally hugged and kissed Ann. "I was going to save it until the party, but I think I should tell you and Freddie now. Go fetch him, will you please?"

"Tell us what?"

"Get Freddie and I'll tell you both at once."

Sally was admiring her appearance in the mirror when Ann returned with her brother. She went to the children, her full skirts rustling as she moved. "Ann . . . Freddie . . . I wonder if you've noticed a change in me these past few weeks."

"I have, Mother."

"And so have I."

"Good. I'm glad. I imagined my attitude was obvious," Sally said. "You see, the fact of the matter is, I've told Mr. Robbins that I will marry him."

"You *what*?" the children exclaimed in unison.

"Does it surprise you?" Sally asked. "I should have thought you would have guessed with him coming so often to visit."

"I was aware that he liked you, Mother," Ann commented.

"Oh yes, he does like me very much, my darling."

"And what of Father?" Freddie asked.

"Your father is gone now, my little one. We must release him and let his spirit go on without constantly holding him in our thoughts," Sally said. "Mr. Robbins tells me that it is wrong to think so persistently of those who have passed over, because we only impede their progress on that side. He had a dream of his late wife, and she beseeched him to marry again and release her."

"A dream isn't reality, Mother," Ann said.

130

"Oh, I know that. But Mr. Robbins is of the opinion that those who are in spirit have a way of contacting the living to give them messages of importance. As in the case of Mrs. Robbins, she has appeared in Mr. Robbins' dreams. I confess I've dreamed often of your father, and it seemed to me that he too was imploring me to find happiness."

"I'm shocked," Freddie remarked. "I thought you would always love Father."

"I will," Sally responded, "in a special way. Just as I will always love my own parents and others who have gone on to whatever comes after this life. But that doesn't mean I must stop living or cling constantly to fading memories."

Ann realized that Freddie was not prepared for their mother's announcement and that he was reacting badly to it. "Oh, Mother, I'm so happy for you!"

"Happy for her?" Freddie questioned.

"Aren't you, brother?"

"Please be happy for me, Freddie," Sally coaxed. "Mr. Robbins has four children of his own. You'll have new playmates and friends."

"Will we?" Freddie asked.

"Why, yes," Sally explained. "Mr. Robbins has a nice house—far newer than this old monstrosity."

"Mother!" Ann exclaimed. "You're not thinking of leaving Falmouth House, are you?"

"Why, of course, we will all move in with Mr. Robbins and his family. In fact, we will all become part of his family," Sally said.

"And what is to become of Falmouth House?" Freddie asked, attempting to curb the anger rising within him.

"Nothing is going to happen to Falmouth House," Ann interrupted. "I know my father's will. I am to inherit the house. It has been arranged."

Sally sighed. "Dear children, this isn't the way I had anticipated it would be. It takes a great amount of money to run a house the size of this. And the place is old, badly in need of repair in many different parts."

"Then I shall see that it is repaired," Ann declared.

"And I'll help her," Freddie echoed.

"But Mr. Robbins feels that if the house were demolished," Sally said, "and a nice new building were constructed—one not quite so large and ostentatious—it would make a perfect family home for all of us."

Ann was fuming. "It's not Mr. Robbins' house to do with. It's mine!" She stormed across the room, then turned back abruptly. "Mother, does Mr. Robbins want to marry you because he loves you, or because he wants to get his hands on this house and property?"

"Why, Ann, what a terrible thing to suggest!" Sally returned.

"I suggest you tell him once and for all that Falmouth House belongs to me. And even if Mr. Robbins attempts to break my father's will, I'm determined to fight him to the end."

"How?" Sally asked weakly.

"I'll go to Cousin Crandall," Ann stated. "And if that doesn't work, I'll travel to Boston and get financial assistance from the Phenwicks."

"Get help from the Phenwicks of Boston?" Sally questioned.

"Why shouldn't she?" piped Freddie. "After all, they're all relatives. Besides, Ann might meet one of the handsome young Phenwicks and find herself a perfect husband."

"Freddie!" Ann exclaimed. "I don't think it's necessary to mention that."

"But it is a possibility, Ann," Freddie said. "Mike told me that both Thadius and John Phenwick are at a marrying age—and both are extremely good-looking. Mike has even been mistaken for John Phenwick—so you know he must be handsome."

"We are deviating from the point," Ann murmured, trying to control the seething tendency within her. "I don't see that this discussion is getting us anywhere. And it's foolish for us to spoil the happiness of Christmas with such bickering." She hugged Sally. "Oh, Mama, I don't want to hurt you or your chances with Mr. Robbins. But wouldn't it be best to know from the beginning if he wants you because he loves you, or whether he really only has ulterior motives?"

"I do believe I love Mr. Robbins," Sally whimpered.

"I only want you to be certain of his reasons. If he truly loves you, Falmouth House won't make one bit of difference to him. If he doesn't, then you will see him for what he is."

Tears had come to Sally's eyes. "I suspect you've inherited wisdom from your father, my Ann. It can't have come from me." She dried her eyes. "As you say, let's not spoil the joy of Christmas. Let us go greet our guests and be jolly."

Due to the holiday, Mike had been permitted to leave work in the early afternoon that day. He had gone to his room, bathed, packed a few things in a small bag and dressed for the party. During the three weeks that had passed since he spent the night at Falmouth House, he had thought much about Ann and the experience he had had during the night. Absent from her, his feelings for Ann increased. If he wasn't in love with her, he was very close to it. How often during that time had he wanted to risk the stormy weather and climb the hill to Falmouth House. Instead, he wrote long letters to Ann, which he never posted. But in writing out his thoughts, he could examine them with perspective.

Mike bundled himself well before he prepared for the walk to the house on the hill, which was close to three miles from where his room was located. Snow had fallen that morning. Now an icy-cold wind was sweeping over the hilly terrain, making the wind-chill factor extremely uncomfortable to endure. His cap pulled low and a muffler wrapped about his neck and face, he began the journey. Generally certain of his way, he wished to make it to the house before dark. Snow changes the look of things and can often make the way confusing to follow.

The snow muffled most sounds. Only distant echoes of wood being cut or a horse pulling a sleigh broke the deep silence. Chickadees swooped down and chattered as they settled in the protective twigs of a bush. Then there was only the hollow whistling of the wind with its biting sting. Mike's eyelashes were fringed with snow.

To keep his mind off the discomfort of his physical experience, Mike tried to hold his thoughts on Ann Ornby and his feelings for her. Ironically, as he thought of the beautiful, gentle young lady and Falmouth House, pictures from his night in the third-floor room came to him. And the words *"You're to become the lion of the Phenwick family."* That was the most enigmatic phrase that he recalled. How often it had repeated in his mind since it was uttered—if indeed it had been spoken and was not just a figment of his imagination, or part of a dream.

Then out of the blue a name came to him. He spoke it aloud. "Ophelia. Ophelia?" He connected thoughts. *"Hamlet.* To be or not to be?" He had only read the play once. Had he? When? He didn't remember. Still he knew it was a play by Shakespeare and he did recognize the names of the characters. Going back over things that entered his mind just prior to uttering the name, the only connection he could make was that one of the Phenwicks bore the name of Ophelia. An odd name, he thought. What had he heard about Ophelia Phenwick? She had recently married a Henry Something-or-other. Had Thadius said she was born and raised in London? Ah! And she had aspired to be an actress. That would be the connection of the name and the play—wouldn't it? He wished he had recalled more of what Thadius had said about his—was it his niece or his cousin? Whichever. *Ophelia* was the kind of name that would come again and again to him, like *piccalilli*

134

and *watermelon seed*; it had a kind of a haunting sound that periodically managed to seep into his subconscious and ultimately erupt into words.

Mike wondered if he had imagined the entire interview he had seemingly had with Augusta Phenwick. And the presence of the cat had caused him to think the ghostly presence had made feline references to him.

Once he had considered what it might be like if he were to go to Cambridge and somehow change places with John Phenwick, somehow dispose of him and assume his name. That was the kind of fanciful thinking one should never mention to anyone else, especially to anyone related to the subject. Still it was a question of whether or not he could take another's place and get away with it. Actually, wasn't that what he was doing anyway? He was taking the place of Michael Black—whoever that might be—instead of acting out the role he was born to play. Or was his amnesia somehow an integral part of that role? Such speculations worried him.

Freddie opened the door to Mike and took his things. "I'm glad you came early. Everyone else is planning to stay over, so naturally we expect you to, too."

"Not unless I can sleep in the room on the third floor," Mike teased lightly. He had cast aside his perplexed attitude.

"I'm certain that can be arranged. Come, we'll take your things up there now," Freddie said.

"Ann?"

"She's still getting ready," Freddie replied. "Actually, I suspect she's preparing for an entrance."

The gray and black cat was in the third-floor hallway as Freddie and Mike climbed the stairs. Startled by their arrival, she scampered into seclusion.

Crandall and Benita Ornby arrived shortly before six. Childless, they often made a point of spending Christmas with different relatives and friends when not entertaining in their home. It was the time of year they most missed not having little ones of their own.

Benita's long, exotic face had a surreal appearance to it. Handsome and startling to behold, she tried to be oblivious to the effect she had on others. A gracious lady, she was kind and outgoing. Instantly she went to Sally and the two chattered like close sisters.

Crandall amused himself until Zebidiah Robbins arrived. The two gentlemen had been friends for a good number of years. Zeb was a tall man with dark hair, a neatly trimmed beard and piercing eyes. He was good-looking, but not extraordinarily handsome. His mouth was higher on the left than on the right and he showed teeth when he spoke. The two men went to the library, where they smoked.

After initially greeting Ann and having a few words with her, Mike excused himself to join the gentlemen with Freddie, while Ann went to the kitchen to help the ladies with dinner.

"I confess I've never felt completely at ease in Falmouth House," Crandall stated. "I suppose I had heard too many ghostly tales about the place when I was a small lad. Fortunately I never had to live here—and only twice as a child did I spend nights in the place. Even tonight I'm a bit apprehensive about staying over."

Zeb puffed on his cigar and laughed. "If Falmouth House were truly haunted, how would your cousins have stood living here all these years?"

"Believe me, that is a question I have often posed," Crandall commented.

"It's simple," Freddie interjected. "We've become friendly with the ghosts. After all, they're really part of the family—sort of."

The men laughed.

"I confess I put no stock or belief in the notion of ghosts," Zeb stated. "Old wives' tales and that sort of thing."

"I'm not so certain about that," Crandall said. "I mean to say, I've heard some very astute members of my family speak of old Augusta and her haunting ways. I was assured she was perfectly harmless, but I don't think I would like to meet her. And the other one that's reported to carry on a spirit watch through the corridors of Falmouth House —what's his name—he was never a member of the family."

"Clayton?" questioned Freddie.

"I suppose that's his name. Well, he was only a friend of the family, I understand."

"He designed and built Falmouth House," Freddie stated.

"Ah, that explains his attachment to it," Zeb commented with laughter.

"I wouldn't be surprised if Clayton were to keep you from destroying the house, Mr. Robbins," Freddie said.

"Me?" Zeb laughed again. "What ever brought that statement on?"

"Isn't it true you would like to get your hands on our property and tear Falmouth House down?" asked Freddie.

Zeb eyed Crandall uneasily. "It is true I've made the statement that I would consider tearing the old monstrosity down if it were mine. That's a perfectly natural statement for one to make. But, believe me, lad, I have no immediate intention of wanting to demolish the old relic."

"Is that the truth?"

"Do you question the veracity of my words?" Zeb questioned. He laughed again. "The fact is, I should say this was very valuable property. It's a tidy piece of land. It's unfortunate, Crandall, that you didn't inherit the house as well as the Medallion company."

"My sister has inherited Falmouth House," Freddie declared. "It doesn't belong to Mother, or to me. It's Ann's." He glared contemptuously at Zeb Robbins.

"Ann's?" questioned Zeb. "I hadn't realized."

"It's quite true, Zeb," Crandall remarked. "I hadn't intended to divulge this information so soon, but it is Christmas and a time for gift-giving. When Cousin John Frederick went off to war, he made arrangements for half of his stockholdings in Medallion to be left to Freddie. It was Cousin John Frederick's belief that the lad could obtain cash interest on their worth, and possibly make a loan against it, using it for collateral. Freddie will be far from destitute when he turns eighteen. Sally owns the other half of the Medallion stock herself, as well as other holdings. This may come as a shock, Freddie, but your mother isn't as badly off, I've recently discovered, as she thought she was. Actually, despite her inheritance of this old house, I suspect Ann has come out the least successful."

"How do you know all this, Mr. Ornby?" Mike asked.

"My cousin had a premonition that he might not return from the war," Crandall said. "We had a long discussion about it and I helped him make arrangements. I've kept track of Sally and her children and determined that they have never really suffered for lack of funds. I suppose it is time the truth was known."

"Very interesting," Zeb commented as he inhaled on a cigar.

"I assume your interest is in the house, isn't it, Mr. Robbins?" Mike questioned.

"I'll be perfectly honest with you. I'm interested in the property, yes." Zeb cleared his throat. "And perhaps I can make an arrangement with Annie to assure her of having a substantial income."

Mike stared at the man suspiciously. Zeb was up to something.

After a hardy meal from which everyone felt uncomfortably stuffed, Sally suggested that they all adjourn to the music room, where Benita would play Christmas carols while the others gathered around to sing. The carol session was short-lived because the room was almost unbearably cold and uncomfortable.

Ann held Mike's hand as the others departed for the sitting room, where a fire was known to be blazing at the hearth.

"We haven't had a moment together alone," Ann said as she held tightly to his hand.

"There hasn't been the opportunity," Mike replied.

"I've missed you dreadfully all these weeks."

"It's only been three, Annie."

"Three? It seems more like three months or three years."

"Hardly that long." Mike laughed.

"I have thought of you all this time."

"And I've thought of you."

She gently caressed his hand as she guided it to her cheek. "I'm now more convinced than ever I want to marry you, Mike."

"Freddie told me of your mother's plans to marry Zeb Robbins, and that Mr. Robbins might try to get possession of Falmouth House."

"He mustn't do that." Ann kissed his hand. "I got angry when Mother first told me about it. I later went to my room. As I was fuming, glaring at myself in the mirror, I was suddenly surrounded by the aroma of violets. Then I knew I didn't have to do anything about it, that Augusta would handle things. And I believe she *is* handling them right now."

Mike kissed her. "No!" he said, stepping back. "It's still too soon, Annie, you must realize that."

"I realize only that I love you."

"I love you, too. Of that I'm certain. I'm simply not certain of myself. You cannot know the confused state I am in. Curiously, little things keep popping into my consciousness, things that must come from my past. Why, on my way up here this afternoon, I suddenly thought of a play by Shakespeare. How I knew the play or even that it was by Shakespeare, I don't know. It's a mystery. I'm certain I haven't read it or even heard of it since I was picked up by Giddeon Phillips in New Jersey. But I knew it, and I even knew the heroine's name: Ophelia."

Ann stared a question.

"It's coming back. I'm certain it is—bit by bit," Mike related. "That being the case, once I'm convinced there is no one—you know—well, then I can think in terms of marriage—perhaps."

"Perhaps?"

Mike told her the entire story about Annie Duggan and how she was shot and killed by Sam Dodsworth; and how it was made to appear that he, not Sam, had shot her. It was Mike's word against Sam's. Besides, the servant Jennings had appeared shortly after Sam left and found Mike with the gun.

"But you don't ever have to go back to New York," Ann protested.

"Not unless they discover where I am. Tim Duggan is a fiery Irishman," Mike stated. "They can become very clannish and vindictive."

"All the more reason why I should go to Boston and visit with Cousin Stuart," Ann declared. "We'll get to the bottom of this once and for all."

"Oh, my dearest Annie." He held her tightly. "If you go to Boston, you must go alone. Frankly, I have a feeling that Thad Phenwick will come to Portland by the time the snows thaw. He can be a liaison for you. You'll like Thad. He's a very nice person."

Ann stood back from him and gazed intently into his face. "I know what you're thinking, Mike. But you're wrong. I wouldn't be more fortunate by marrying my cousin Thadius. How could I possibly be? You're the man I love—and the only one."

"How did you know—I mean, what makes you think—?"

"Who can say what it is that causes one person to love another?" she asked. "Who can explain what magic ingredient attracts two people out of a world of strangers to

140

each other? Do you think I could be content married to a rich cousin whom I didn't love when I feel as I do toward you?"

"Annie, there's always a chance—"

"Don't! Please don't say it again. I don't want to hear about it. If there is someone else when your memory returns, then we'll face that at that time."

Mike smiled understandingly, covering his own doubts and feelings of being ill at ease. "We'd better get back to the others. I'm certain your mother is about to announce her engagement to Zebidiah Robbins."

"Wait," Ann said. She went to the bookcase. "I want you to take this book with you and read it. Not tonight, but when you're in your room down in town."

The Mysteries of Rosea Hackleby?"

"I won't tell you anything about it," Ann said. "I want you to discover it for yourself."

"Rosea Hackleby?" He ran his hand over the book cover.

"One kiss more—please."

He kissed her. "Merry Christmas, Annie."

"Merry Christmas, dearest Mike."

Another gentle kiss before they walked hand in hand from the music room. They hadn't even noticed the faint scent of violets.

Chapter 12

1866

George Tomlin was a man in his early thirties with distinguished features and a good physical structure. Sandy hair and light blue eyes weakened his features; still he was a man who could attract his share of attention from the ladies. A businessman and working his way upward in a stock investment firm, he was considered the most eligible man in Portland society. He was from a good family, from which a consciousness of wealth had been passed on to him.

Crandall Ornby had met George Tomlin several years before when they were both taken in as members of the Athletic Club at the same time. Later Crandall introduced George to Zebidiah Robbins. Ultimately Zeb and George became associated in a business way and were in the process of considering a firmer merger of their talents. George was practical with a good head for business. He was Zeb's kind of man.

When Zeb announced that he had set the date of his wedding to Mrs. Sally Ornby, George was asked to be best man. And, since Ann Ornby was to be her mother's maid of honor, she was introduced to and regularly thrown into the company of George Tomlin.

The thaw had made the streets muddy and streams of water flowed in the gutters. Green was sprouting everywhere, but the mud and wet still kept people from getting out. Mike had only made two visits to Falmouth House during those months of severe winter. It was decided that that space of time would do well for both he and Ann to consider their feelings. During that time Mike read and reread *The Mysteries of Rosea Hackleby* until he knew much of it by memory.

In the back of the book, Jane Ornby had sketched a record of family members as best she knew. The Ornby side was pretty well represented. The record of her own brother Edward, who had also been adopted as a Phenwick, included his marriage to Patricia, their two children, Susannah and David; and Susannah's adopted children, Marcia and Gregory. Mike knew that Marcia had been Stuart Phenwick's first wife and that their children were Daniel Charles and Ann Marie. He wrote those names in.

Following the lineage of Daniel Charles Phenwick I, the son of Augusta, was a little more difficult. There had been one illegitimate son, Elias, two other sons and a daughter: Alexander, Peter and Rachel. Rachel had died as a teen-ager. Alexander had married his cousin Susannah. Peter had twice married and had fathered four children with each wife. Augustus, Peter's eldest son, was the father of Stuart and Gordon; neither Jane nor any of the others in Portland had known of Prentise Phenwick's children, Peter's second son. The third son, Joshua, had five children: the names of the two eldest were included. Peter's only daughter, Joanna, had remained unwed. By his second wife, Nancy, Peter had fathered Thadius, John, Paul and Daniel Louis.

Besides the names of Thadius and Paul, Nancy's sons, the name that stood out and seemed to leap off the page at Mike was that of *Joanna Phenwick, actress*. Had Thad mentioned that his half sister was an actress in London? Perhaps he had. Under Prentise's name, Mike penned in the name of his eldest son, Jim.

Then Mike examined the name of Joshua, his wife

Olivia and his daughter Ophelia. Again he got a strange reaction from that last name. The other child listed was Arnold Leon. The numbers 3, 4 and 5 were left blank. He said aloud, "I believe Thad told me their names were Carrie, Elizabeth and David Charles." After writing them in, he looked up. "When did Thad tell me that?" Then he thought if he were to take the name of Phenwick and perhaps become an adopted brother of Thad, Joshua would be his half brother, too, sort of. *But that wouldn't be right.* Why? The thought puzzled him.

Mike, who rarely received mail, got two letters in one day. The first was from Thad, saying that he had intended to visit Portland that March, but his half sister, Joanna, had arrived from London and he would have to postpone his visit until May or June.

The second letter contained an invitation to the wedding of Mr. Zebidiah Robbins and Mrs. Sally Ornby. Ann had included a brief note saying that she had missed not seeing him and hoped that he would come to call again soon. She went on to mention that she would be in the wedding party.

The next day Mike was called into Crandall's office at Medallion.

"You wished to see me, Mr. Ornby?" Mike questioned, wiping his hands self-consciously on his trousers.

"Mike, I'll come directly to the point," Crandall said, puffing on a cigar. "I've been watching you, observing your work and the way you relate to the men."

"I hope my work has been satisfactory, sir."

"Don't interrupt," Crandall snorted. "Word arrived this morning that my supervisor, Nate Hazelton, passed away last night. He wasn't an old man, just in his forties. A tragedy. I'll have to take his young son on—don't know what he can do, but I can't leave the family without an income. That's neither here nor there. I have to replace Nate. In my estimation, there's only one man for the job. You."

144

"Me, sir?"

"It'll mean a considerable increase in salary," Crandall announced. "It will also require a change of life-style. You'll want to take a house somewhere, perhaps consider buying one. And naturally, although I don't wish to rush you, it would be advisable for you to consider taking a wife. Family men are dependable."

"I'm overwhelmed, sir."

"Don't be, Mike. I've known from the day you first stepped into this office that you were destined to move up in Medallion. It was only a matter of time and the skill you showed at familiarizing yourself with the company. Well, the time has come." He extended his hand to the younger man.

"Mr. Ornby, I've been thinking," Mike said shortly thereafter, "that I've decided to change my name."

"Change your name?"

"Yes, sir. You see, I can't very well consider marriage if I don't have a legal name, can I?"

"There is a point to that."

"I had written a month ago to my friend Thadius Phenwick of Boston," Mike continued. "And he has sent word giving his consent, along with that of his mother and his cousin Stuart, for me to take the name of Phenwick."

"Phenwick?" Crandall threw his head back with a roar of laughter. "You wish to become one of the notorious Phenwicks?"

"Notorious, sir?"

"They have been known to be." Crandall wiped his eyes. "With the thousands, nay, millions of names available, I can't imagine why you would want to become a Phenwick. Of course, I'm a Phenwick several times removed—and I add, thank God for the removal! The Phenwicks are a strange lot who seem to attract more than their share of notoriety. I've never put any stock in all the superstitious nonsense surrounding them and all that. But I suppose if you have the blessings of Stuart and Thadius

145

—was it?—then I can only add more power to you. However, maybe I'd better give second thoughts to allowing you to become too powerful at Medallion in Portland. After all, Medallion is basically a Phenwick company."

"I have no personal designs on the company."

"Why not? Unless young Frederick proves to want to take control of Medallion in time, it will fall into other hands. I have no heirs—at least none close enough to want to follow in my footsteps," Crandall stated. "Oh, I have a nephew or two—somewhere. The Ornbys have spread out, many have gone West or at least to the Midwest. Who can blame them? These winters are severe. Sometimes I think if I didn't have the business I would leave Portland too. But Benita's family is here and she has strong ties with them." He laughed. "Listen to me rambling. I suppose that is my way of saying I approve of you becoming a Phenwick."

"Thank you, Mr. Ornby." Mike shook the man's hand and left.

Crandall stared at the door after Mike had closed it. He admired Mike Black. Life was pretty much ordinary and unexciting for Crandall. If Mike did become a Phenwick, a new dimension of intrigue could well develop in connection with Falmouth House. While he was firmly associated with Zebidiah Robbins, Crandall felt that he would tend to side with Mike in the matter. It could prove to be interesting.

George Tomlin had called several times at Falmouth House. Charm seemed to be his middle name. He was full of fun and liked to make clever remarks, usually based on a pun. Ann found him highly amusing. His youthful good looks were like a breath of spring long before spring indicated it was near. He had a large repertoire of stories with which he amused the Ornbys.

Because of the inclement weather and nasty conditions as a result of it, George was invited to take a room in the home of Zeb Robbins. It was a short walk from there to

Falmouth House. Zeb would drive George into town for business, and usually take him along when he went to call on Sally Ornby.

"What ever do you find to occupy your time in this old relic?" George asked Ann one evening when they were left alone in the first-floor sitting room. "I should think this old house would get on your nerves."

"I suppose it might if I hadn't been born and raised here," Ann replied sweetly. She found herself charmed by the man and sometimes caught in the aura of masculinity and fascination that surrounded him. "I often write. I keep a diary and I've started a journal. Lately I've even written a few short stories, and I'm giving thought to composing a novel."

"A novel? How can you possibly write about anything but this gloomy environment?" questioned George.

"How? Very simple. I use my imagination. That's the most important attribute a writer can possess, I believe. Why, with an active imagination, I can travel anywhere and create all sorts of people and situations," Ann said.

"Ah, you live life vicariously, then."

"Perhaps," she returned. "And what do you do to amuse yourself, Mr. Tomlin?"

"I work, which is something I greatly enjoy. My family is well-to-do, I suppose you might say. I've grown up with affluence and privilege, but I've also been impregnated with a knowledge and desire to accumulate greater wealth. Industry is the coming thing, and I expect to have created my own private fortune before I'm forty."

"That is very ambitious of you, Mr. Tomlin."

"Ambition mixed with determination and conviction, Miss Ornby," George replied. "Those are essential factors. As a boy I dreamed of becoming well established in business before I considered taking a wife and starting a family. My father is a wise man. He has done very well. He has recently advised that I would do well to start a family while I am still young. Then my·sons will be able to follow in my footsteps while I'm still able to guide them."

"You seem to have it all planned out, Mr. Tomlin," Ann commented, curiously watching him.

"Very much so." George grinned confidently.

"Now all you have to do is find a wife, is that it?"

"Precisely. And I've discovered the girl I intend to marry."

"How very interesting. Is she aware of your attentions?"

"She will be within the next few minutes," George replied. "Miss Ornby, I wish *you* to be my wife. I want to marry you."

Ann had not been taken by surprise, since the direction George Tomlin's conversation was taking had appeared quite obvious. She fluttered her eyelashes and looked down at her hands. "That's very interesting, Mr. Tomlin; but you seem to overlook an important factor. I'm not in love with you."

"Love will happen in time, if you set your mind to it," George returned. "Respect and admiration are very important between two people. How many people actually marry for love anyway? I should imagine very few of them do."

"I suspect that is a naïve theory, Mr. Tomlin," Ann commented.

"A very practical theory, Miss Ornby." He took her hand. "Will you marry me?"

Ann gently eased her hand from his. "No, I think not, Mr. Tomlin. At least, not for the present. Perhaps if I discover I've developed an emotional attachment to you, or even become convinced that I have fallen in love with you, that will be another matter. Until such a time, I cannot encourage you. I suspect that I'm as coldly calculating about love and marriage as you are about business, Mr. Tomlin."

"May I continue to come call on you?" he asked, not to be discouraged.

"If you like. I enjoy your company. And as long as you are to be Mr. Robbins' best man, we will be associated in the wedding arrangements."

On the night before the wedding, Zebidiah Robbins called at Falmouth House without George Tomlin. Freddie opened the door to him and led him to the second-floor sitting room.

"My dear Mrs. Ornby!" Zeb exclaimed as he rushed to her after Freddie disappeared behind the closed door. "You must be filled with excitement and anticipation for our big day tomorrow."

"I am, Mr. Robbins, oh, I very much am," Sally replied. "I wonder if I looked on my first wedding day with such anticipation."

"It would be selfish of me to wish not," he returned. "But we both have matured since our individual first nuptials, haven't we? That is understandable. And I know my love for you will never be the same as the love Mr. Ornby had for you—I don't wish to attempt to take his place. That would be foolish of me."

"Nor do I desire to be a replica of the first Mrs. Robbins," Sally remarked. "It is important that we understand that, isn't it?"

"Quite." He kissed her. "I do dearly love you, Mrs. Ornby. You must know that. And I admit I'm resolved to accepting the fact that your children do not wish to come and live in my house. It's understandable, seeing that Falmouth House does belong to Ann Rose. We will be close enough. Chances are, by fall the children—or at least Frederick—will be disposed to coming to live with us. It would be my wish—for your peace of mind and my concern—that Ann Rose will marry before long. A husband with her in this old mansion would give her a sense of security and take much of the worry from us."

"Yes, I see what you mean," Sally said. Zeb had broached this matter before in a casual way.

"From a practical point of view," Zeb continued, "I

feel we should give much consideration to a marriage arrangement for Ann Rose. Family, wealth, position, all these are important. With recent medical discoveries, and inherited healthy traits, I feel it is wise to consider the family into which one is marrying—for the sake of the children of the union. Family is important. And a person would be smart to marry into a healthy rather than a sickly one."

"Ann Rose and Frederick have always enjoyed remarkably good health conditions," Sally explained. "I suppose I should be extremely thankful about that."

"Ah, yes."

"I suspect you have a family in mind," Sally stated, "into which you think it would be correct for Ann Rose to marry."

"I have known the Tomlin family for years," Zeb said. "They have been the pictures—all of them—of robust physical specimens. Furthermore, they have wealth."

"George Tomlin?" Sally blinked. "I thought as much."

"George is a fine young man. And, I might add, a trusted business associate in many ways. I cannot recommend him too highly."

"He would be your choice then?"

"Unconditionally."

"I wonder." Sally sighed. "The suggestion can be made to Ann Rose, but she will have to make the final acceptance."

"That will not be the case with my own daughters," Zeb declared. "I intend to make all arrangements for their marriages when the time comes. I believe that is a father's duty. Furthermore, I expect to make similar arrangements for my son. I'll not have any of my children marrying into poverty or anything less than affluence. I would like to think that your love for me was so strong that you would trust me to handle the mating of your children, too, my dearest."

Sally stared at him before a smile came. "I do love you,

Mr. Robbins. But, were you to know Ann Rose well, you would be aware that she has quite a mind of her own. I doubt that her own father—had he lived—would have been able to enforce a marriage on her that was not acceptable to her."

"Well, we shall see, shan't we?" Zeb returned.

John and Kate Collier arrived from Greenfield for the wedding. Handsome John walked with a slight limp incurred from a Civil War wound. Their eldest child, Nellie, was eleven. She saw to the welfare of the three younger Colliers: Elizabeth, George and Rupert. Kate was the granddaughter of Patricia Phenwick and the only member of that side of the family to attend. It was easier for Kate to travel from nearby Greenfield to Portland than to go to Boston. Hence, she had kept a family closeness with the Ornbys.

John Collier walked with a cane at that time of the year when the ground was moist and the fresh green grass was slippery. He could normally walk without it while indoors. The reception was held at Falmouth House, a place John had curiously investigated from time to time. Not one for much extended socializing, he wandered off to the library to browse through the dusty books. Believing that he would be the only one out of the swing of things to retreat to that place, he was startled to discover that another had arrived at the library before him.

"Don't tell me there's more than one person who finds these wedding receptions a bother," John exclaimed. "I'm John Collier. I don't believe we've met."

"How do you do, Mr. Collier. I'm Mike—uh—Black."

"There seems to be some indecision there."

"I'm in the process of changing my name—legally," Mike related. "I know that you're somehow connected with the Phenwick side of the family, so I'm hesitant to mention that I've filed papers to change my name to Phenwick."

"Ah, so you're the one! I believe Annie mentioned something about that—or was it Freddie?" John shook Mike's hand. "So it's to be Michael Phenwick, heh? I don't believe there's been a Michael Phenwick. There was once a Michael O'Plaggerty, brother-in-law to the first Daniel Phenwick. Mike and Danny were great friends. There's a curious story there, if you're ever interested." He chuckled. "Why, may I ask, have you escaped from the celebration?"

"I know few of the people present," Mike replied. "It's kind of a strange atmosphere. Besides—" He looked down and sighed.

"Something bothering you?"

"Only a personal matter," Mike said. "I may have been a bit premature in filing to change my name."

"Why so?"

Mike explained about his amnesia. "But my principal reason for wanting to become a Phenwick is so that I can marry Ann Ornby. She is determined to become a Phenwick woman."

"Ah, the improbable Phenwick women!" John laughed. "My wife, Kate, is a Phenwick woman. Or so she claims. So was her mother, Rebecca. I never could see what remarkable distinction the title gave any of them."

Mike explained about Ann's alleged reasons and her inheritance of Falmouth House.

"So that is your motivation," John stated. "Well, I reckon it is good enough. But something is troubling you."

"It's one thing to take the Phenwick name, and another to become a kind of adopted brother to Thadius," Mike explained. "It is still another to be a man without wealth, although I do have a promising position with the Medallion company."

"I should think you had some remarkable recommendations."

"The Phenwicks will be only an adopted family, just as the name for me is only assumed," Mike said. "I'm hardly competition for George Tomlin, scion of Francis Tomlin, one of the more affluent men of Portland. The Tomlins have a clean health record. For all I know my own mother was tubercular and my father an epileptic—or goodness knows what other maladies they might have been afflicted with."

"I take it George Tomlin is romantically interested in Annie," John commented.

"He seems to be. I suspect it's part of a plot to get control of the Falmouth House property, and perhaps inadvertently to get a foothold into the Medallion company," Mike said. "That's just a hunch I have—I mean about the Medallion company."

"And are you in love with Annie?" John questioned.

Mike looked up. "Yes. Yes, I am. You're the first one I've actually admitted that to—you, a stranger."

"In that case, it would seem you should confide your feelings to Annie. I'm only a casual bystander. She's the lady in question."

Mike spoke of his fear that the return of his memory might divulge that he had had an unsavory past filled with complications.

"But suppose your memory does not come back," John suggested. "You may well have lost a lifetime in worrying about it. And, even if it does, and you discover you had not previously been married, wouldn't you feel foolish and perhaps deeply depressed to think that you had lost Annie? And, if there is another wife, she may have considered you legally dead by now and remarried."

"Until I know the truth about myself, I will constantly live under a shadow," Mike stated.

"True. Such a shadow will only be as significant as you let it become," John returned.

"I see what you mean."

John put his hand on the young man's shoulder. "Our doubts and fears are our own worst enemies, Michael. I know that only too well. It is easy enough to say this, it's quite another matter to conquer such emotional reactions.

Dr. Joseph Ornby taught me that. I've never been happier than since I've been married to Kate. Our love is beautiful and our four children are the greatest blessing of my life. I might have been defeated early on if I had bowed to the fact that I was a poor man and couldn't hope to find happiness among the wealthy Phenwick clan. That was nonsense. As far as I'm concerned, the man who doesn't marry for love is a fool—and will rue the day he married for any other reason."

The two men were interrupted by the arrival of pretty little Nellie, John's eldest daughter.

"Papa, I've been looking everywhere for you," the child said.

"And now you've found me, my darling," John returned, catching her in his arms. "This is my little princess, Michael. Nellie, may I present Michael Phenwick?"

"I'm pleased to make your acquaintance, Mr. Phenwick," Nellie responded, with a slight curtsy. "Papa, Mama is waiting for you."

"Will you excuse me, Michael?" John said and left the room, holding tightly to his daughter's hand.

Mike lingered in the library for fifteen minutes before he resolved to confess his love to Ann and ask her to marry him. He departed from that room with determination and confidence.

Chapter 13

On the same day that Sally Ornby married Zebidiah Robbins in Portland, young Paul Phenwick, in Boston, was going about his usual interests and his part-time work for the Medallion company when he encountered a tall stranger. The man was bull-like, with a hard, heavy face and a menacing expression.

"Your name is Phenwick, ain't it?" the man gruffly asked.

"I'm Paul Phenwick, yes, sir."

"I think you and me're gonna have a talk," the man stated. "Come with me."

"To where?"

"Never mind that. I'll not harm ya if ya give me the answers I want."

"Please, sir, I don't know what this is all about," Paul protested. "I've got to get back to the office. I'm on an errand."

Paul was taken to the Commons to a secluded area behind shrubbery.

"Who—who are you?"

"It don't matter who I am."

"It does if you want me to tell you anything."

The man squinted one eye. "Oh, yeah? Well, my name's Sam. That's all ya need to know."

"Sam?"

"I'm lookin' for a man, who I understand stayed with you people last year," Sam stated. "A man who goes by the name of Mike Black."

"What do you want with Mike?"

"He's wanted for murder—and there's a reward on his head," Sam declared. "And I intend to collect it."

"Mike hasn't been in Boston for a long time."

"I know that. I've asked around. But I've got a feelin' you know where he went," Sam said.

"I only know he was headed for Portland, Maine," Paul related. "That's all I know."

"What was he going to do in Portland?"

"There's a Medallion company—I mean—I don't know. I think you'd better talk to my brother Thad if you want to know anything else. Please, you're hurting me."

Sam glared, then shoved Paul to the ground. "Ya'll tell no one about this, or I'll come back and give ya worse—much worse."

"Yes, sir." Paul held the side of his face where he had been brutally pinched.

"And if you've lied to me—well, ya better not have, that's all I've got to say."

"I didn't lie."

Paul watched as the man skulked off. He was about to get to his feet when he saw a small envelope nearby. Reaching it, he read the name of Sam Dodsworth and a New York address on the front of it.

"I can't say yes now," Ann had said that afternoon when Mike had mustered the courage to ask for her hand in marriage.

"Why not?"

"You must give me time to think about it," Ann had said. "That is only proper."

"But I thought—"

George Tomlin had interrupted them, saying that he had come to get Ann at her mother's request.

Ann had smiled hope at Mike, but he felt she could have been more encouraging. The presence of gregariously smiling George Tomlin didn't help ease his apprehensive feelings.

Mike gave Ann two days to consider his proposal, during which time he put in long hours at work and returned to his small room in a state of exhaustion.

On the third evening he went to call at Falmouth House. When he arrived, he was greeted by Freddie, who informed him that Ann had a caller, George Tomlin.

"Are you going to let that discourage you, Mike?" Freddie asked.

"How would you react if you were in my place?"

"I don't know." Freddie scratched his head. "You wait here. Promise?"

"Sure."

Freddie dashed into the house and went to the sitting room, where his sister was in conversation with George Tomlin. Freddie interrupted with a whispered message to Ann.

"Tell him to come back in an hour," Ann whispered.

Freddie returned with the message. "But don't go away, Mike. Come on in and I'll entertain you while she's busy."

Mike was ready to go back down the hill and mope in his room, but not until he stopped at a tavern and had at least a bucket of beer. However, he was fond of Freddie and enjoyed his company.

"Where are you taking me?" Mike asked.

"To the basement," the boy replied. "You've never been down there, have you? I don't go down much in the wintertime because it's too cold, but I've always played in the basement during summer and the warmer months."

"I guess I'd been told there was a basement," Mike commented as they climbed down the steps.

Freddie carried a lamp which gave a flickering, eerie glow.

"What's down here?" Mike questioned.

"Just things. Old rooms, old furniture and clothing. Just things." Freddie led the way. "This is a very long corridor. Actually, it's a tunnel that leads all the way to the hill opposite Back Bay. It's been partitioned off, but you can get through it if you know the way.

"Why such a long tunnel?"

"Falmouth House was built before the Revolutionary War," Freddie explained. "Old Augusta must have constructed a means of escape should the house be attacked." He pointed to his left. "That room is where old Rosea Hackleby wrote much of her book. It's been burned. I don't know the circumstances. I guess the manuscripts weren't there when it happened."

They went into the room which had been Rosea's laboratory. Freddie put the lamp on the table and got another lantern.

"I used to play in this room. My father did when he was a little boy," Freddie said.

"Freddie, did your father tell you about Falmouth House?" Mike questioned as a curious thought came to him.

"He told me much."

"Did he ever mention a man by the name of Ben Strothart?" Mike asked, sitting on a shaky table.

"Ben Strothart? I don't think so," Freddie replied. Then he snapped his fingers. "That wouldn't have been Old Ben, would it?"

"I don't know. Who was Old Ben?"

"My father said he was a pirate."

"A pirate?"

"He was the uncle of Augusta, if I remember right," Freddie remarked. "I don't remember too much about it, except that Old Ben supposedly told Augusta where his

158

pirate treasures were buried. It's all pretty fanciful, if you ask me. But legend has it that Augusta found the treasures —or at least part of them—and it was with that wealth that she built her Phenwick fortune."

"I'll say that sounds pretty fanciful," Mike commented, "and a bit like an old adventure story."

"If that Old Ben was Ben Strothart," Freddie commented, "that's all I know about him. I recall I used to pretend I was a pirate, and naturally I was Old Ben. But Clayton said—I mean—"

"Clayton?"

Freddie crossed his fingers. "Well, I have an imaginary friend I call Clayton."

"I thought you once told me that Clayton was a ghost."

"Oh. Well, I guess I did." Freddie sighed. "Maybe he's still imaginary, then."

"What did Clayton tell you?"

"That part of Old Ben's treasure was still buried down here," Freddie said. "Clayton said he himself had buried it under direct orders from Augusta."

Mike thought a minute. "When was the last time you encountered your friend Clayton?"

"Two or three weeks ago, I think it was. Why?"

"I think maybe I'd like to see him sometime."

"Clayton's particular."

Mike laughed. "Come, show me the rest of the basement."

When they turned to the first floor, both Mike and Freddie took time to wash up. The basement was dusty, with dirt floors and walls that had been constructed of rocks and mud.

"So you've been prowling with Freddie in the basement, have you?" Ann said when she went to greet Mike.

"What did George Tomlin want?" Mike asked after acknowledging her first statement.

159

"He again asked me to marry him," she replied.

"Oh."

"He has much to offer." Ann was sitting in a chair by the window. "He comes from a very wealthy family and he is an excellent businessman."

"A fine recommendation."

"Mother would be pleased if I were to marry him," Ann went on, watching Mike's reaction. "Mr. Robbins is a good friend of Mr. Tomlin, as you well know. So naturally Mr. Robbins has persuaded Mother that Mr. Tomlin would be the right man for me."

"I can see where that would appear to be the case." Mike ducked his head. "It would seem that luck is on his side all the way around."

"Except—"

"Except?" Mike looked up.

"Except I don't love him," Ann stated. "Nor do I believe I could ever force myself to do so."

"Why not? He has everything."

"For one very good reason; I'm in love with someone else," Ann stated, smiling brightly.

"In love?"

She rose. "With Michael James parenthesis Black Phenwick." She gently reached for his hand. "I do love you, Mike. And I'm still as determined as ever to marry you—if you still want me."

"Want you?" He had his arms about her and his lips touching hers before she could catch her breath.

Ann was still tingling with excitement nearly ten minutes later when Mike thought it prudent to be less demonstrative of his romantic feelings. She could have continued in his passionate embrace, but she respected the wisdom of his decision.

"Will June be too soon?" Ann asked, whispering as she nibbled at his ear.

"Too soon?"

"For the wedding."

"No. Maybe not soon enough. I may burst with anticipation until then."

"Two months?" She giggled.

"Annie—no matter what, I want you to know that I love you more than anything or anyone else in the whole world," Mike said. "Past or present, I know I could never have loved anyone as greatly as I love you at this moment. If there is another—"

"Shh. Don't speak of it. That's a bridge we may never have to cross." Ann was back in his embrace, lifting her lips to his.

Crandall Ornby was working late at Medallion, trying to get a few loose ends tied together in preparation for a trip to Boston and a business conference with Stuart Phenwick. Benita had been warned to hold supper for him. He was expecting Zeb Robbins to stop by with some papers for him to sign.

When the rap came at the outer door, Crandall believed it to be Zeb. He was alarmed to see a hulky shadow outside and a large, brutish face when the man stepped into the light.

"Yes? What is it? We're closed," Crandall stated.

"I'm looking for Mike Black," Sam Dodsworth said as he glared fiercely at Crandall.

"Mike? What do you want with Mike?"

"He's a Confederate deserter and a murderer," Sam stated, pulling a soiled paper from his pocket. He thrust it at Crandall. "Five thousand dollars reward for his return, dead or alive. Read that description. Is that the Mike Black who works for you?"

Crandall read. "It could possibly be. It's Mike's general description—but it could also describe a half a dozen other men of my acquaintance."

"It's the same person. I know. Where is he?"

Crandall shrugged. "Who are you?"

"The name's Dodsworth," he said as he reached a meaty hand at Crandall, connecting with his lapel.

"He—that is—he went on an errand for me to Yarmouth," Crandall lied. "He won't be back until sometime tomorrow."

"Where's Yarmouth?"

"North of here. Not far."

"I'll wait. Where does he live?"

"Over on High Street, I think. He moves around, going from one rooming house to another."

"You'll go over with me and show me," Sam said, tightening his hold on Crandall's coat.

"I have business to attend to here."

"I've come clear from New York on business with Mike Black," Sam snorted, "and I'll be damned if I'll wait."

"Just let me finish this list and I'll gladly accompany you," Crandall stated, not certain what advantage stalling would have.

"All right, you've got ten minutes, that's all," Sam declared.

Sam Dodsworth had made several inquiries around town before he had located the Medallion company. In the course of interrogating several persons, he mentioned he was looking for Mike Black. What he hadn't realized was that when he was in the Wardlow Tavern Mike had been seated in the shadows and had recognized him.

Mike went immediately to his rooming house, gathered a few things and begged the landlady to say that he was out of town and that she did not know when he would return.

Under the cover of night, Mike was able stealthily to make his way to Falmouth House. Lilly Gore met him

162

at the front door and said she would announce his presence.

When Ann arrived, she was ready for another romantic interlude. But that had to be postponed while he explained the urgency of his situation.

Chapter 14

Satisfied with the rooming house keeper's story, since it coincided with Crandall's, Sam Dodsworth decided the only thing he could do was wait until the next day.

"I've got a hotel room with a double bed," Sam stated.

"I trust you'll sleep comfortably," Crandall returned, feeling terribly on edge in the company of the menacing individual.

"You're going to spend the night with me, Mr. Ornby," Sam declared. "Furthermore, you may remain with me until I've got Black in my custody tomorrow."

"I have a wife who is expecting me home."

"Would you rather we go to your house?" Sam asked.

"No! For God's sake, no!"

"Then we'll go to my room." Sam stared threateningly at Crandall. "Incidentally, I have a gun and I'm a very good shot. Do ya get my meaning?"

"Yes, I believe I do," Crandall stammered. He was trembling with fear.

Nearly an hour later, when Sam Dodsworth and Crandall Ornby were ensconced in the hotel room, Freddie left Falmouth House on their best horse. He went to the rooming house and inquired for Mike.

"He ain't here. You're the second one that's come lookin' for him. There were two of 'em the first time. If

I'd 'a known he was in some kind of trouble—" the short, stout landlady said.

"Did you hear anything the other two men said?" Freddie interrupted to ask.

"Only that they were going to spend the night in a hotel—something like that," she related.

Freddie gave her a dollar. "Thank you. I'd be obliged if you didn't mention that I had been here."

From the rooming house, Freddie rode to Crandall Ornby's fashionable home in a newer wealthy section of Portland. Ascertaining that Crandall was not home and that Benita had begun to worry over her husband, Freddie left and went to the Medallion company. It was stoutly locked. He deduced that one of the men who had appeared at the rooming house must have been Crandall—and, if so, he must have been under the coercion of the man Mike referred to as Sam Dodsworth.

After reporting to Mike what he had discovered, Freddie was sent to spend the night with Benita.

"I don't believe there will be any problem tonight," Mike said as he tried to relax.

"What does all this mean?" Ann questioned.

"That Sam Dodsworth has come up with a little scheme of revenge," Mike explained. "Chances are he gave the authorities in New York a cock and bull story about me and the incident of Annie Duggan's death. I don't know where the five-thousand-dollar reward came from, but he probably instigated that, too. My belief is that his intention is to capture me and shoot me before he takes my body back to collect the reward."

"No! Oh, Mike, no!"

"As gruesome as it seems, that undoubtedly is what he is up to," Mike said. "He can't afford to take me back alive. My side of the story could raise suspicion toward Sam. He's obviously a ruthless man who will stop at nothing to get his way."

"Oh, Mike, what will we do?" Ann asked, clinging to him.

"We'll spend the night here," Mike related. "That will give me time to formulate a plan."

"Stay together tonight?" Ann questioned, gently caressing him.

"You in your room, while I spend the night on the third floor," Mike stated. "I love you dearly, and I respect marriage vows."

"I suspect you're morally much stronger than I am," she whispered.

"My darling," Mike sighed, "if you could realize how much I want to be with you always, how deep my love is, you would not question why I must conform to standards which have been dictated as being right."

"Who would know other than you and me?" she asked.

"No one. But *we* would know." He kissed her. "Believe in my love, Annie, please believe in it."

Shortly after Mike left Ann alone in her room, the clock struck the hour of ten. She had been instructed to lock the door from the inside and remain within her room until he came for her the next morning. It would have been more convenient for Mike to have occupied Freddie's bed, if he had not had that peculiar desire to spend the night again in the third-floor room.

The night was comfortably warm. Mike remained seated beside the open window for nearly an hour, staring out. No light was burning. He tried to sort his thoughts and formulate a plan of action. Going to the police was out since he had overheard Sam Dodsworth speak of the reward bulletin with Mike's description on it. Assistance from Zeb Robbins, who was extremely disappointed that Ann had chosen him over George Tomlin, was only a vague possibility.

When Mike finally stretched out on the bed, his mind still whirled with thoughts of Sam Dodsworth. The one

166

contemplated plan that kept returning to him was to lure Sam into an out-of-the-way place, kill him and bury his body where it might never be found. But Mike was not the kind of person who could commit such an act. He didn't believe it was possible for him to kill any man. If it came to his security and the welfare of the girl he loved, he felt he might be able to take desperate measures.

At some time he had drifted off to sleep. Somewhere in the old house the chiming of three o'clock seemed to arouse Mike. He opened his eyes and stared into the darkness in an attempt to identify his surroundings. Then he remembered.

The faint gray light appeared near the door. The scent of violets caused him to sit up.

"You've come up here in hopes of seeing me again, haven't you?"

The outline of the lavender light he took to be Augusta Phenwick began to take on finer definition. "Yes."

"I seem to have brought little force with me. Therefore, this must be brief. You are in trouble. I know that. I've been watching."

"Ben Strothart was your uncle, wasn't he? And he was a pirate."

"That is true, but not pertinent to this moment, my big pussycat. There is danger surrounding you. Once you are free of that you can come back and we'll discuss Uncle Ben."

"Have you any suggestions?" Mike asked.

"Yes. You're to go to the basement. I had specially designed. A partition has been placed in the tunnel, but there is a way to get through it. Beyond there are several small rooms—hardly more than caves. You can hide in one of those until danger has passed."

"Can you see what the outcome will be?"

"I can. But there are reasons why certain things must be played out. I can tell you no more about that."

167

"Why must they be played out?" Mike asked.

"The whole purpose of being born into flesh is to learn a series of lessons. Some are born into one circumstance while others into entirely different ones. That is obvious. But what is not so clear to see is the fact that one takes on outer garments and circumstances to learn his special lessons. Let me tell you a story. I believe I am permitted that much."

"A story?"

"A spirit was born into a wealthy family as a male child. He was pampered and spoiled. While not the eldest child, he was the oldest male. And it would have appeared that he was on a self-destruction course. But that was not his mission in this life. He had to change and drastic measures had to be taken to bring about that conversion. Perhaps he could have effected the desired alteration of his circumstances if he had been aware that such a change was necessary. However, because he was an older soul, it was deemed necessary that he be taken from his earlier environment and be forced into an entirely different set of experiences."

"Without memory of his previous experiences?" Mike questioned.

"I see you have quickly grasped the point."

"But is he never to know of his past?"

"There is no such thing as never. Ultimately all things arrive at a natural solution."

"But his memory—will it return?"

"Ah, I see you perceive the precise point I'm attempting to make. You display an interesting identification. Of that, too, I am proud."

"Can't you tell me my name?"

"It will be revealed when you are ready to know it."

"In this life?"

"If you are ready."

"But I must know. It's very important to me. Why must my past remain so enshrouded in mystery?" he asked.

"The cloud is lifting. You've been given certain clues. Think back, my big pussycat. It has been no accident that you've been led the route you have come."

"I can see you intend to speak only in riddles on that matter," Mike commented. "Well then, let me ask another question."

"One only. My energy is fading."

"You have surrounded Ann Ornby with the scent of violets," he stated. "Does that mean that she is destined to become a Phenwick woman? And, if so, will the fact that I have set the legal processes into work to change my name to Phenwick satisfy your requirements?"

Augusta laughed with a chuckle of amusement. *"One of my husbands, the first Joshua Phenwick, adopted the name of Phenwick. I made certain it was legal after we were married. You may draw your own conclusion in that respect. As to Ann, the gentle child in the lineage of my Jane, I readily admit it is my intention that she become a Phenwick woman. I cannot allow Falmouth House to fall into the hands of strangers. I have selected you, through whom my precious Phenwicks will continue at Falmouth House. I'll be near."*

"But how can your precious Phenwicks continue through me?" he asked.

The light had faded and only a wisp of the scent of violets remained.

"Wait! I have so many more questions to ask you."

A tinkle of laughter seemed to move on the faint breeze.

"Augusta?"

Silence prevailed.

What had she said? Did her words have some sort of cryptic meaning? Or had she existed at all—other than in his mind? Had he actually been conversing with himself? Impossible!

Mike traced back over the words he had heard—or

thought he had heard. Confusion scrambled around in his mind; thoughts collided with one another; yet from that stew of puzzling ideas a kind of logic began to formulate. He was glad he had returned *The Mysteries of Rosea Hackleby* to Falmouth House. He only regretted that he had not taken the book with him that night to the third floor.

A lip-reader could easily have read Sam Dodsworth's thoughts since his lips moved constantly in reaction to the things that entered his mind. Sometimes he mumbled, other times he whispered, most of the time his lips silently formed words. Aware of this condition, Sam took pains to hide his affliction by wearing a large walrus-like moustache that covered his upper lip. Brawny and coarse, his undisciplined appearance was both comical and menacing. He was no physical match for Crandall Ornby, who, while not completely delicate, had certain gentlemanly refinements that did not include brute strength.

Crandall had attempted to catch the room clerk's attention as Sam directed him to the stairs and the room he had taken on the second floor. The room clerk had cordially nodded back and gone about his job.

"How long do you intend keeping me here?" Crandall demanded to know.

"Well now, I reckon that is goin' t' be up t' you, Mr. Ornby," Sam replied as he removed his coat and vest. "Ya might as well pull off some 'a your clothes and make yourself comfortable."

"I beg your pardon."

"That's quite all right, Mr. Ornby. You're wearin' woolen trousers and coat," Sam allowed, "and I don't take much t' the idea 'a sleepin' with someone who's wearin' scratchy things."

"Sleeping with?"

"In that bed." Sam laughed. "I'm a light sleeper. But

170

t' take righteous precautions, we'll spend the night with our ankles tied together."

"A most disagreeable prospect," Crandall snorted, sniffing and reacting to a disgusting aroma that emanated from the rowdy man. "What is it precisely you wish of me?"

"Information. Namely, the whereabouts 'a Michael Black."

"I told you he was in Yarmouth."

"Well, I don't know Yarmouth," Sam said. "I'm not a stupid man. I was in the war—a good soldier. And, I might add, I killed my share 'a Confederate men. Hence, I believe ya should know, I would have no qualms about killin' another one or two. I suspect ya get my meanin'."

Crandall sighed. "What more can I possibly tell you?"

Barefoot, Sam had peeled down to his underbreeches. His hairy chest and back gave him the appearance of a bear. "Ya gonna pull outa them things, or am I gonna have t' cut them off ya?" He brandished a knife.

"Good Lord!" exclaimed Crandall. "You're barbaric!"

"I never claimed t' be otherwise, did I, Mr. Ornby?"

Reluctantly Crandall disrobed down to his underthings. As he did, Sam watched out of the corner of his eye and, at the same time, went to get a bottle of whiskey he had left in the closet.

"We'll have a few belts and get t' know each other better, Mr. Ornby," Sam stated as he poured liquor into two soiled glasses.

Crandall was so unnerved that he eagerly took the whiskey and drank it down in two swallows. He coughed in reaction.

Nearly two hours later, ankles tied, the men reclined on the uncomfortable bed. Sam had produced a second bottle after the first was emptied. By then Crandall felt no pain, if he felt anything at all.

"Before ya go t' sleep, Mr. Ornby," Sam said, pinching Crandall's cheeks with a firm grip of his meaty fingers,

I want ya t' tell me where this Falmouth House is that ya mentioned."

Crandall could not focus on the man. He sighed and passed out.

Sam Dodsworth was gone the next day when Crandall awakened to find himself securely tied to the bed, a roll of cloth stuffed into his mouth. His head was pounding and he was unable to recall anything that had happened the night before.

Freddie left the Ornbys' house early the next morning on instructions from Benita and went directly to the Medallion company. It was Saturday and only a few men were scheduled to work. When he found them waiting to get in, he advised that if Mr. Ornby didn't arrive within an hour they should take the day off.

From Medallion, Freddie went directly to Falmouth House, where he found his sister still locked in her room. He reported that Crandall was missing.

"You'd better get back and stay for a while with Cousin Benita," Ann advised. "If she is of the opinion you should notify the authorities, then you must do so, but not without her consent."

"Cousin Crandall is missing—"

"Nevertheless, it is Cousin Benita's place to notify the police," Ann interrupted.

"And what of you?"

"I will remain here with Mike."

Shortly after Freddie left to return to the Ornby house, Mike appeared from the third floor. He greeted Ann with a kiss.

"I'll fix breakfast for you," Ann said a few minutes later.

"I'll take some cheese and bread and apples with me," Mike returned, "and go down to the basement."

"The basement?"

Mike explained about his conversation with Augusta.

"I'll show you the way," Ann instructed after gathering a basket of food in the kitchen.

Lantern in hand, Ann led the way down the stairs and into the musty-smelling basement.

"I should imagine I could find my way around down here in the dark," Ann commented as they moved through the dark corridor. "Freddie and I have often played here. The rooms beyond the partition are pretty much barren. We can take chairs and a table from these other rooms. There's even a cot or two you can put back there."

"I'm not planning on setting up housekeeping," Mike commented. "I'm of the opinion that Freddie should go immediately to the police and tell them about Crandall Ornby's disappearance. It's what I should have done when I first realized Sam Dodsworth was here in Portland."

"I've been formulating a plan," Ann stated a short while later as they reached the partition in the tunnel. "Come, we must go in this room to the left. There's a secret opening into the room beyond. That's the only way we can get to the other side of the wall."

"What plan do you have?" Mike asked as he caught her in his arms just before reaching the obscure entrance to the next room.

"I'll tell you, but the price will be a kiss," she teased.

The fee paid, Ann pulled him through the passageway and into the room that was hardly more than a cave. "You'll stay here until night. By then I will have arranged for transportation—perhaps a boat. I'll come down then and we can go to Boston together."

"How can you arrange that?" asked Mike.

"I'll go to Mother, explain the situation and get her to help me," Ann explained. "Mother can get Mr. Robbins to assist us."

"And what do you propose we do in Boston?"

"Go to the Phenwicks. Surely Cousin Stuart will be able to do something. He has much influence," Ann remarked. "In the meantime you will be out of reach of Sam Dodsworth."

"Temporarily," Mike augmented. "I suppose it is worth a chance."

Together Ann and Mike moved a few pieces of furniture into the far room. In a short while it was relatively comfortable.

"There are other things I should get from upstairs," Mike said.

"Such as?"

"Extra fuel for the lamp and a robe of some kind. It's quite cold down here," he said. "And another thing, I would like to read some more in the book by Rosea Hackleby. I'll have the whole day and it will occupy my time."

Together they returned to the steps leading to the first floor.

"I think it would be best if I went above," Ann stated, "and you remained here. I can manage all those things."

Lilly Gore was puttering around in the kitchen when Ann arrived. The servant assisted by getting the oil and a heavy greatcoat that had previously belonged to Ann's father.

Mike met her at the top of the steps to take the fuel and the book after he had donned the greatcoat.

"You needn't go back with me," Mike said at the foot of the stairs. "I can find the way."

"One kiss, then," Ann coaxed, "and I'll get on with what I have to do."

Mike encompassed Ann beneath the greatcoat with him as he kissed her more passionately than he had ever kissed anyone before.

Freddie had ridden directly to Benita Ornby and soon convinced her of the need to engage the police in finding Crandall. Benita quickly agreed and desired to accompany the boy to police headquarters.

174

It was not until four o'clock that afternoon that the hotel management became suspicious of Sam Dodsworth, who had registered under the name of Sam Johnson. He had been seen leaving midmorning and, although the room had been taken for another day, it seemed that Sam had taken everything he had brought with him. Moreover, singular sounds had been heard coming from the room he had rented. The maid had refused to enter, claiming Sam had given her intimidating looks which constituted a personal threat.

When the manager opened the door in the company of the maid and a houseman, he was astonished to find Crandall bound to the bed. The maid was sent out while the men untied him and helped him into his clothing.

"I must get to the police at once," Crandall stated.

Upon discovering who Crandall was, the hotel manager was most apologetic and offered to do whatever he could to assist.

"Your wife was here around noon, Mr. Ornby," the police captain said. "We've had four men scouring about looking for you."

"Well, they looked in the wrong places," Crandall stated. "In that case, I wish you to send one or two men along with me while I ascertain that Mr. Ornby has not been molested by that fiend."

"Can you give us a description of the man?"

"I can, but I believe it is imperative that we get to my home in the shortest length of time," Crandall stated.

While two men were found to accompany him, Crandall gave a vivid description of Sam Dodsworth to the police. Crandall was assured that other officers would be on the lookout for the man they knew as Sam Johnson.

Crandall had a tearful reunion with Benita as Freddie stood by and watched. Then the lad excused himself and went to speak with the police officers.

"I'll want to go to my company," Crandall stated a short time later, "and see that Johnson has not returned there to do damage. As a matter of fact, I suggest that both of you men come with me."

"I want to go along, too, Crandall," Benita declared. "I can't possibly stay here alone knowing that creature is out there somewhere."

"Very well, my dear. Come along. Freddie can stay in the carriage with you," Crandall said.

Freddie had a premonition that he should get back to Falmouth House, but he knew he was needed with Benita Ornby. He did not express the creeping fear that was coming over him, but he could not rid himself of the terrible uneasy feeling he had.

Chapter 15

Mike had plowed through as much of *The Mysteries of Rosea Hackleby* as he could during that day. He had found several references to Ben Strothart and the alleged buried treasure that was reputed to be still unlocated. Rosea had written that Augusta, in her zeal, had reburied remaining parts of the treasure in several secret places in each of her different old houses. And, as near as the writer could discover, Ben had left other treasure maps that had not been explored.

While Mike found information about Ben Strothart interesting, he was perplexed as to why Augusta had mentioned the old pirate to him—unless she meant for Mike to locate part of the old man's treasure. That was a possibility, but quite unlikely, he thought.

Mike became intrigued with Rosea's accounting of the possession of Rachel Phenwick, Augusta's granddaughter. The child allegedly had been possessed by the spirits of two old witches. And it was Rosea's belief that, after Rachel's death, she was reincarnated as Rebecca Phenwick. A strange case, indeed. Rosea's philosophy about reincarnation absolutely fascinated Mike.

Even more fascinating to the young man was Rosea's opinions about ghosts. She had devoted several pages to the history of Clayton Latshaw, the architect of Augusta's houses. The man had been both preacher and teacher to the Phenwicks back in the eighteenth century. A queer sort, Clayton was killed in the basement of Falmouth House, where his ghost had been seen on several occasions by others besides Rosea, notably by none other than Dr. Johnny Ornby, Jane's second son.

Rosea had had several encounters with Augusta's ghost, to whom she had devoted an entire chapter. It was the writer's opinion that Augusta had condemned herself to be earthbound by her desire to supervise the Phenwick women. But Rosea also believed that Augusta would rue the day she made such an arrangement as she would become bored with the tedious monotony of such an existence.

There were many other things included in the book that captured Mike's imagination. One name leapt out at him: Joshua Phenwick. It seemed to awaken a familiar note within him. At the back of the book, where Jane had written a brief genealogy, he discovered the name of Joshua Phenwick three times. One, the second husband of Augusta. Two, the name taken by Charles Signoret, Augusta's third husband. Three, the name of Peter Phenwick's youngest son.

A feeling of compassion came over Mike, eerie and perplexing. And there was the name of the third Joshua's eldest daughter: Ophelia. Again the surge of emotion within him.

Mike put the book aside and stretched out on the cot he had carried from the other basement room. A peculiar image flashed into his mind's eye: a magnet, the sort a young boy might have as a plaything. He opened his eyes. How had he known that object was a magnet?

Because of lack of sleep the night before, Mike eventually closed his eyes again and fell unconscious. His dreams were more vivid and equally more confusing than they had ever been. Several times he subconsciously thought he should awaken and try to remember what he had dreamed.

When he finally came to consciousness, all he could recall was the thought of wanting to awaken and remember—not the content of the dreams.

The day had been overcast and by afternoon rain had begun to fall. At first it had been a persistent drizzle, then great dark clouds were blown in from the ocean. After Crandall had had a look about the Medallion company, he suggested that they all return to the house, where he wanted the police to remain.

Freddie would return with them and wait until the storm subsided. Still he was frantically concerned over his sister's well-being; he was that certain she was in danger.

Ann had to do considerable talking to get her mother to cooperate in the plan she had presented. Ultimately Sally had agreed and, instead of going directly to Zeb Robbins, she made arrangements for Ann to take money which she herself had saved.

Arriving back at Falmouth House at five-thirty, arrangements made for a carriage to be waiting at the gravestone exit to the underground tunnel at eight, Ann was wet and exhausted.

"Lilly!" Ann called as she entered the creaky old house. Her voice had a muffled echo.

Lilly Gore did not respond.

Ann went to the kitchen and, not discovering the servant there, she went to Lilly's room. Still no sign of the woman.

After looking about the first floor and unable to locate Lilly, Ann climbed the stairs to the second floor as a feeling of morbid apprehension came over her. It wasn't like Lilly to leave the house unless she had to run errands, and she never went out at night. Then it occurred to Ann that the woman might have become uneasy being alone in the house and had gone to the Robbins' place to be with Sally. That thought only temporarily soothed her. The fact is it would be illogical for Lilly to go out in the bad weather.

Ann changed from her wet clothing, pulled into a simple gown and robe.

A door slammed somewhere in the house.

"Lilly?" Ann called as she went to the door of her own room.

No answer.

A flash of terror went through her as another slamming noise came from the third floor. Why the fear? She crept to the stairway leading up and was able to climb the first three steps before her nerve left her.

"Lilly? Lil—Lilly! Is that you up there?" she called.

No answer.

Somehow Ann felt frozen in her tracks. Although she could neither see nor hear it, she sensed movement up above. Her pulse was pounding frantically and she could not get her foot to return to the step below. Abject horror ripped at her nerves as she sensed the movement getting closer to where she was standing. Why hadn't she brought a lamp with her? Or a candle?

A gust of wind blew down the stairs from the third floor. Ann could not find the voice to scream. In the next terrorized moment she felt something touch against the skirt of her robe. Then she was able to scream, but it was more a squeal than a full-voiced yell. She put her fingertips to her mouth and bit on them to keep from making further noise. Trembling, yet still unable to move, she closed her eyes and braced herself.

"Meow."

Meow? she thought. The cat. It was the cat! She managed to lower herself into a stooping position and reached in the darkness to find the animal. "There you are, Leona. You gave me a terrible fright, do you know that?"

"Meow."

As Ann picked up the delicate gray and black striped cat, she could feel that Leona was lactating, the fur on her belly was loose. "Oh, Leona, you've had kittens, haven't you? Where have you hidden them?"

180

The cat purred.

"Shall I put you back down to go to your babies?" Ann asked as she walked toward her room.

Two black eyes were watching her. Lips were moving with the diabolical thoughts churning in the malevolent head. Meaty fingers tensed as Ann was observed stroking the animal.

Leona spit, tensing with alarm.

"Now what is it, kitty? Did I hurt you? Stroke you the wrong way?" Ann put the cat to her cheek. "Do be calm, Leona. You'll have me all in a state, too."

The cat hissed again, ears laid back.

A footstep cracked the floor behind Ann. She pivoted about as a dark, terrifying shadow lunged forward, hands clawlike to snatch at her. Leona sprang, scratching her nails into the attacker's face. He swore.

Ann ran toward her room while Leona scampered through the hallway and back up the stairs to the third floor where her kittens were waiting.

Inside her room, Ann bolted the door. She could hear heavy footsteps clomping toward her room. A moment later a thud crashed against the door.

Ann's room had a connecting door to the chamber next to it. Mind racing to find a solution, she recalled that her mother had kept loaded pistols in her room. Had Sally taken them with her after she had married Zeb Robbins and went to live with him? It was a chance she had to take.

The door splintered with the weight of the husky shoulder against it. At the same time Ann went into the next chamber and quickly to the hallway door.

No more had Ann begun to run down the corridor than she heard the dreadful thud of heavy feet running behind her. She had the sensation of running through newly made bread dough, her progress seemed that slow. Her pursuer was gaining on her. Confused, she was unable to sort her thoughts enough to determine what her next move should be. Even if she reached Sally's old room, would she be able

181

to locate the pistols in time for them to be effective against the man close on her heels? And if she went into that room, might she only trap herself?

She heard a loud clatter and verbal reaction to falling. The footsteps behind her ceased momentarily as the air was salted with vile profanity. The attacker had obviously slipped and fallen.

Ann had reached the cabinet where the pistols were kept and was having difficulty opening the drawer when the door to the room crashed open. Rain was beating against the windowpane. A bright flash of lightning slashed across the hideous, bleeding face. Sam Dodsworth was far from being a handsome man; now his appearance was drastically altered by the scratches Leona had applied to his large, cruel face.

Ann screamed as she tugged at the drawer.

Sam instantly wrapped his thick hand around her wrist and jerked her, flinging her across the room until she sprawled on the bed. Before she could catch her breath, Sam took hold of her arm and snapped it into a hammerlock. He was breathing heavily and blood dripped from his face onto hers.

"All right, girl, we've had enough of a chase!" Sam exclaimed. "I'll not harm ya if ya tell me what I want t' know."

"What do you want of me?" Ann questioned, gasping.

"Tell me where Mike Black is."

"I don't know."

"I'm not above slapping a girl silly if'n she don't tell me what I want t' know," Sam roared.

"Mike isn't here."

His hand cracked across her cheek. "You're lying!"

"Are you going to beat me senseless?" she cried. "I can't tell you something I don't know."

"We'll see about that," Sam snarled. "Your cousin told me ya was sweet on Mike Black, girlie. All right, if'n anyone knows where he is, it must be you."

Tears of fright and pain were streaking down her cheeks. "Then go ahead slap me until I'm unconscious, for all the good it'll do you," Ann said defiantly. She wondered how much of his abuse she could take.

Sam clutched his hand about her wrist and jerked her to her feet. "I've searched the house top t' bottom, he ain't here. So we'll just have t' try another tactic, won't we?"

"Where are you taking me?" Ann demanded to know.

"First t' the kitchen," Sam replied. "Then—well, that's for me t' know and your Mike t' find out, ain't it?" He laughed sinisterly.

When Ann resisted, Sam practically threw her ahead of him. She lost her balance on the back stairs and fell down three before his huge hand connected with her arm and she was jerked back into standing position.

"My brother will bring the authorities here!" Ann stated, hoping to convince Sam.

"Thanks for the warning, girl," he returned, a grisly grin on his bitter mouth. "But I ain't plannin' on stayin' around t' greet them. Nor are you, Miss Ann Ornby."

Ann realized too late that she shouldn't have mentioned the possibility of her brother coming to Falmouth House. Still it appeared that Sam Dodsworth had already made other plans.

In the kitchen, ropes were tied about her wrists behind her, and around her ankles. As she protested the indignity, he stuffed a piece of cloth into her mouth and tied a gag around it. If that wasn't bad enough, a blindfold was put over her eyes. She wiggled and vainly tried to resist. He was too overpowering and strong.

Once Ann was securely bound, Sam lit a lamp and washed the blood from his face. The cat scratches had not gone deep.

A short while later a tarpaulin was thrown over Ann before Sam hoisted her onto his shoulder and carried her from the house. In the rain, she was lashed onto the back of a horse and tied securely in place. She ached all over and her position on the animal was so uncomfortable she thought she was going to die at any minute. It was even more horrendous when the horse began to move; and she prayed to lose consciousness when the horse trotted.

As Freddie approached the gloomy old house about forty-five minutes later, shivers of fright went through him as he observed that every window was dark. The house had never looked so sinister or forbidding before. He would have preferred not to enter and go back to the Ornbys' or to Zeb Robbins'. But he had had that tremendous premonition about his sister.

Stealthily he entered the front door and went around lighting as many lamps as he could. Within a few minutes he had scoured the first and second floors. No Ann. No Mike. No Lilly.

Apprehensively he climbed to the third floor, a lamp in his hand. He pushed open doors and held the light high before he entered. He was too frightened to examine any of the closets. And when he left the third floor, he moved as if a ghostly horde of hounds were snapping at his ankles.

Freddie was not about to go into the basement. Nor did he have the courage to remain longer in the old house. He must immediately get help. Leaving many of the lamps burning, he closed and locked the front door behind him and hastened as quickly as he could to the house of Zebidiah Robbins.

Chapter 16

Ann listened for unusual sounds as she lay in that terribly uncomfortable position on the horse. Mostly she was aware of the animal's hooves racing through large puddles of water. Twice she identified the hollow sound of the hooves as they crossed wooden bridges. She had no sense of direction.

Lightning jaggedly was thrust at the horses. Tree branches snapped as they were hit. Then the ground had a muted texture of sound, different from that made while in the city. Had they gone into the woods? That was conceivable since the land around the outskirts of Portland was heavily wooded. The faint scent of wet pines, an aroma Ann knew well. Other wet forest odors. It seemed they rarely rode on level ground: a continual climbing and going down.

The ride seemed hours, although in actual time it took less than twenty-five minutes. When the horse stopped, Ann could hear the persistent sound of rain on the tarpaulin. In all her anxiety and turmoil, she thought it was kind of Sam to have covered her to keep from getting wet. Then she realized his gesture was not out of kindness at all, but to keep her from being recognized should they have encountered anyone along the way.

Just to be lifted down from the horse's back was a minor

185

relief. Then Ann was flung up onto Sam's shoulder. She detected the sound of footsteps across wooden boards. A porch. A door was opened. Her head was banged against the doorjamb as she was carried through it. She welcomed the pain at her temple as a means of having a place to focus away from all the other discomfort she had endured.

Sam climbed one flight of stairs, walked across a wooden hallway and climbed a second group of steps. He sounded winded as he carried her through a second hallway and into a room. Unceremoniously she was pitched onto a bed. The fall was only slightly broken and Ann felt as if several of her bones had been crushed.

Moments later, she could hear Sam's footsteps leaving the room.

At first there was awful silence, then the rumble of thunder and a cloudburst of rain falling on the roof. She calculated that she had been taken to a three-story house, somewhere remote from the city of Portland, probably in the forest. Cold with fear and trembling from the excruciating experience through which she had just been, she resolved that she was helpless and completely at the mercy of Sam Dodsworth.

Although her vision was entirely blocked, when Sam returned she perceived he had brought a lamp. How long had he been gone? Ten, fifteen minutes? She had lost all concept of time.

"Now, girl, you're safely away from Falmouth House," Sam muttered as he removed the tarpaulin. "Sorry for the inconvenience. No doubt you've traveled under better conditions. But this is one ya can tell your grandchildren about—if'n ya live t' have grandchildren, that is." He untied the gag and pulled out the cloth that had been stuffed in her mouth.

The cloth had absorbed all the saliva and Ann was parched with thirst. "Please, may I have some water?"

"Oh, I've brought that for you," Sam said. "I ain't all heartless, ya see." He chuckled. "But I ain't all heart

186

either." He put a rusted tin cup to her lips. "Take just a little and spit it out after ya rinse your mouth. Then ya can take a good swig."

"Thank you." Ann did as she had been instructed, pretending to ignore the rust she could decidedly feel against her lips.

The lamp was turned up to full flame before Sam removed the blindfold from her eyes. She blinked, but could only see a dark shadow looming behind the intense glow of light. She turned her head to the side to shield from the glare.

"Roll onto your side and I'll untie your hands," Sam instructed. "But your ankles will remain tied."

Ann used her freed right hand to stand off the glare of the light. She waited.

"Ya know, girl, I was a Yankee soldier in the Civil War," Sam said after a period of silent contemplation. "I don't know exactly how many men I killed. After ya kill the first one, the rest are easy, so t' speak. And after a dozen or so, it's just as mechanical as any other job. And I killed a few women, too—women what were aidin' the rebels. And when we'd go in an' take over a town or a village and sack it, I wasn't above slittin' a few throats 'a kids who tried t' resist us. I don't mind a-tellin' ya that I got so I enjoyed killin' about as much—but not quite—as I did rapin' them rebel women. There was a thirteen-year-old girl near—"

"Stop it!" Ann shouted. "Have you no decency?"

"Very damned little," Sam replied. "I could tell ya stories that'ud curl your hair."

"I don't want curly hair."

Sam laughed. "Ya ain't lost all your wits, have ya, girl?"

"And stop calling me girl; my name is Ann."

"Ann? I prefer callin' ya girl."

"Why?" Ann fired, believing she sensed a weak spot.

"Why?" Sam ducked his head and pulled up a rickety

187

chair, which he straddled backward. "I ain't a sentimental man—as I suppose ya've figured out."

"Sentimental is the last thing I would accuse you of," Ann said, rubbing her wrists where the ropes had cut into her flesh.

"But there was a time—long before the war and I learned t' kill people," Sam uttered, "when I had some ideals. That may come as a laugh to you, but it's true. My mother was religious as sin. But she was a hard woman, too. I'll admit she was the only woman I've ever been afraid 'a."

"Oh, I imagine you would have got over your fear of her, too," Ann dared to say.

"It's not so."

He did have a soft part. "How could you do such terrible things to other women if you had such a deep love for your mother?"

"I didn't say nothin' about love. I feared her. And maybe I was a-tryin' t' get even with her by doin' what I done," Sam said.

"Then actually you did want to kill your mother—and possibly—"

"No! That ain't true. You're confusin' me," Sam said.

"Haven't you ever loved any woman?" Ann asked, trying to get a closer look at his face.

"Why should you wanta know that?" Sam picked at his fingers. "It's for that very reason I'm gonna continue callin' ya girl."

Ann tried to remember the name Mike had told her. "Oh, I see."

"Ya see *what?*"

"You were in love with Annie Duggan."

"No. I liked her and she was promised t' be my wife," Sam stated, "but I never loved her. At least, I reckon I didn't. Who th' hell knows what love is anyway?"

"I believe you must have had some feeling for her," Ann said. "Didn't you?"

"I was gonna marry her, wasn't I?" Sam charged. "Then he killed her."

"Who did?"

"Mike Black! And I intend t' get him for it."

"Mike didn't pull the trigger that killed Annie Duggan."

"What difference does it make? If'n he hadn't been meddlin' with her and foolin' around—well, hell, it don't matter none. He killed her and he's gonna pay for it."

"*You* actually pulled the trigger, didn't you?"

"He held the gun on me. I got it away from him. Then when I went to shoot him, Annie—"

"Annie stepped in the way."

Sam rose and stood close to the bed where the light caused a gruesome expression in shadows on his face. "Ya know, ya shouldn'ta told me ya knew that. An' I shouldn'ta admitted it t' ya. 'Cause now ya leave me only one thing t' do."

"Hadn't you planned to kill me anyway?" she asked.

"No. I mighta left ya here t' starve t' death, but I wasn't gonna outright kill ya," Sam said, almost a pathetic whimper in his voice. His lips moved in a silent utterance of profanity. "I ain't gonna fool around, girl. D'ya hear me?"

"Quite clearly." Ann tried to remain outwardly calm.

"I'm gonna ask ya again, and I want a' answer—or I'll get nasty. Where is Mike Black?"

"I don't know how you could possibly get nastier," she commented.

"Don't ya?" Sam growled. "Where th' hell is Mike Black hidin'?"

"I told you I don't know."

"And I told you I think you're lyin'!" Sam fumed.

"But you don't know that for a fact," Ann countered. She ached in every part of her body, but she managed to keep a sweet, gentle expression.

"Ya know, when I was in the army," Sam stated, changing his tactics, "before we marched into Atlanta, several Confederates were captured. It was cold and cruel, but

189

we tortured them into givin' us the information we needed t' know about the city. There's ways 'a torturin' men t' make them talk. Ya might call it inhuman treatment, but it works. And I ain't above usin' the same techniques 'a torture on a woman—meanin' you."

"How can I tell you something I don't know?" she asked.

"But I think ya do know where Black's hidin'."

"And what is to happen to him if you find him?"

"There's a reward on his head—dead or alive," Sam declared. "I don't much cotton t' the notion 'a carryin' a corpse back t' New York, but that seems the logical thing t' do."

"You want Mike so you can kill him?"

"He's gonna die one way or the other," Sam said. "A hangman or a firin' squad, it don't make much difference. And if'n he's dead when I take him back, he won't have no chance of escapin'."

"Why is there a reward on his head?"

"I told you, because he shot Annie Duggan."

"No, you told me you shot Annie Duggan," Ann remarked. "You want to kill Mike to cover up for your own transgression. Have you no conscience?"

"No! None! I gave up havin' a conscience when I enlisted t' be a soldier. And we won the war, didn't we?" Sam sounded irrational.

"If the country is now filled with self-righteous men like you," Ann whispered, "I would just as soon be dead. Go ahead, kill me."

"I can't just yet. In the first place I don't like takin' my pleasure with a stiff corpse," Sam related. "And secondly, I want Mike Black—and you know where he is."

In the next half hour or so Sam Dodsworth performed several gross forms of torture on Ann. At times the pain was so excruciating that she nearly lost consciousness. His familiarity was so humiliating and denigrating that Ann began suffering more from mental and moral anguish than from actual physical pain. She cried and screamed. Twice he pressed his knife so hard against her flesh that he drew blood. The nature of his means of torture ultimately became so obscene that it defied description.

"One last time," Sam grunted disgustingly; "tell me where Mike Black is or I'll rip you wide open with this knife!"

Fully aware that he intended to carry out his vile threat, Ann broke. "No, don't! Unless I could be certain that that one thrust of your knife would kill me—and it well might eventually—I'll tell you where he is. He's hiding in the basement of Falmouth House."

"I searched the basement."

"There's a partition at the end of the tunnel," Ann weakly related. "Go into the room on the left. You'll find an alcove—a kind of closet. There's a door in the rear of it that opens into another compartment. He's there. God forgive me!"

"I didn't look there," Sam snorted.

"Now kill me! Please!" Ann begged.

"No, not yet," Sam returned. "I'll let ya stew in what ya been through. And if'n Black ain't where ya said he was, I'll come back and give ya even worse than I've given ya so far."

"Can there be anything worse?" Ann moaned.

"That's a wrong question t' ask a man like me, girl," Sam sneered. He took the pitcher of water he had brought upstairs and poured the remaining contents on the rope at her ankles.

"Why did you do that?" Ann feebly questioned.

"Water'll make that rope shrink and cut into ya," Sam replied diabolically. "There ain't no way you're gonna untie it. And if'n your feet ain't numb now, they will be soon, so ya ain't gonna get outa that bed."

"I told you where Mike is. I've betrayed him. Why don't you kill me and have it done with?" she pleaded.

Sam laughed menacingly and strode from the room.

Pain pounding throughout, Ann listened as Sam's footsteps went downstairs. The rain was still falling, but she was certain she could make out the sound of the horse's hooves as it rode away.

"Oh, Mike, Mike, why was I so weak," she cried. "I simply couldn't endure any more of the pain. I couldn't. Forgive me. Please forgive me!"

The oil was burning down in the lamp.

Ann tried to sit up and brace herself on her elbows. What an empty, desolate sensation came over her. She scanned the barren room and sobbed.

A flash of lightning stabbed at the window, causing the pane to reflect the electric torment of the storm. The steady downpour of rain fortunately kept the other sounds that were part of the old house from taunting her—for the present.

She screamed, squealing sounds of panic and forlorn neglect. Her torment was devastating.

Chapter 17

Mike had put *The Mysteries of Rosea Hackleby* aside and had fallen asleep. He sensed more than actually felt the presence of a hand on his shoulder. Awakening, he looked to his right shoulder, which still seemed to have an imprint of a hand. No one was there. The lamp had burned low, creating an even more eerie atmosphere than had been in the room while Mike had been reading.

He stared up at the ceiling trying to recall the dream he had been awakened from. All he recalled was a ship and a storm. Why couldn't he remember?

Again he sensed the imprint of a hand on his shoulder as if it were tapping. When he looked to his right, he detected a faint glow that appeared to take on the form of a hand.

Trembled confusion went through him. He tried to move his shoulder, but it seemed to be held down. Then, as he watched with uncanny terror, the hand took on full dimension. Following from the hand, Mike saw a lace cuff and a satin coat sleeve. He managed to jerk back and get a better view of the apparition that was standing beside the cot. It was the figure of a man—a pear-shaped figure, he thought, dressed in eighteenth-century attire and with a pigtail at the back of his head. The face was somewhat comical, almost a caricature of a priggish-looking, somewhat affected gentleman.

Mike sat up. The apparition did not alter its position.

"Who the devil—?" Mike questioned.

"Possibly . . . just possibly."

"I must still be dreaming."

"It would be easier for you to take if I were but a dream, I have no doubt."

"Who are you?"

"It would be more to the point to ask who I was."

"Well then—?"

"You wouldn't believe it any more than any of the others have. I simply don't know why Augusta is so good at this sort of thing, and I'm not."

"Augusta?"

"Augusta Phenwick. Is there any other Augusta?"

Seeing his attitude, Mike became less apprehensive. The image he saw was a gentle, convivial sort. "You're trying to tell me that you're as ghostly as Augusta Phenwick, are you?"

"Not as ghostly. Far from it. She appears and people believe in her. I appear, and I'm taken less seriously than I was when I walked around in flesh like you. Correction. I never boasted the handsome garment of flesh you wear. Fate was not that generous with me."

"Are you Clayton?" Mike asked, recalling the name he had heard.

"How brilliant of you to have guessed!"

"I was told the basement was your haunt, but I hadn't hoped to meet you," Mike said, trying to be congenial.

"That is because you don't believe in me."

"Why should I?" questioned Mike.

"Because you see me!"

"I suspect I really just imagine you."

"Nonsense, I'm perfectly real. But let us not bicker about trivia. I don't have that much power and you may

194

shortly find yourself speaking with a blank space. Ta-ta. The fate of one in my position."

"Very well, get to the point of your visit."

"Not so fast. Would you like me to tell you who you really are?"

"Yes. Can you?"

"No. That is, I know who you are, but I'm forbidden to tell you."

"Who has forbidden you?" questioned Mike.

"Just because I'm in spirit doesn't mean I have that much freedom. Goodness no. Fact is, I've far more restrictions on me now than I ever had. It's because I willed myself to be earthbound to this house. I think it's one of the loveliest of my creations, don't you? Well, perhaps you've not seen Phenwick House in Greenfield. And that silly Patricia had my original Barrywell House in Boston torn to the ground. But she did have the good sense to have the new Edward House constructed after my designs for the original Boston manor. You see, vanity over accomplishment continues on this side."

"You didn't answer my question."

"I can't, I told you that." The vision moved about the room. *"But look here, just to prove I'm real, I'll show you a thing or two. Come this way. Oh, you needn't be afraid, I won't bite you. How could I? I don't have teeth."* He laughed. *"I don't know why mortals are so afraid of the likes of me. Ghosts are merely spirits who hover close to the living because we haven't been able to relinquish our hold on earth and our dealings with mortals. Alas."*

"Are you seeking pity from me?" Mike asked.

"No, I should think not." He pointed. *"You see that niche in the wall? It's just a slight indentaion."*

"What of it?"

"If you were to dig into it about seven or eight inches, you would find a very interesting surprise. Augusta has

195

assured me that the contents of it will be yours if you dig for it. It's hers to give, you know."

"Did Augusta send you?" Mike questioned, almost believing in the experience through which he was going.

"Yes, she did. And, as a matter of fact, there isn't time for you to dig for the treasure. Oops, I let that slip. Well, never mind. You can come back for it. I was sent to tell you three things."

"Three things? And they are?"

"A. If you go through this door it will lead you to another chamber which is directly behind the partition in the tunnel. Actually, it's a second wall and the rest of the tunnel lies beyond it. But to get through it you've got to go into the room across from this, which is rather like a maze. In the far left corner you'll find a little passageway, oh, terribly narrow, I fear, and it will wind you back to the tunnel. At the end of the tunnel is an exit I skillfully devised which leads through a mock tombstone. There's a lever to the right about knee-high from the ground. I'll try to be around to generate enough energy to assist you when the time comes for you to go through."

"That sounds very complicated."

"Oh, you see, I was a very complex person—extremely."

"You said there were three things."

"Ah, yes. The second is that someone with the initials of S.D. has purloined your lady friend, abducted her from this house and is now on his way back to get you. He knows you're down here."

"S.D.? Sam Dodsworth?"

"That would seem a logical guess, wouldn't it?"

"Sam has taken Ann?"

"Grievously, yes."

"To where?"

"I cannot answer that. Oh dear, I'm fading out, aren't I?"

"Then what was the third thing you were to tell me?"

"Why, that Leona has given birth to five kittens."

"What? What kind of information is that? Who is Leona?"

"Your little pussycat friend on the third floor."

It took Mike a moment to remember the cat who had befriended him the first night he slept at Falmouth House. When he looked back to where the apparition had been, it was gone. "Clayton?"

In the basket of food he had brought down from the kitchen, Mike found a knife. The apparition's appearance may have well been his imagination or part of a dream. One thing might prove that the incident had actually happened. He took the knife to the indentation in the wall and scratched at the hard dirt.

After several minutes of digging, Mike was ready to give up when the knife touched a casket made of metal. No matter what was in the container, it was in a way proof that he had been visited by Clayton Latshaw. He could therefore assume that what he had been told about the passageway was true, as well as the fate of Ann Ornby and the imminent arrival of Sam Dodsworth.

But why had Clayton bothered to tell him about the cat? It was a riddle. On one hand, Mike thought he should investigate the end of the tunnel; yet, on the other, he had a curiosity to go back upstairs. If Ann was up there, the finding of the casket might have only been a circumstantial accident.

Carrying a lantern, Mike hurried through the underground corridor until he reached the steps. On the first floor, he went around the hallway to the back stairs, which he took all the way to the third floor. He went directly to the room in which he had slept.

What was he looking for?

A tiny squeaking sound attracted his attention. That was followed by another and still another. The noise came from under the bed. Crouching down on all fours, he reached his hand under until he touched a tiny furry object. A moment later he was observing a baby kitten with its eyes not yet open.

Holding the light so he could see beneath the bed, Mike counted five kittens. As he rose to his feet, the mother cat entered, leaping up onto the bed and going to him to be petted.

"So you're Leona, huh?" Mike smiled as he stroked the affectionate animal.

Mike left the room and went toward the front stairs. Leona followed him. "Go back, your kittens want you."

Leona rubbed against his leg.

"Are you hungry? Hasn't anyone fed you?" he asked. About that time he heard a faint groaning sound coming from a closed room. Upon entering he discovered Lilly Gore tied in a chair.

"Thank God you found me," Lilly exclaimed. "I was certain I was about to meet my Maker tied to that chair. What's going on here, anyway?"

"I was about to ask you the same question," Mike returned.

"Ah, poor Leona," Lilly commented as the cat brushed against her. "No one has fed the poor thing with me being tied up here."

"Who tied you?"

"He was a big man with a gruff voice," Lilly responded. "A brute, he was."

"Sam Dodsworth?"

"He didn't give his name, and I never asked for it," Lilly said. "Come along, old dear, Lilly'll give you something to eat."

"You do that, Mrs. Gore," Mike instructed. "Then you must go to your room and lock yourself in. Is that clear?"

"Lock myself in? What ever for?"

"I haven't time to explain. Go down the back stairs.

But be sure to let the cat come back up here. She has newborn kittens."

"Ah, have ya, Leona?" Lilly said as she went toward the back stairs.

Mike had begun to descend the front stairs when he stopped. Clayton had been right on two facts: the casket and Leona's kittens.

Leona? Leona? Why did that name sound familiar to him? A faint flash of memory beamed into his mind, then as quickly disappeared. Had he known someone by the name of Leona in the past? If he had been married before, could that have been the name of his wife? Questions, questions.

Footsteps were heard coming up the front steps from the first to the second floor. Mike held his position until he saw Freddie rounding the balustrade.

"Freddie. Over here."

"Mike?" Freddie ran to him. "Where've you been?"

"I've been in the basement all this time. Where've you been?"

"I just came from seeing my mother and convincing Mr. Robbins to get the police," Freddie related. "Do you know where Ann is?"

"No, I don't," Mike admitted. They were standing outside the door to Ann's room. "Come on, let's check in her room."

"I was there earlier," Freddie replied. "But it won't do any harm to look again."

While in the room, Freddie's attention went to the sound of approaching horse hooves. He stepped to the window. "It's a solitary rider."

Mike was quickly to the window and watched as Sam Dodsworth dismounted from his horse. "It's Sam! I've got to get away from here."

"The tunnel through the basement."

"Come on." Mike pulled Freddie through the second-floor hallway. As they reached the stairs going down,

199

the front door was heard opening and slamming closed. "I'll try to make it down below. You go to the kitchen and get Mrs. Gore to her room. Stay low. I'll find my way."

Leona was just finishing her meal when Freddie entered the kitchen. Lilly Gore was not there.

As Freddie reached the door, it swung open and Sam Dodsworth blocked the way.

"Who are you, boy?"

"It would be more to the point to ask who you are and what you are doing in my house," Freddie returned.

Leona arched her back, laid her ears backward and hissed.

"That damned cat!" Sam roared and charged toward Leona. As he moved, Freddie extended his foot, tripped the man and sent him sprawling. Leona raced over Sam's back and out the door. Freddie followed the cat.

Sam was soon back on his feet. As he reached the kitchen door, he saw the door to the basement being closed. Moments later he was taking the basement steps as quickly as he dared and followed in the direction of Freddie's footsteps.

In the meantime Mike had reached the chamber in which he had spent several hours during that day. He crossed through the adjoining hallway and into the far room with the mazelike passages. Several times he came to dead ends and had to retrace his steps. Ultimately he found himself back where he started.

As Mike was preparing to go back in, he heard Freddie's voice followed by Sam's incoherent reply. Mike knew he had no other choice but to find his way through the maze.

When Sam reached the chamber wherein Mike had spent so much time, Freddie in tow, he looked about angrily. "He ain't here."

"I told you he wasn't," Freddie said.

Sam shoved the boy through the door into the inner

hallway. "Not here either. All right, boy, you're comin' with me: Now I've got two hostages."

Mike had heard Sam's words. He hurried through the tunnel and tried to find the latch at the tombstone exit Clayton had mentioned.

Chapter 18

Leona had heard the approaching sound of Sam Dodsworth as he forced Freddie up the basement stairs. She had lingered in the shadow of the rear steps to the upper floors of Falmouth House until the burly man and defenseless boy appeared. Then she scampered to the third floor to protect her kittens.

"If'n I had the time, I'd find that damned cat and wring its neck, I would," Sam stated as he stomped through the first-floor hallway. "I never did much like animals anyway."

"What're you planning to do with me?" asked Freddie.

"Take you t' join your sister and hold ya both for ransom," declared Sam. "I'll smoke Mike Black out one way or the other."

Sam permitted the boy to get a coat in the hallway before they left the old house.

"You'll ride on the horse with me," Sam stated. "I ain't takin' no chances with ya."

"Why're you doing all of this?" Freddie inquired as Sam got on the steed behind him.

"Don't ask so many questions. Ya'll just have t' wait and find out," Sam said. "But I'll tell ya this, if'n I don't get my hands on Black, one way or the other, both you and your sister are liable t' end up as bloody corpses."

"You would kill us?"

"Gladly if you don't cooperate."

Sam kicked the horse as he held the reins with his arms securely about Freddie. The rain was falling heavily. The horse raced through wide puddles, splashing as it sped with pain. Several times the animal was startled by flashes of lightning and the rumble of thunder seemed to terrify it. Sam had difficulty keeping it under control and had second thoughts about Freddie in front of him. More than once he considered disposing of the boy, but that would be careless and would leave unnecessary evidence behind.

Freddie could well see the way they were headed. While unfamiliar with the area, he had heard of it. He made mental notes of guideposts along the way. As they crossed the second bridge, he made special note of the sharp turn to the right from the main road. The path through the forest was overgrown and more than once the horse darted in the wrong direction before Sam was able to get it back on the trail.

Limbs slashed at boy and man as thick patches of fern obscured the pathway. One limb hit Freddie with such force that he fell back against Sam, and the latter thought the boy had been knocked unconscious. Freddie pushed his weight against the man and realized he was no physical threat to Sam.

A while later the horse was directed up a muddy road. The going had actually been easier in the woods, where years of fallen leaves had made a compost matting to absorb water and mud. The horse was uneasy in the mud and, despite the beating Sam administered, it slowed down to a cautious speed.

By the time they reached the old house nestled back in the wooded area, the horse was on the verge of exhaustion. It was tied to a shaky hitching post.

"What place is this?" Freddie asked as he was shoved to the splintery front steps.

"Who knows, it's just an old abandoned house," Sam said. "I came upon it by chance. I reckon no one ever comes this way, and, if'n they did, they wouldn't see it from the road."

The water-soaked steps were rickety and the porch had several loose boards, making walking across it a hazardous adventure. The interior of the structure was desolate and water dripped in through paneless windows or where the glass was broken. No furniture.

Freddie was taken into a back room on the first floor wherein were only the remains of an old trunk. The boy was soon tightly bound and gagged.

"I may be the last person in the world ya see," Sam taunted. "It's your last chance t' tell me where Mike Black is. Are ya goin' t'?"

Freddie shook his head.

"You're a fool, boy, you're a fool," Sam blurted. "Maybe after you've given the matter some thought ya'll change your mind."

Freddie stared at the man with frightened eyes. Then when he was alone, he wanted to cry. He fought against it, reasoning that if his nose were to become clogged, he would be unable to breathe with the gag in his mouth. How long could he endure?

Mike had spent nearly two minutes searching for a means of opening the tombstone exit to the tunnel. Using his fingers, he clawed at the soil around the large stone. Finally he found a rusted latch, but he couldn't force it to move. Dare he return to the house so soon? Finally, with the weight of his shoulder against the stone, he was able to budge it. Ultimately he managed to push it open far enough to permit his body to slip through.

From the road by the old tomb, Mike ran up the hill as best he could, since his feet slipped in the mud. He arrived at the wall as Sam and Freddie were going through the front gate. After observing the direction in which they

204

went, he made his way to the stable and got the only horse that was there. Frantically he rode in the direction the others had gone.

His mount was an older animal, but it was surefooted and Mike exercised great patience with it. Only occasionally did he catch glimpses of Sam and Freddie.

It was not until he crossed the second bridge that he lost the trail. Mike had earlier noticed that hoofprints were in the mud as he followed. On that road there was no indication that a rider had gone that way. He turned back. No hoofprints in the opposite direction. Then he noticed a broken limb going through the woods. He walked the animal as he tried to find indications where the other horse had gone. Fern was trampled in several places and once in a while he discovered a fresh hoofprint. The leaf compost was spongy and few tracks had remained.

Finally he became aware that he had completely lost the trail. He tied the horse under a large tree and went to scout about for a possible path. Using his knife, Mike made occasional cuts on tree trunks so he could find his way back to the horse.

The rich, earthy smell of the wet forest added to his apprehension at being lost. Periodically a bird would call and another would answer. The sound of the trickle of water came from a distance, but it well could have been runoff, not a stream.

Mike found an overhanging rock above a shallow cave. At least it was protection from the rain. He could use the time to put his thoughts into order and formulate a plan.

No more had he settled on a boulder and leaned back against another one than Mike was alarmed by a distant growling sound. A bear? A wildcat? He filled his pockets with rocks and gathered several sticks of substantial size in case he needed to beat off an attack. Then he went back to his resting place.

It would be night before long, he thought. At most there would be about forty-five minutes of light. There wasn't enough dry wood around to start a fire to keep wild animals away.

The growling sound came again.

A mountain lion? Were there such animals in this part of the country? He didn't know. But the thought caused him to associate with another as a picture of Leona came to his mind.

"Leona's a strange name for a cat," he said aloud with an amused chuckle. He wrote the name out in the wet ground, using a twig. Then he said, "What better name! Cat—lion—leo— Leona was obviously taken from the word 'lion.' Well, the little thing is somewhat like a lioness. However, I don't believe Leona would be much help against a wild animal attack. Leona. Leona?"

What was so very familiar about that name? Why did it seem to haunt him?

Very indistinct at first, but gradually increasing, the fragrance of violets seemed to surround Mike. He was so busy considering the cat's name that he didn't notice it at first.

"Augusta? Are you here?" he called.

The scent of violets became extremely pungent, then began to fade.

Mike rose and went in the direction the odor seemed to move. He was about to call out again when he became aware of a distant sound of horse hooves. Hiding in the underbrush, he waited as the sound got closer. His heart was racing in anticipation.

A few moments later the figure of Sam Dodsworth appeared emerging through the trees. He was alone. The horse was permitted to take its time through that wet jungle.

Sam passed within a few feet of where Mike was crouched. The horse slowed and Sam looked suspiciously around as if he had a premonition that he was being watched. Then impatiently he kicked the horse and urged it to pick up speed.

"It'll be dark before long now," Sam muttered. "If I have t' come back again tonight, I'll have t' bring a lantern or two."

Mike waited until Sam was well out of sight before he emerged from the brush. His first impulse was to go for his horse, but he thought it best to move on foot and try to pick up Sam's trail from the direction he had come.

Periodically Mike dropped a rock and made a cut in a tree trunk as he trailed the path of horse hooves a distance of about five hundred yards to where he discovered a mud road. He then went back for his mount, following the dropped stones and notches in the tree trunks.

Night was only moments away by the time Mike arrived back at the mud road with the horse. It was too dark to see hoofprints from a riding position, so he pulled the animal forward as he detected the horseshoe outlines.

Only because the prints came from that direction did Mike know where to turn off the road onto the compost-covered path that led to the old house. A flash of lightning startled the horse, causing it to bolt away from his hold. But the lightning flash had also silhouetted the outline of the old house a short way ahead.

Mike went after the animal, which led him a bit of a merry chase before he was able to catch it. Then, realizing the jittery condition of the creature, he tied it securely near the back of the house.

Chapter 19

Shortly after Sam Dodsworth had left her on the third floor of the deserted old house, Ann became aware of the shrinking of the rope about her ankles. Her feet had gone numb. She still felt terribly weak and despondent over the treatment she had received at the hands of such a villain. The physical pain was bad enough, but the deep gashes he had psychologically caused in her mind were more profound and agonizing. The scars to her body would heal, she reasoned, but the depth of fear he had caused, the humiliation and indignation might never be erased.

It was some time before she was able to pull herself together and become rational enough to attempt to view her situation objectively. She was cold. The tarpaulin was hardly enough to give her warmth. The lack of circulation in her feet made her feel chilled through and through. Wind and rain came through the open windows. Few panes of glass were left in any of them.

At the next bolt of lightning and the thunderous downpour of rain, the reflection of the light hitting a windowpane caught Ann's attention. A thought came to mind. It would be a desperate chance, but perhaps she could manage it.

Pushing the tarpaulin from her, Ann put her legs to the side of the bed. Her feet touched the floor, but there was no sensation of feeling within them. No way she could walk, she determined to lower herself to the floor and crawl to the window.

Crawling was impossible with her ankles bound. She wiggled and twisted and finally resolved to roll toward the wall. She could see certain bits of debris on the floor, so she would have to go slowly and push the objects aside as best she could.

The process of rolling from the bed to the window was agonizing. Several different objects pierced into her, causing sharp pain. She inched her way until she reached the wall. Then, getting onto her knees, she reached up to the sill, connected with it and hoisted herself up. Most frustrating was the fact she could not stand. As a result, she fell back to the floor. It was then that she tore a piece of her gown large enough to wrap around her fist in several layers.

Hoisting herself upward again, Ann managed to brace herself with one hand while she plunged the covered hand through the glass. Still bracing herself, she was able to dislodge a small piece of glass, which she protected as she fell back to the floor.

Turtlelike she crept back to the bed with the piece of glass. After pulling herself onto the bed, she began the torturous maneuver of attempting to cut the rope with the piece of glass. She cut her hands and feet more often than she cut the rope, and bit by bit the tedious job began to show signs of progress.

It was close to dark by the time Ann had severed enough of the rope that she could pull it free from her ankles. Then came the terrible sensation of pins and needles. She massaged her feet as best she could, but they were bleeding both from the glass she had used on the rope and from where the rope had cut into her flesh.

Once circulation was restored to her lower extremities, Ann used the piece she had torn from her gown to cover the wounds. She had to tear additional material to fulfill her needs for bandages.

The rain suddenly had stopped as if a valve had been turned off somewhere. Only the dripping of water from the eaves continued. Still an ominous silence seemed to hover about Ann as she remained on the bed. She had heard sound on the first floor at the time Freddie had been bound, although she had no idea what had caused it. Now that eerie lack of sound, except for the dripping water, caused a terrified reaction to come over her.

Now that she was free of the restraining rope, what could Ann do? She felt she must get away from that room. Her shoes were gone. How far through the woods could she get shoeless? Perhaps she could rip enough of her gown in pieces to bind about her feet, but how much protection would that be against jagged sticks and rocks in the forest?

The thing to do, she finally decided, was to search about that old house and see what she could find. It would be naïve to hope that she might find a pair of boots, but there might be something.

Her feet ached as she attempted to walk across the room. As she reached the door, she scraped a splinter into her foot. After removing it, she tore strips of material from her gown and wound them about her feet.

From the room in which she had been held, Ann went across the hall to the chamber opposite. It was barren. She went to examine the other two rooms on that floor. The next she reached was also empty and appeared charred at the far corner where it once had caught fire. The fourth room had several pieces of loose wood strewn over the floor.

Ann went in to examine closer. She lifted several of the bits of wood, which appeared to have been wall studs, possibly the remnants of a partition that had been removed. Finding one of sufficient bulk, but light enough that she could handle, she carried it with her. Should she en-

210

counter Sam Dodsworth again, she would strike with all her might—hopefully catching him by surprise—without bothering with conversation. He had hurt her; she wanted to retaliate.

Wood in hand, Ann slowly took the steps down to the second floor. More than once she nearly lost her balance; and she quickly learned not to trust the wobbly banister.

A sound coming from the first floor caused Ann to freeze in her tracks. It was a dull thud. To find protection, she charged into the nearest room, only to discover that the doorway was covered with a gossamer spider's web. She screamed as it seemed to wind around her. Then as she held her hand over her mouth, she heard the thudding sound again coming from below.

She went to a second room near the head of the stairs. Using the piece of wood she carried to prod the doorway, she ascertained that the spiders had not been so industrious in that room.

Darkness had completely surrounded the old house. Ann could no longer see her way. Due to heavy black clouds overhead, there was no source of light whatsoever. It only she could find a lantern or a candle. Even if she did, what would she use for matches? She felt as if she were trapped in darkness. That being the case, she wasn't certain she wanted to remain in that mysterious room without knowing precisely what was in it—if anything.

"Hoo! Hoo!"

It was all Ann could do to keep from screaming again. Yet she quickly identified the sound as that made by an owl. But what if the bird were in the room with her? She wasn't certain if owls were known to attack human beings or not. Although she thought she would never wish for such a thing, she prayed for lightning. At least in that momentary brilliant flash she might be able to see the condition of the room.

Anticipating another vocalization from the owl, Ann stood near the door and determined that she would control fear. All she heard was the fluttering of wings. Apparently the owl cared no more for being in her proximity than she relished being in his. She sighed.

No more had the breath expired from her lungs than Ann heard the definite sound of footsteps on the first floor. She was certain it was Sam Dodsworth returned to take up the torture where he had left off. She gripped the wood in her hands tightly. Quickly she decided to beat him at his own game. Even if he had a lantern with him, she schemed that she could wait for him at the top of the stairs and surprise him with a crashing blow to the head. She reasoned that he must have come on horseback, therefore she hoped to stun him long enough for her to make an escape, get the horse and ride back into town.

Everything depended on the force with which she swung the wood. Without being able to see where she was aiming, she realized she would be taking a gross chance. Still it was one she must take.

Either her eyes had become accustomed to the darkness, or a tiny amount of light was coming from someplace. That was fortuitous, she thought, as she made her way to a position beside the head of the stairs. She made several trial swings, just to be certain she could take aim.

The footsteps were at the base of the stairs. Ann could see the vague shadowy outline of a man as he began the climb. He did not have a lamp and appeared to be blindly groping his way up the banister.

Waiting until she could hear the heaviness of his breathing, Ann positioned herself for the crucial blow. He came forward, higher and higher, nearer and nearer. The wood was over her shoulder, her stance was right. Then, with all the power she could muster, she swung. The wood exploded with an awful cracking sound as it connected with the intruder's skull. He cried out, staggered.

Fearing he was only stunned and would lurch at her any second, Ann swung again, catching the wood across his cheek. He moaned, then fell backward and rolled down

212

the stairs, making a hideous clomping noise as he did.

He lay deathly still, motionless. Had she killed him? Or had the fall down the stairs caused the final termination?

Ann remained at the head of the stairs, not daring to move for several moments. It seemed an eternity. The thought that she might have killed a person—even Sam Dodsworth—caused a fitful churning sensation in the pit of her stomach.

Then she heard the thudding sound she had heard before. It was persistent, as if someone were kicking against the floor. Ann braced herself. Did she have the nerve to climb down the steps? If so, might she not find that Sam Dodsworth was still conscious below and waiting to even the score?

She held the piece of wood on her shoulder as she inched her way down the steps. Only as she neared the bottom could she see the sprawled figure of the man in a contorted position. She tiptoed and sidestepped around the balustrade. Then she stood frozen as she stared into the darkness at that mass of humanity that was unconscious—or dead.

The thudding sound came again.

Carrying the piece of wood, Ann forgot about her immediate desire to escape. Besides, it had occurred to her that Sam had brought back a second captive with him. On one hand she prayed that it wasn't Mike; on the other, she wished that it was he.

The dark clouds temporarily drifted over to expose the nearly full moon. Moonlight shone in through the windows. Ann could almost see her way as she followed the thudding sound.

There was no mistaking that the body in the room she had entered was tied, his heels causing the thudding sound on the floor. Ann tripped over the broken trunk and nearly fell on top of Freddie before she caught herself. The moonlight was sufficient for her to identify her brother.

"Freddie!" she exclaimed as she untied the cloth holding the gag in his mouth. "Freddie, what're you doing here?"

"I'll explain when you've untied me," her brother replied.

Clumsily Ann released his hands. Because of the cuts and bandages, she was unable to work any faster. The force of wielding the wood as a club had caused her hands to bleed again.

While Freddie untied his ankles, he briefly explained how he happened to be in the old house and that Sam Dodsworth had apparently returned to Falmouth House to find Mike.

Ann related her devastating experience with Sam, only intimating the extent of the horrors he performed on her in an attempt to make her tell the whereabouts of Mike. She was seated on the floor beside her brother when she remembered.

"Freddie, we've got to get out of here!" she exclaimed, explaining what she had done just prior to finding her brother. "He must have a horse tied out front."

"Come on, let's go, then," Freddie urged. "If he regains consciousness, we'll be in for it."

"I can't! I can't get up! My feet are sore, they won't hold me," Ann declared. "Both my feet and legs have gone numb."

"I can't carry you."

"You can get me to my feet and support me," Ann replied.

"Yes, but—"

"What is it?"

"Suppose he's out there waiting for us."

"Oh, Freddie, what will we do?"

"You wait here. I have some matches in my pocket— if they're not wet," he said. "I'll go see what condition he's in, then, if he's still unconscious, I'll go see if I can ready the horse. You wait here."

"There's a tarpaulin upstairs."

214

"We can't bother with that. I wish we had a candle," Freddie said as he hobbled from the room.

Ann rubbed her feet to get circulation into them. When she still could not rise, she crawled toward the door. She was resting beside the door when Freddie returned.

"Is he—is he dead?" Ann questioned.

"No." Freddie was trembling as he stood staring down at her. He struck a match and crouched beside Ann.

"Look, there's a bit of candle," Ann said.

Freddie reached for the candle and lit it before the match burned down. "He's unconscious—and bleeding."

"Serves Sam Dodsworth right for doing what he did," Ann exclaimed. Then her triumphant expression changed as she tried to interpret the look in Freddie's face. "What is it? What's wrong?"

"That isn't Sam Dodsworth out there," Freddie stated; "it's Mike."

"Mike?"

"I don't know how he got here," Freddie commented. "I'm scared, Ann. He's breathing funny, gasping for air. I think he may be—"

"No! Oh, God, no! Help me to my feet, Freddie. We must help him, if we can," Ann stated. "Oh, I hate myself for hitting him."

"You couldn't help it, Ann. You didn't know who it was," Freddie stated as he lifted her to a standing position and permitted her to put her arm about his shoulders.

Upon examining Mike by the dim candlelight, Ann tore off the remaining part of her gown skirt, then divided it and instructed Freddie to go out and get it wet.

In his quest for standing water, Freddie went around the side of the house and discovered where Mike had left the horse tied. He returned to Ann with the wet cloth.

"Mike must have got out of the basement," Freddie said as he watched Ann mop the cloth over the injured man's face, "gone around to the stable and got Molly. She's tied outside."

"Then you'd better ride instantly to the home of Crandall Ornby," Ann instructed, "and get help."

"But what if Sam Dodsworth returns?" questioned Freddie. "And worse yet, what if I encounter him en route?"

"That's a bridge we'll have to cross when we get to it," Ann declared. "You must go as fast as you can."

"If I can find my way."

"You'll find it, Freddie, I know you will."

"Are you certain you'll be all right?"

"I'm not certain of anything at this moment, except that I know we need help—and we've got to get Mike away from here," Ann said.

"I don't like leaving you alone."

"Freddie, for goodness' sake, go!" Ann yelled.

Then he was gone and Ann sat on the floor, holding Mike's head in her lap. She had checked and hadn't discovered any broken bones. Blood came from his temple, but she had managed to cover the break in the skin and cause coagulation to begin.

In the dim candlelight Mike briefly opened his eyes. They didn't seem to be focused on anything. *"Leon-a."*

"Leona?"

"Leon-a. Great . . . big . . . pussy . . . cat . . ."
He sighed and lost consciousness.

"Mike? Leona?" Ann realized that he was not going to speak again. Gently she soothed his brow. Tenderly she hugged him as tears began to flow down her cheeks. She had forgotten about her misfortune, her pain, the terrible experience with Sam Dodsworth. She thought only of the love she had for Mike.

And she prayed that that beautiful man would recover and would not suffer permanent damage from the blow she had inflicted. She could not believe that she had been able to swing with such force; yet she knew that during a time of panic or emergency she was able to muster unusual strength. The exertion spent in that final attempt to protect herself had taken its toll on Ann.

Freddie had been able to guide Molly back to the mud road. He was lost. The only thing he could do was to follow the road until he came to a house, wherever that might be.

Chapter 20

Freddie did not discover a house along the road. If people lived in that area, their houses were well off the beaten track. However, after traveling for several hours, he came across a signpost with an arrow pointing with the logo of Portland, 8 miles. He had been going in the wrong direction.

He stopped by a brook long enough for Molly to drink. He didn't know if he would have the strength to ride on to Portland without rest. A few minutes later, after he, too, had taken a drink and washed his face, he continued.

Weary and blurry-eyed, Freddie finally arrived in the city limits and went directly to the Ornby home. Dawn was just beginning to lighten the sky. A sleepy servant answered the door and reluctantly delivered the message to his master when Freddie appeared determined to persist until his mission was accomplished.

Crandall appeared a short time later, wrapped in his dressing robe, the nightcap still on his head. "Freddie, what is it?"

"Mike is unconscious and Ann is on the verge of fainting dead away," Freddie explained. "We've got to get them to a doctor."

Crandall rallied to the cause and began giving orders to

his servants. The three men who worked at the house were hustled into their clothing and given guns in case they should be surprised by Sam Dodsworth. Benita insisted that she go along. Crandall rode in the carriage with his wife, while Freddie sat on the wagon seat with the stableman and directed the way.

Benita had brought several items she thought might be needed, including smelling salts, alcohol and bandages. Crandall had a flask of brandy, from which he took two large swigs en route.

A makeshift stretcher was made of the tarpaulin and two straight tree limbs. The three servants and Crandall hoisted Mike's limp body onto it and carried it to the wagon. He was made as comfortable as possible under the circumstances.

Benita had applied the smelling salts to Ann and she became more alert, but it was obvious that she was suffering great physical discomfort. Bandages were tied about her bleeding ankles after alcohol was used as a disinfectant. She was dazed and her body ached. She could only walk with the assistance of Benita and her brother.

Once inside the carriage, Ann threw her arms about Benita and cried.

"There there, Ann Rose, your ordeal is over now," Benita soothed. She had a rich, comforting voice.

"Is it?" Ann asked, staring with eyes that still reflected the horror of her experience. "Has Sam Dodsworth been caught?"

"We don't know, dear," Benita replied. "We've not had a report."

"Then it's not over until he is captured and properly dealt with," Ann said. "Oh, hold me, Cousin Benita, please hold me! I'm still very frightened. And I do believe I hurt in every part of my body."

Crandall and one of the servants rode in the bed of the wagon and did their best to keep Mike from jostling around too much. It was a difficult job. Freddie sat on the seat beside the driver, directing the way.

By the time they reached the hospital in Portland, the sun was well up and bright. Typical of New England, after such a violent storm, the sky was cloudless and a vibrant cerulean. White seagulls soared, sweeping down and around. Ann saw neither the sky nor the birds. Only with effort and assistance was she able to make it into the smelly building. She was quickly placed on a stretcher and wheeled into an emergency receiving room. Mike was taken to another.

Word was sent to the home of Zebidiah Robbins and both Zeb and Sally hurried to the hospital. In a state of exhaustion, Freddie was placed in a hospital bed and given a sedative after Zeb assured him that Sam Dodsworth had been apprehended by the police. It seems that Sam had arrived at Falmouth House and had charged into the basement. After thoroughly searching the tunnel and not finding Mike, he had returned upstairs about the time the authorities arrived. Ironically, however, as he was hunkered down by the window preparing to shoot the approaching officers, he was brutally attacked by Leona. The cat struck with a vengeance, as if her attack had been prompted by Augusta herself. One of Sam's eyes was badly scratched and his ear had been severely ripped. The police had been alerted by the man's screams. Leona fled. Angered and in pain, lowering his guard, Sam went after the cat. The police had him surrounded and he surrendered.

"The girl has been badly shaken up," the doctor informed Crandall and Sally, "and she has a few nasty cuts and scratches, but I find nothing critical. It's her mental condition that might have been impaired. Only time will tell how she will manage with that. She is still very young and undoubtedly will get over the horrendous experience with only a few minor scars."

220

"My poor baby," Sally moaned. "What can we do?"

The doctor said, "My suggestion is that she stay in the hospital for a few days and remain under observation." He frowned. "The situation is not as promising with the young man. I have tried all that I know, and I've called in two colleagues. He doesn't seem to respond to anything. In a word, he's comatose."

"Does that mean he'll not pull through?" questioned Crandall.

"It could if his vital signs weaken before he regains consciousness," the doctor said. "We're convinced he has a brain concussion. And if he remains in a coma for too long a period of time, he could well expire from lack of nutrition. We'll do what we can, but we don't have the specialists here in Portland to handle such cases."

"What can we do?" Sally asked after the doctor left.

"If he makes no improvement in a day or so," Crandall answered, "I'll wire my cousins in Boston and see what they suggest. After all, both Joseph and Augustus specialize in mental conditions and problems with the brain."

"Then wire them immediately," insisted Sally.

"We must wait at least a day and see if he responds to the treatment the doctors here can give him," Crandall said.

Charges were filed against Sam Dodsworth, including three counts of kidnap, assault and battery and grievous harm inflicted with intent to commit murder. He was held in jail without bond until a case could be properly prepared against him.

The jail conditions left much to be desired. Filth and vermin were part of the prevalent situation. Dodsworth was isolated in a small cubicle. Only after he had shrieked with persistent pain had attention been given to the wounds given him by Leona. The examining doctor believed it was doubtful that his eye could be saved. But no definite action would be taken with it until his fate was decided.

Late that afternoon Dodsworth had a mysterious visitor.

"Unless he can get me outa here, I don't want t' see him," Sam groaned as he lay upon the hard pallet in his cell. However, after second thought, his curiosity up, he consented to see the man.

"My name is George Tomlin. I know you don't know me."

"Are ya a lawyer?" Sam asked.

"No." George chuckled softly. "No, I'm a business-man."

"Then what is your purpose 'a disturbin' me?"

"I am curious to know why you have come to Portland clear from New York, Mr. Dodsworth," George said, not favorably reacting to the offensive odors of the place.

"I have my reasons."

"Mr. Dodsworth, I carry a certain amount of weight around Portland," George continued, "and I have many influential friends and associates in high places."

Sam pulled the reward bulletin from his pocket and thrust it through the bars for George to read. "I come after him t' get the reward."

"Ah, I see. And how did you know he was in Portland?"

"I traced him t' Boston from New York," Sam replied. "And there I discovered he was in Portland. I was a soldier and learned how t' get information."

"I see. So Michael Black is a Confederate deserter and a murderer," George mused. "That could well make a difference in your defense, Mr. Dodsworth."

"What is your interest in this, Mr. Tomlin?"

"It's personal and I wouldn't want it known that I had

222

come to you like this, nor that I will exercise what influence I can in your behalf."

"Personal? In what way?"

"I believe that is not your concern, Mr. Dodsworth," George replied, returning the reward notice to the prisoner. "But let me assure you I have much to gain if Michael Black is extradited from Portland and brought to justice. Perhaps I shall make a little trip to New York and see what I can do about that. Do you know who put up the money for the reward?"

"Yes. It was Captain Roderick Wellington," Sam stated. "I went t' him and explained that Annie Duggan was destined t' become my wife. I even took her father with me—Tim Duggan, who had promised me her hand. Ya see, I arrived at the stable minutes after Black shot and killed Annie. By the state 'a dress they each were in, I suspect that he had attempted t' rape her; take her by force, and when she resisted, he shot her. I wrenched the gun from his hand—it only had a single bullet. I slipped and he somehow overpowered me and escaped. When Captain Wellington heard that story, he was furious because he knew for a fact that Black had also been messin' around with Mrs. Wellington."

"Are you certain of all this?" George Tomlin questioned.

"As certain as I'm sittin' in this lousy cell."

"I see. Yes, I see." George smiled smugly. "Can you give me the address of this Major Wellington?"

"*Captain* Wellington," Sam corrected. "And yes, I can."

Later that evening George Tomlin went to the home of Zebidiah Robbins. He was shown into the library.

"I think this is a matter that should be discussed in the presence of Mrs. Robbins," George stated.

"If you will tell me the nature of the news you have,"

Zeb replied, "I'll decide if it's suitable for Mrs. Robbins to overhear."

George explained the information he had. Sally was immediately sent for and the data was repeated.

"Mike a Confederate deserter, a murderer and possibly a spy?" Sally questioned. "I can't believe that."

"That seems to be the case, Mrs. Robbins," George said. "It is my suggestion that I go to New York and get this matter sorted out."

"Can't you simply contact the authorities here in Portland?" she asked.

"I'm of the opinion that it would be wise to interview Captain Wellington and Mr. Tim Duggan personally in New York. If their stories coincide with Sam Dodsworth's, we may find it necessary to drop charges against him due to extenuating circumstances. After all, Miss Ann Rose was aiding and abetting a criminal."

"*If* Mike is indeed a criminal," Sally stated. "You will excuse me, Mr. Tomlin, Mr. Robbins. I have had a most distressing day. Both my children are in the hospital and I must take a sleeping draft and retire. Good evening."

"She is deeply distressed, as you can see, George."

"Yes, quite so."

Zeb poured two glasses of brandy. "You appear to be attacking this matter with a great amount of zeal, George."

"The reason for that should be obvious, Zeb."

"Ah, to eliminate the competition," Zeb commented. "Quite so. Have you really become so smitten by Miss Ornby that you would resort to such measures?"

"I believe I—well, have strong feelings for her," he admitted. "And, as you yourself know, she is a prize."

"Quite a prize, quite a prize indeed," Zeb sighed. "But don't you fear Miss Ornby's reaction when she discovers that you had a hand in bringing the man she loves to justice?"

224

"She needn't know of my involvement," George replied.

"But Mrs. Robbins knows. The mother and daughter are quite close," Zeb remarked. "It was foolish of you to insist that Mrs. Robbins be present. You may have defeated your purpose." He raised his glass. "But I wish you well in your endeavors. You'll be going to New York then?"

"Yes, tomorrow, I should think," George returned, "once I've had time to consult several acquaintances here on behalf of Sam Dodsworth. The man can be arranged to be taken care of in the end. He's a born felon, so there's no question he won't ultimately be brought to justice."

"I only hope, George, that his justice is not at *your* expense," Zeb said quietly.

Ann was kept under heavy sedation for three days. A slight infection had developed in her right ankle, but with adequate care it seemed to be healing. Freddie was only hospitalized one day, but he spent as much time as he was allowed going from Ann's room to Mike's.

The doctor said, "Your friend, Mr. Black, shows no signs of regaining consciousness. I don't like to give up hope, but I must say it doesn't seem promising."

"You can't let him die," Freddie exclaimed.

"We are equipped with neither facilities nor knowledge to deal with his condition," the doctor explained. "We're baffled."

After conferring with Ann in her dazed state, Freddie went directly to the Medallion company and spoke with Crandall Ornby. "Please wire Boston. Mike will die if he doesn't get proper help."

"It might be best if he did," Crandall returned, not looking directly at the boy.

"What? How can you say that?"

225

Crandall explained that George Tomlin had already gone to New York.

"Mike is not guilty!" Freddie declared.

"How do you know?"

"He told me."

"Do you think he would honestly admit his guilt under the circumstances?" Crandall questioned.

"You know Mike, he's worked for you. Do you think him capable of doing the things he has been accused of?" Freddie asked.

"I wouldn't think so, knowing the kind of man he is. Still there is that matter of amnesia. Mightn't that be a convenient ploy to cover past deeds?"

"No! Because I believe in Mike's sincerity," Freddie stated. "And I intend to take Mike to Boston and get help for him, both medical and legal."

"And how do you intend to manage that, Freddie?"

"I think you will help me. You can loan me the money, Cousin Crandall, against my stock in Medallion."

"George Tomlin is an associate of mine," Crandall argued.

"And I'm your cousin. Mr. Robbins won't help me, but I think you will because I know you like Mike—and he likes you."

"Let me think about it, Freddie."

"Please don't think about it too long, Cousin Crandall. Mike might not hang on unless he gets the proper care."

"But to move him now might prove to be fatal."

"And to leave him here wouldn't be?" Freddie questioned.

Crandall could not give the boy a definite answer that day, but asked him to come around the next morning. When Freddie was gone, Crandall sat in meditative silence for nearly an hour. Above all else he had to admit that he liked Mike and could not believe that he was a felon or even capable of committing such acts as those of which he had been accused. Furthermore, since he

226

had personally been abused by Sam Dodsworth, the thought of that beast being permitted to go unpunished for his behavior was intolerable to Crandall. But what he would do, he would do in secret.

Chapter 21

Freddie had had a long talk with Benita Ornby and she persuaded her husband to make arrangements to get Mike to Boston. Crandall arranged for a compartment on the train to Boston. Assured that Ann Rose was well enough to travel, she and her brother were destined to accompany the comatose patient.

The train departed early in the morning and arrived in Boston that afternoon, where it was met by Dr. Joseph Ornby and Thadius Phenwick. By the time Zeb Robbins discovered that Mike had been taken from the hospital, it was too late for him to do anything immediately about it.

"Cousin Ann, you and Cousin Freddie must come and stay with us," Thad Phenwick stated after introducing himself. "I consider Mike a good friend, and I will personally see that everything possible is done for him."

Reluctant to leave Mike's side, but convinced that Dr. Joseph would do his best for the invalid, Ann agreed to accept Thad's offer and went to meet Nancy and his brothers, Paul and Daniel Louis.

"John will be home this evening," Nancy informed Ann. "There are those who say Michael Black bears a strong resemblance to my son John. But I suppose a mother never sees the physical side of her children as others do."

Freddie took an instant liking to his cousin Paul, and the feeling was apparently mutual. After spending the following morning at the hospital, Freddie persuaded Paul to take him to the Medallion office.

"This is my nephew, Stuart Phenwick," Paul introduced as they stood in the presence of the handsome man. The usual explanation had to be made about their ages and why Stuart was so much older than his uncle.

"I'm pleased to meet you, Freddie," Stuart said as he shook the boy's hand. "What brings you to Boston?"

Freddie explained precisely why he was there and the circumstances around Mike.

"It's peculiar that this should come up now," Stuart commented. "Just the other day I was speaking with my wife, about the situation at the home of Captain Wellington in New York. On my last visit there, I had heard of the reward placed on Mike's head. Captain Wellington was quite irrational in his thinking, if I may say so."

"I'm as certain as I'm standing here," Freddie stated, "that Mike did not kill Annie Duggan. He just wouldn't have. And, even if he did pull the trigger, it surely must have been an accident."

"Seeing that you have such a strong belief, Cousin Fred," Stuart commented, "I have to travel to New York on business before long—I could alter my plans and go in the next day or so. Maybe I can uncover some information that will help Mike."

"Oh, if you only can," Freddie declared.

That evening, when John Phenwick arrived home from Cambridge, Ann was remarkably impressed by his likeness to Mike. "Apparently I have more than one double in this world," he remarked. "People are always telling me I look like someone else."

"You only look like John Phenwick to me," Nancy

stated. "But to whet my curiosity, I believe I'll have a look at your hospitalized friend, Ann."

"You won't see much now," Ann replied. "He's swathed in bandages."

"It's such a lovely evening, Ann," Thad said a short while later. "Would you enjoy walking to the hospital with me? I promised Joseph I would stop by this evening."

"Just to prove that my ankles are strong enough, I'll accept," Ann returned lightly. She liked Thad.

"So you've fallen madly in love with Michael Black, have you?" Thad questioned as they walked down the tree-lined street.

"I do believe so," she confessed.

"I'm sincerely fond of Mike," Thad said. "We had become such good friends. It's funny about me. When I was younger I got a terrible crush on Ruth Eldridge. Well, I was very immature and, out of desperation, I joined the navy. I don't really regret my sojourn in the service, for it helped me to become a man. But during that time I was quite lonely, and, I thought, friendless. My only close companion died in my arms when we were under attack."

"How terrible!" exclaimed Ann.

"I grieved for weeks. Fact is, I still think of that time," Thad admitted. "Anyway, the point is I was truly ripe for Mike's friendship when he came along. Then, because of all this trouble, Mike had to leave Boston. I should have gone to Portland with him. Maybe not. As you know, I had planned to come up to visit this spring, except that my half sister, Joanna, arrived from London two weeks ago. She's gone to Philadelphia on a trip right now, but we expect her back in another week or two. Joanna's your distant cousin, too. I'm certain you will like her. She's the actress of the family."

"I notice you're quite close to your brother John."

"Johnnie and I have always been very near to each other," Thad said. "At least we were before I flew off to the navy and he remained at home. Oh, we Phenwicks are a mysterious lot." He laughed. "Joanna told me some fabulous tales about the family. And my niece and her husband will be here in a day or so; you'll like them."

"Your niece?"

"She, like all the Phenwick women, recently underwent several harrowing experiences," Thad related. "First she was lost at sea, then washed up onto a deserted island; rescued, then held captive for ransom in Charleston. But, obviously, she managed to escape. The fate of her brother is—"

A carriage came rumbling past, the horse out of control. Thad grabbed Ann in his arms and carried her out of the path of the frantic animal.

"Whew! That was close, my dear Ann," declared Thad.

"It seems I've been through enough harrowing experiences alone to qualify as a Phenwick woman," Ann commented, still in Thad's firm embrace.

He released his hold and stood back. "So that is why Mike so desperately wished to become a Phenwick." He laughed. Then his expression changed. "And what if Mike should not recover?"

"Then I would want to die, too," Ann stated. "I swear I'll take my life if need be."

"But there are other Phenwick men around, available to—"

"No. I've decided on Mike," Ann replied. "What were you saying before the horse came at us?"

"I forgot."

After looking in on Mike, Ann and Thad went to Dr. Joseph Ornby's private office in the hospital. Hospital aromas seeped into that place.

"Well, his vital signs are improving," Dr. Joseph said as he entered the room. "I'm encouraged."

"Have you reached any conclusions?" Thad asked.

"Only that he is suffering from an acute brain concussion," Joseph said. "You must pack a tremendous wallop, young lady."

"I didn't know it was Mike I was hitting."

"Of course, of course," Joseph remarked. "I didn't mean to bring that up. It was unthinking of me. Well, I've conferred with my brother, Aug, after he examined the patient. We're both of the opinion that an operation would not be called for at this time. Fact is, nature simply has to take its healing course with him. By the look of his vital life signs, I would judge he might be coming out of the coma in another few days. These things take time."

Ann and Thad sat in the room with Mike for nearly an hour. Neither spoke much, just sat and observed.

Shortly before they were ready to leave, Mike's lips began to move. "Ooooo-ffff. Oooooo-ffff-eeee." He sighed.

Thad stood by the bed. "What is it, Mike? What're you trying to say?"

Mike opened his eyes. They apparently did not focus on either Ann or Thad. "Leee . . . ooooon . . . a . . . great . . . big . . . pusssssss." He closed his eyes and became quiet.

"What do you make of that?" asked Thad.

"I don't know what he tried to say at first," Ann replied, "but it sounded like he was trying to say Leona. We have a cat at home named Leona. And Mike told me that in alleged conversation with Augusta, she had called him a great big pussycat."

"Then I suspect he's beginning to come around."

"I wonder. Oh, Thad, I wonder," Ann commented. "It's funny about Leona. She just appeared one day, not at the door, but up on the third floor of Falmouth House. Nobody admitted to letting her in. She could have possibly climbed a tree and jumped over onto the house—but there aren't any trees close to the house that reach the third floor. I believe the cat took an instant liking to Mike. And, from all accounts, she was instrumental in helping to

232

thwart some of Sam Dodsworth's activities while he was at Falmouth House."

"A curious animal. I should like to meet her someday," Thad remarked. "I think it best we go now."

"Yes." Ann stared back at Mike, then went to kiss him on the cheek above the bandage. Then she turned and smiled at Thad.

Chapter 22

The day was hot and humid when Stuart Phenwick arrived in New York. After taking care of initial business, he went directly to the Wellington house, where he was welcomed by Thelma Wellington.

"Ah, dearest Stuart," Thelma exclaimed, "this is an unexpected surprise."

"I was in town on business," Stuart said, "and I couldn't resist the opportunity to call upon you and Roderick."

"How exciting to have you here," Thelma remarked. "But I do see a look in your face that tells me your visit isn't as casual as you pretend it to be."

"You're very perceptive, Mrs. Wellington," Stuart returned. "Very well, I've come about Michael Black."

"Michael?" Thelma gasped and put her hand to her breast. Her sigh and her facial expression betrayed her emotions.

"Were you responsible for placing the reward on Mike's head?"

"Me? No. Never," she said quickly. "Believe me, I fought against it. It was Captain Wellington's doing, not mine."

"Why? Surely not only because of the murder of Annie Duggan, a trollop of a chargirl."

Thelma paced to the window and stared down into the

street below. "No. That wasn't it at all, of that I'm certain. Before Michael left, Roderick had become suspicious of his relationship with me, but, of course, he could prove nothing. Well, after Annie Duggan died, her fiancé and her father came around determined to cause trouble."

"And they obviously did," Stuart commented.

"Annie had apparently told her father a thing or two about events that happened in this house—events unknown to Roderick," Thelma said. "To enlist my husband's assistance in seeking revenge against Michael, Mr. Duggan informed Roderick of the things Annie had told him."

"What sort of things?"

Thelma turned. "Shall we say, intriguing indiscretions."

"About Mike?"

"Yes. And—well—"

"You?"

"They were hardly more than innocent flirtations—at least on Michael's part," Thelma confessed. "Oh, Stuart, you know how desperately lonely I was with Roderick away. And then when I learned he had been badly wounded and—well, he's not been a husband to me since he returned. I am still a young and vital woman, Stuart. How could Roderick possibly be jealous in his physical state?"

"I should think he would have even more reason than ever since he has become incapacitated," Stuart remarked. "Surely his physical limitations have caused drastic emotional and mental conflicts within him. I should imagine, were I in the same condition, that I would be equally as possessive and jealous of any man who even looked at my wife." He patted her on the shoulders. "Now, I think I should like to have a word or two with Captain Wellington."

"I'll not go with you, Stuart," Thelma sighed. "You know the way. Do stop back before you leave . . . please."

Stuart left Thelma Wellington in the parlor and went upstairs. He was fond of Thelma in a platonic way. She had come to rely on his visits and conversations while her husband had been away at war. They were good friends, nothing more. At least that had always been Stuart's attitude.

Stuart explained the reason for his visit to the invalid Roderick Wellington in the presence of his attendant, Harry Stiles. Wellington reacted violently to his words.

"But have you concrete proof against Michael?" Stuart asked.

"What more proof do I need? I know why Thelma hired him here in the first place," Wellington stormed. "She wanted to get her hands on him. That's why, when I hired Harry Stiles here to be my attendant, I made certain he was the sort who had no desire whatsoever for women. Isn't that so, Harry?"

The short, bald man with the comical face blushed and barely nodded his head.

"Then with the testimony of Tim Duggan about what his poor dead daughter told him concerning the goings-on in this house," Wellington raged on, "and the testimony of Sam Dodsworth of when he found Annie and Black in the stable and in their disgraceful condition—well, what more proof do I need?"

"But do you know that Mike pulled the trigger, causing the death of Annie Duggan?" Stuart questioned.

"I had given him that gun, Stuart," Roderick argued. "I identified it when the police showed it to me."

"That still doesn't prove Mike shot Annie."

"It does in my book, Stuart Phenwick. And that's all I'm going to say about it—now or ever," Wellington fired. He motioned for Harry to turn his chair to the window. "I think our visit is over, Mr. Phenwick."

Stuart stopped in the parlor for a few brief words with Thelma, then excused himself, claiming he had business to which he had to attend before the end of the day.

As Stuart reached the entrance hallway on his way out,

he heard his name whispered. Turning about, he saw Harry Stiles creeping stealthily down the stairs.

"Ah, Mr. Stiles. Did you wish to speak with me?"

Harry Stiles nodded. "There is a small tavern around the corner, Mr. Phenwick. I would be honored if you would join me there."

"Join you?" Stuart was skeptical.

"I believe I have certain information to impart which might be of vast interest to you," the male nurse said.

"Come along then."

The floor was sawdust-covered and the clientele was rowdy, consisting mostly of workmen. Harry led the way to a small corner table and motioned for the waiter to bring two beers.

"Now then, what is this all about?" Stuart asked.

Harry waited until the beer was served. "What Captain Wellington said about me is quite true. I have no personal interest in physical encounter with ladies. I have perverse desires. I'm what is known as a voyeur. Do you know what that means? I like to watch other people, you know, being intimate."

"I see."

"I have a record with the police. That is how Captain Wellington found out about me. I thought it was curious that he should have engaged me as his nurse. I confess I try to behave myself. But there are times when I just can't—well, I lose control. Such was the case the time I saw Miss Annie Duggan sneak down to the stable to be with Michael Black."

"You saw the two of them together?"

"On many occasions," Harry admitted. "The first time I only observed Annie go in. But after that, I discovered a place where I could hide to watch what was going on. And I'll confess, for the most part I was disappointed. Annie was in love with Michael, and it seemed he was in love with her. Annie's the one who wanted to do things . . . you know . . . Those Irish immigrant girls are like that. Why, I recall—er—never mind that."

"Why have you told me this?" Stuart asked.

"Because I was present, in my hiding place, on the day that Annie Duggan was shot," Harry related.

"Ah, then who actually killed Annie?"

Harry looked down at his short stubby fingers. "Mr. Phenwick, I'm a poor man. And because of my record, it's difficult for me to get good positions. I'm lucky to have a job with Captain Wellington. And if I were to tell the truth about what happened in the stable that day, I've no doubt Captain Wellington would discharge me on the spot. Are you beginning to comprehend what I'm getting at?"

"Quite so, Harry. How much will it cost me to know who actually pulled the trigger?"

"Only a hundred dollars for me to tell you, sir," Harry replied, "but for me to give testimony in court and compromise myself by disclosing my unorthodox behavior, naturally, I would expect a great deal more . . . a great, *great* deal more."

Stuart thought a moment. "Very well, I believe we can come to substantial terms in this matter." He lifted his wallet from his pocket. "Did Mike pull the trigger?"

"No, sir, it was Sam Dodsworth."

"Will you testify to that in court?"

"Will you pay me what I demand?"

Stuart smiled.

Mr. and Mrs. Henry Ashton had been on holiday at Cape Ann, Massachusetts. They were met at the train station by John Phenwick, who greeted his niece and Henry warmly.

"If you don't mind," John said boyishly, "I would prefer to make a detour before we go back to our house."

"Whatever you say, Uncle John," his niece said mischievously. She called him uncle despite the fact that she was three years his senior. "But I will be delighted to slip into a hot tub of water and relax from the tiring journey."

"I just want to stop by the hospital and see how our invalid is coming along," John returned. Circumstances had put curious notions in his head and he was playing a hunch.

Dr. Joseph Ornby had met his cousins in the hallway as they were approaching the room in which Mike was residing. "If he regains consciousness, I would like to attempt using hypnosis on him to see if we can't get into his background."

"He must be coming along pretty well," Thad said, "if you're considering such means."

"He's much improved," Joseph replied. "Now, you must excuse me, I've other patients to see."

Freddie walked a few steps behind his sister and Thad. Twice that day he had been to the Medallion office inquiring about word from Stuart. There was nothing.

No more had the three entered the room than Mike blinked his eyes open, rolled them about and squinted in their direction. A faint smile came to his lips.

"Mike?" Ann questioned as she reached to touch his hand.

He frowned, closed his eyes and opened them again. "Where am I? I say, what am I doing here? And what are all these bloody bandages about?"

"You're in the hospital, my dearest Mike," Ann whispered. "I'm afraid you've had a terrible blow on your head."

"Rather," he said, attempting to raise his head and reacting to pain. "It's a bit of a bore, isn't it?" He stared curiously at Ann, then at Freddie and Thad. "I don't believe I know you people."

"Don't know us?" Ann questioned.

Freddie quickly slipped from the room on a mission to find Dr. Joseph.

"I'll tell you, I'm bloody hungry, that's what I am," Mike said after again looking questioningly at both Ann and Thad.

Thad stepped nearer the bed. A thought had come to him. "Aren't you Michael James Black?"

"Who the bloody hell is Michael James Black?"

"Up until a few days ago, you were," Thad replied.

"Nonsense."

"Then who are you?"

Mike stared, closed his eyes and frowned. It was several moments before he opened his eyes again. "I say, isn't that peculiar, I can't remember."

"Don't you know me?" asked Ann, a queasy feeling coming over her. "Don't you remember me?"

"Should I know you? His frown turned to a brief smile. "I suppose I should, shouldn't I? I can only assume that by the expressions on your ruddy faces."

"I'm Ann Ornby."

"Ann? I knew an Annie once—wherever was it? I simply can't recollect."

"And I'm Thadius Phenwick."

"Oh, that name is familiar, too. Phenwick? Phenwick?"

"We're an old and well-established family in Boston."

"Boston?" Mike scowled. "Boston in America?"

"Boston, Massachusetts," Thad corrected.

"How the devil did I get to Boston? This is a queer one, isn't it?"

"The Ornbys are part of the Phenwick family from Portland, Maine," Ann said, then added, "United States of America."

Mike chuckled with amusement. "Go on, you blokes are putting me on. Excuse me, miss."

"Ann."

"Yes, Ann. A very pretty name. We had a queen by that name."

"Are you British?" Thad questioned.

"I should think I was, wouldn't you?" Mike returned.

240

"Blimey, I know *that*, but I'll be blasted if I can remember my name."

Freddie returned with Dr. Joseph. The doctor pushed his way to the bed.

"So you've decided to open your eyes, have you?" Joseph stated. "Well, that's an encouraging sign."

"And who's this?" Mike asked.

"I'm Dr. Joseph Ornby."

"Of Portland?"

"No, of Boston. There are Ornbys in Boston, too," Dr. Joseph informed him. He turned to the others. "Would you mind excusing us for a few minutes while I examine the patient?"

"You mean me, don't you?" Mike asked. "I'm the bloody patient."

"Quite right."

"Oh, I say."

Thad took Ann's arm as he helped her from the room. Freddie was directly behind them.

"That blow on the head has jarred his memory again," Thad remarked as they reached the corridor. "Now he seems to have forgotten who he was during the time of his amnesia."

"But he doesn't seem to know who he is now," Freddie inserted.

Tears had come to Ann's eyes. "He doesn't know me, doesn't remember how much we were in love. It's my fault. I hit him."

"There there, dear Ann," Thad comforted. "You couldn't help what you did. It was a matter of circumstance."

"Still I feel to blame," Ann cried.

Thad led Ann to a bench and motioned for Freddie to sit with her. His attention had gone to the entrance of his brother John. "Wait here."

"It'll be all right, Ann, I know it will be," Freddie

persuaded. "This is probably only a temporary setback. At least he's conscious."

After greeting the Ashtons, Thad pulled John aside and explained what had occurred.

"I want to try a little experiment, Johnnie," Thad said at last. "And I want you to help me."

Shortly thereafter Dr. Joseph emerged from the hospital room and went to speak in private with Ann, questioning if she needed a sedative. He tried to sound comforting, reassuring, but she was not convinced.

Thad entered Mike's room with his hand on his brother's shoulder. "Since you don't recall your own name, do you mind if we call you Mike?"

"I should think that would be quite all right," Mike responded. He stared strangely at John. "I say, don't I know you?"

"Do you?" John asked. "I was wondering if you might."

Mike put his hands to his own face as if to get an impression of his features. "Come nearer to the bed, old boy, if you don't mind. You'll forgive my familiarity, but I'd like to—" He stroked his nose to feel the dimensions of it, then reached up to touch John's nose. "I say! I have the sensation of looking at myself."

"But how do you know what you look like?" Thad asked, motioning John to get a mirror from the bureau.

"I don't," Mike said. "No, I do. He has my face."

"He is my brother John. John Phenwick," Thad stated.

John handed the mirror to Mike. He watched a moment while Mike examined his face, that part of it that was not bandaged. Then John slipped from the room.

"Oh, excuse me," Dr. Joseph was saying. "How thoughtless of me. Miss Ann Ornby and Master Freddie, may I present your distant cousins, Mr. and Mrs. Henry Ashton."

"If we're cousins, you mustn't call us Mr. and Mrs. This is Henry and I'm Ophelia," John's niece said.

"Ophelia?" Ann questioned, slowly rising to her feet.

242

She looked from Ophelia to the doctor, then to John. "Ophelia . . . not Portia . . ."

"My dear niece," John interrupted, "if I might drag you away for a moment, I think you should come with me."

"Yes, I think she should," Ann stated, brightening.

"And you see," Thad was saying as the others entered the room, "we were in the process of legally changing your name to Phenwick."

The beautiful Ophelia held her skirts as she glided into the room. Henry lingered behind with Freddie and Joseph. John directed her to the bed.

A look of recognition came to Mike's eyes. "Ophie?"

"Oh, my Lord! I don't believe it!" Ophelia exclaimed. She turned to Joseph. "Where can I kiss him that I won't hurt him?"

"On the right cheek."

"Ophie, is it really you?" he questioned, lifting a hand to touch her face.

Henry stepped forward. "I say, is it Leon?"

"Leon?" Mike questioned. "He was the second mate on the *Silver Belle*."

"He's now my husband," Ophelia stated.

"Yes, I am Leon, aren't I? Arnold Leon Phenwick," Mike said.

"We had given you up for drowned at sea," Ophelia remarked, teary-eyed.

"No wonder he looked like a Phenwick," Thad commented. "He *is* a Phenwick." He went to the bed. "Perhaps I had better reintroduce myself. I'm your Uncle Thadius. And this is your Uncle John."

"You get your good looks from me," John teased.

"How could he possibly?" Ophelia questioned. "He's at least two years older than you, Uncle John."

"Well, it can't be the other way around, can it?" John asked.

"John, Thadius," Dr. Joseph interrupted, "may I suggest that you take Henry and Ophelia and Freddie outside for a few minutes? So much excitement is liable to scare his memory away again." He laughed.

When the others had left, Joseph took Ann's hand and led her to the bed. He patted her tenderly, then quietly walked away.

Ann was staring down and could not muster the courage to look into his face. Gently she reached over to touch his hand. "You don't know me, do you?"

"You're Ann Ornby," he said coldly. "We've met."

"You've forgotten Falmouth House and Mother," she said, "and the Christmas party and the beautiful times we had together. Why, I imagine you've even forgotten about Sam Dodsworth and Annie Duggan, too. It's all as dark now as your previous life was when you were in Portland. You may be Leon to them, or Arnold, or whatever, but to me you'll always be Mike."

An expression of compassion crossed his face.

"And, Mike, I love you very much—and I always will."

Chapter 23

Because he wanted to believe that Mike was guilty of the murder of Annie Duggan, Captain Wellington remained stubborn and hard to convince otherwise. Still Stuart persisted and, with or without Roderick Wellington's approval, he took steps to clear Mike's name. The testimony of Harry Stiles was the decisive bit of evidence needed, although such testimony cost Harry his job. Benevolently, Stuart compensated the man for his disclosure and, in a sense, confession of his peculiarities. Harry emerged a richer man for coming forth with the truth.

The ultimate fate of Sam Dodsworth was yet to be decided. Stuart would eventually travel to Portland to take further steps to prosecute the man with the aid of Crandall Ornby. Needless to say, Sam would receive extreme retributive action for the crimes he had committed.

Summer had come to Boston. While there were many pleasant days, generally the weather was hot and humid. With the uncomfortable heat, Mike (or Leon, if you wish) was relieved to have the bandages removed from his head. He had been daily visited by his sister Ophelia, and, of course, by Ann. Ophelia had taken time to get to know her pretty cousin from Portland. Although they had little in common, they became well acquainted.

Nancy Phenwick had taken Ann under her wing from the time she had arrived in Boston. The matriarch was convinced that if Mike didn't renew his feelings for Ann the girl would make an appropriate wife for one of her sons. She thought Thad showed a remarkable interest in her; but she realized, because of his resemblance to Mike, John might prove ro be her choice. Nancy was determined that the wives of each of her boys would become Phenwick women.

Mike was eventually permitted to leave the hospital. He was invited to stay with Nancy and her family. He rejected the offer in favor of going to Edward House, where his sister and her husband were staying with Stuart and his family.

Dr. Joseph Ornby spent many long hours with Mike. He was technically recovered from the brain concussion; the physical aspect had healed. But he was psychologically confused, especially about the dark period of two years during which he had been known as Michael James Black.

"Do you refuse to recall those days, Leon?" Joseph asked, "If so, why?"

"I simply have no recollection at all," Mike said. "I've been told of all the hell I endured during that time; perhaps that is why I don't care to remember."

"There were beautiful experiences as well," Joseph remarked softly. "I believe if we could somehow lift that veil of confusion that you would find those were the happiest days of your life."

"I was perfectly happy in London with my family and friends," Mike stated. "When Aunt Joanna returns, I intend to go with her, even if Ophie and Henry remain here."

"You might not find it the same once you're back," Joseph said, "Things and people change. That's one of

246

the true blessings we have. None of us really has to go on in a static existence."

"My existence in London wasn't static. I say, I rather enjoyed the life of being a playboy."

"Let me see your hands, Leon." Joseph reached to take them. "These are not the hands of a playboy. They've become coarse with labor, strong as your body has become strong. While I suspect you were never a weakling, your own sister attests to the fact that you were devoid of any great physical strength."

"I was born to wealth, Joe, it suits me well," Mike returned.

"There is someone else we must discuss," Joseph continued.

"You mean my cousin Ann Ornby, don't you?"

"Have you no feelings for her at all?"

"I find her quite pretty and obviously devoted to me," Mike replied. "But I feel no depth of emotion toward her. I suppose in time I might develop a different attitude. She is certainly as pretty as any girl I could hope to find. The thing is, Joe, I have given little thought to marrying. I like the life of being a bachelor, don't you know. It's a way of existence that I find most satisfying."

After Freddie Ornby had observed the change in Mike with the emergence of the true character of Leon Phenwick, he at first became despondent. Then he had several long conversations with his cousin Paul. Paul did not have the physical beauty of his three brothers, but he had a kind of innate wisdom and sense of adventure that none of the others possessed.

"I want to go to Falmouth House," Paul said after Freddie had told him about the mysteries therein. "Mother will allow us to travel together. I believe the answer to Leon's problem lies in that house."

Freddie didn't quite comprehend what his cousin was

getting at, but because they had become such close friends, he was willing to try anything. Nancy gave permission and they went for a weekend visit to Falmouth House.

"Leon was never a lady's man," Ophelia told Ann. "He was always very close to Aunt Joanna and she pampered him. I believe Father was disturbed by Aunt Joanna's influence over him—and Cousin Susannah was just as bad. Once you meet Aunt Joanna you'll be able to comprehend my meaning. I love her dearly, but she is flamboyant and eccentric. And, I suspect, Leon patterns himself in some ways after her."

"I feel so helpless," Ann whispered. "Mike is friendly toward me—perhaps I should say cordial—but that old look and attitude haven't returned. It's ironical that I so desperately wanted his memory to return—and I did, because the thought of him living with his past a blank was unbearable for me. Now I know there was no wife and family left behind—but I hadn't expected to find him quite as indifferent as he is."

"Leon's foppish," Ophelia remarked. "I believe that is an appropriate description of him. My younger brother, David, is quite different—or at least he was."

"I still love him, Ophelia," Ann sobbed. "No matter how he has changed, I can't stop loving him."

"It's funny; I never thought I would be capable of love," Ophelia commented, "until I fell in love with Henry. Then everything changed. If only there were some way to make Leon, as he really is, fall in love with you."

"Love cannot be coerced," Ann cried. "I tried to become interested in other men when Mike was away during the winter. It was useless. I knew then that the only man for me was Mike—or perhaps I should get used to calling him Leon now."

Ophelia went to her and took her in her arms. "There there, Annie, it'll be all right, I'm sure." She breathed deeply to brace herself. "Hmm. I like your perfume. Violet, isn't it?"

Ann sniffed through stuffed sinuses. "I'm not wearing perfume. I thought it was yours."

"Not mine. I've been fond of the scent of violets ever since—" Ophelia stopped. Both girls got the message at the same time and they began to laugh.

Freddie and Paul returned from Portland the following Monday. Carrying a large basket, they went directly to Edward House and asked to see Mike. The butler announced the boys and they were shown to Mike's room.

"Well, I say, this is a surprise, my lads," Mike said in a fairly jovial mood. His spirits were getting brighter. "What have you in the basket?"

"Something for you," Freddie answered, shoving the basket toward him.

"A gift?" Mike laughed and almost seemed his old self to Freddie. Aware of the pranks boys are known to play, he cautiously lifted the lid.

"Meow," came the voice from within the basket.

Mike stared at the gray and black cat, glanced up at the boys, then returned his attention to the animal. *Something happened!* He put his hand down to stroke the animal. "It's Leona. Dear little Leona." He removed the cat and held it to his cheek as he caressed. "And you've splashed her with perfume—far too much. It's almost overpowering."

"We didn't put perfume—"

Paul kicked Freddie.

"Where are your kittens, Leona?" Mike asked.

"Mrs. Gore is looking after them at Falmouth House," Freddie explained. "They're big enough to drink from a saucer and they're very much all over the place."

Mike gazed steadily at Leona, then glanced up again

at the boys' expressions of anticipation. "Freddie . . . Paul . . . go tell Dr. Joseph that the curtain has gone up—the veil has been lifted!"

The boys left and Mike hurriedly changed into his finest apparel, while Leona watched. When he stood before the looking glass to adjust his cravat, he thought he heard the sound of a woman's amused laughter; but when he turned around, he saw only the cat contentedly washing herself.

Thad greeted Mike at the door. Nancy was a short distance behind him.

"You've brought a cat," Thad commented.

"I've come to see Ann—if she'll see me," Mike said.

Thad ran up the stairs to get Ann.

"Why, Leon, you sound your old self again," Nancy observed.

"I've remembered how to speak without an English accent, Miss Nancy," he said contritely. "I suddenly remembered a lot of things."

Nancy kissed him on the cheek and showed him to the parlor. "Welcome back, Michael."

A few moments later Ann appeared at the parlor door, Thad directly behind her. But, seeing the situation, discreetly Thad stepped back and closed the door, leaving the young couple alone.

"Annie—"

"Mike?" She accelerated her speed as she moved to him. "Mike—?"

"I may be Leon or Arnold to the others," he said softly, "but I'll always be Michael to you, won't I?"

"I don't understand."

He kissed her, taking her in his arms and holding her as he had done during those momentous interludes at Falmouth House. He didn't have to tell her; Ann knew that his memory had returned.

"How——?" Ann asked as they broke long enough to gaze into each other's loving face.

"You can blame my return of memory on Leona."

"Leona?"

"You know Leona, don't you?"

Ann reached to pet the cat. "I don't understand."

"Neither do I. And perhaps I never will. Freddie and Paul brought Leona to me," Mike explained, "and I suddenly remembered. It happened in a flash—as Joe suggested it might. I also recall my life before I was Michael James Black—excuse me, Michael James Phenwick. Stuart brought word this morning that my name had legally been changed. And here I was a Phenwick all along."

Ann kissed him, embracing him tightly. Then she gently put the side of her face to his chest and stroked his arm. "Perhaps it's brazen of me, but I must tell you that I'm very much in love with you."

Mike pulled her face to his. "And I love you, my dearest Annie."

They kissed and kissed again, becoming totally involved in each other.

"Do you smell violets?" Ann asked a short while later.

"Although Freddie and Paul denied it," Mike replied, "I suspect they doused Leona with violet perfume."

"Oh. Is that what it is?" Ann held her lips to be kissed again.

"That's a logical explanation," Mike answered. "Then again, maybe the boys were telling the truth. It doesn't matter. I only know I love you. And I think I should tell you that you have a choice."

"A choice?"

"You can become either Mrs. Arnold Leon Phenwick," he said merrily, "or Mrs. Michael James Phenwick, now that I legally have two names." He laughed.

Ann laughed with him until the sound of laughter could no longer be heard as their lips met again and again.

A sunbeam shone through the window. Leona leapt to a table by the window to enjoy the afternoon warmth. Contentedly she purred as she washed her paws and kept a satisfied watch on the young lovers.

KATHERYN KIMBROUGH'S
Saga of the Phenwick Women

Spellbinding novels in the greatest series of gothic romances ever conceived.

☐ AUGUSTA—Book 1	00271-9	1.25
☐ JANE, THE COURAGEOUS—Book 2	00278-6	1.25
☐ MARGARET, THE FAITHFUL—Book 3	00286-7	1.25
☐ PATRICIA, THE BEAUTIFUL—Book 4	00294-8	1.25
☐ RACHEL, THE POSSESSED—Book 5	00304-9	1.25
☐ SUSANNAH, THE RIGHTEOUS—Book 6	00312-X	1.25
☐ REBECCA, THE MYSTERIOUS—Book 7	00320-0	1.25
☐ JOANNE, THE UNPREDICTABLE—Book 8	00347-2	1.25
☐ OLIVIA, THE TORMENTED—Book 9	00365-0	1.25
☐ HARRIET, THE HAUNTED—Book 10	00382-0	1.25
☐ NANCY, THE DARING—Book 11	00399-5	1.25
☐ MARCIA, THE INNOCENT—Book 12	00413-4	1.25
☐ KATE, THE CURIOUS—Book 13	00430-4	1.25
☐ ILENE, THE SUPERSTITIOUS—Book 14	03181-6	1.50
☐ MILLIJOY, THE DETERMINED—Book 15	03204-9	1.50
☐ BARBARA, THE VALIANT—Book 16	03228-6	1.50
☐ RUTH, THE UNSUSPECTING—Book 17	04037-8	1.50

Buy them at your local bookstores or use this handy coupon for ordering:

All Time Bestsellers

- [ ] THE AELIAN FRAGMENT— George Bartram — 08587-8 — 1.95
- [ ] THE BERLIN CONNECTION— Johannes Mario Simmel — 08607-6 — 1.95
- [ ] THE BEST PEOPLE—Helen Van Slyke — 08456-1 — 1.75
- [ ] A BRIDGE TOO FAR—Cornelius Ryan — 08373-5 — 1.95
- [ ] THE CAESAR CODE— Johannes M. Simmel — 08413-8 — 1.95
- [ ] THE CAIN CONSPIRACY— Johannes Mario Simmel — 08535-5 — 1.95
- [ ] DO BLACK PATENT LEATHER SHOES REALLY REFLECT UP?—John R. Powers — 08490-1 — 1.75
- [ ] THE HAB THEORY—Allen W. Eckerty — 08597-5 — 2.50
- [ ] THE HEART LISTENS—Helen Van Slyke — 08520-7 — 1.95
- [ ] TO KILL A MOCKINGBIRD—Harper Lee — 08376-X — 1.50
- [ ] THE LAST BATTLE—Cornelius Ryan — 08381-6 — 1.95
- [ ] THE LAST CATHOLIC IN AMERICA— J. R. Powers — 08528-2 — 1.50
- [ ] THE LONGEST DAY—Cornelius Ryan — 08380-8 — 1.75
- [ ] THE MIXED BLESSING—Helen Van Slyke — 08491-X — 1.95
- [ ] THE MONTE CRISTO COVER UP Johannes Mario Simmel — 08563-0 — 1.95
- [ ] MORWENNA—Anne Goring — 08604-1 — 1.95
- [ ] THE RICH AND THE RIGHTEOUS Helen Van Slyke — 08585-1 — 1.95
- [ ] WEBSTER'S NEW WORLD DICTIONARY OF THE AMERICAN LANGUAGE — 08500-2 — 1.75
- [ ] WEBSTER'S NEW WORLD THESAURUS — 08385-9 — 1.50
- [ ] THE WORLD BOOK OF HOUSE PLANTS—E. McDonald — 03152-2 — 1.50

Buy them at your local bookstores or use this handy coupon for ordering:

Popular Library, P.O. Box 5755, Terre Haute, Indiana 47805 B-5

Please send me the books I have checked above. Orders for less than 5 books must include 60c for the first book and 25c for each additional book to cover mailing and handling. Orders of 5 or more books postage is Free. I enclose $_____ in check or money order.

Name _____

Address _____

City _____ State/Zip _____

Please allow 4 to 5 weeks for delivery. This offer expires 6/78.

Reading Fit For A Queen

QUEEN-SIZE GOTHICS are a new idea. They offer the very best in novels of romantic suspense, by the top writers, greater in length and drama, richer in reading pleasure.

- ☐ THE FOUR MARYS—Rinalda Roberts   00366-9   1.25
- ☐ GRAVE'S COMPANY—S. Nichols   00252-2   1.25
- ☐ GRENENCOURT—I. Charles   00264-6   1.25
- ☐ THE HARLAN LEGACY—
Jo Anne Creighton   03206-5   1.50
- ☐ THE HEMLOCK TREE—E. Lottman   00235-2   1.25
- ☐ INN OF EVIL—J.A. Creighton   00224-7   1.25
- ☐ ISLAND OF SILENCE—
Carolyn Brimley Norris   00411-8   1.25
- ☐ ISLAND OF THE SEVEN HILLS—Z. Cass   00277-8   1.25
- ☐ KEYS OF HELL—L. Osborne   00284-0   1.25
- ☐ THE KEYS TO QUEENSCOURT—
Jeanne Hines (Empress)   08508-8   **1.75**
- ☐ THE LAZARUS INHERITANCE
(Large type)—Noel Vreeland Carter   00432-0   1.25
- ☐ THE LEGEND OF WITCHWYND
(Large Type)—Jeanne Hines   00420-7   1.25
- ☐ LET THE CRAGS COMB OUT HER
DAINTY HAIR—J. Marten   00302-2   1.25
- ☐ LUCIFER WAS TALL—Elizabeth Gresham   00346-4   1.25
- ☐ MIDNIGHT SAILING—S. Hufford   00263-8   1.25
- ☐ THE MIRACLE AT ST. BRUNO'S—
Philippa Carr (Empress)   08533-9   **1.75**
- ☐ OF LOVE INCARNATE—Jane Crowcroft   00418-5   1.25

Buy them at your local bookstores or use this handy coupon for ordering:

Popular Library, P.O. Box 5755, Terre Haute, Indiana 47805   B-10

Please send me the books I have checked above. Orders for less than 5 books must include 60c for the first book and 25c for each additional book to cover mailing and handling. Orders of 5 or more books postage is Free. I enclose $_____in check or money order.

Name _____

Address _____

City _____ State/Zip _____

Please allow 4 to 5 weeks for delivery. This offer expires 6/78.

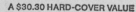
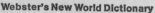